Trespassers!

A Tribute to Benny Rothman and All Fighters for the Freedom to Roam

Malc Cowle

Published 2012
by

**NORTHEN GROVE
PUBLISHING PROJECT**
27 Northen Grove
Manchester
M20 2NL
www.malcsbooks.com

Copyright © 2012 by Malc Cowle
ISBN-13: 978-1479238514

All rights reserved by the publisher.
This title is sold subject to the condition
that it shall not, by way of trade or otherwise,
be lent, resold, hired out, or otherwise circulated
without the publisher's prior consent in any form of
binding or cover, other than that in which it is
published and without a similar condition
including this condition being imposed
on the subsequent purchaser.

No parts of this publication may
be reproduced, stored in a retrieval system
or transmitted in any form or by any means,
electronic, mechanical, photocopying,
recording or otherwise without
the express permission
of Malc Cowle.

For Tom Cowle,
his heirs and successors,
and in fond memory of Benny Rothman.

THE day was just ending as I was descending,
By Grindsbrook, just by Upper Tor,
When a voice cried, Eh you, in the way keepers do,
He'd the worst face that ever I saw.
The things that he said were unpleasant,
In the teeth of his fury, I said,
'Sooner than part from the mountains
I think I would rather be dead!'

HE called me a louse and said, 'Think of the grouse!'
Well I thought but I still couldn't see,
Why old Kinder Scout and the moors round about,
Couldn't take both the poor grouse and me.
He said, 'All this land is my master's!'
At that I stood shaking my head.
No man has the right to own mountains,
Any more than the deep ocean bed!"

From *The Manchester Rambler* by Ewan MacColl

Trespassers!

Originally published as three short stories comprising

No Man Has A Right To Own Mountains,

Connie Gartside's Triumph

and

The Bicycle Frame Builder's Apprentice.

"DEMOCRATIC RIGHTS are like public footpaths. Neglect their use and they will be fenced off, ploughed up and built on. When you really need them to protect your liberties and those of others, you will find they have been taken away."

Benny Rothman in conversation with Malc Cowle

No Man Has A Right To Own Mountains

A Tale of Land Theft for Feral Children of All Ages

Chapter One

"OME on Rosie. It's time for bed!"

"Aw Mam. I'm not tired."

"Never mind you're not tired! You *will* be in the morning, if you don't get your beauty sleep!"

"But it's Saturday tomorrow. Can't I stay up late?"

"No. I've lots to do tomorrow and I want you up early young miss!"

Rosie glanced at her mother. Realising she'd be wasting her time arguing, she decided to change tack. Maybe some subtle diplomacy could win her more time.

"If I get ready straight away can Granddad tell me a tale?"

"Aye - as long as he's happy about it."

"Will you Granddad?"

The old man shook his mane of white hair with a chuckle.

"Go and lave yer face and hands lass; put yer 'jamas on and we'll see."

Rosie's cheeks dimpled, and, with a flashing grin on her impish little face, and a sweep of her long dark brown hair, she was off up the stairs at a fast trot.

"Now Dad, just make sure you don't get her too excited. I really do need her up fresh in the morning. I've all the shopping to do and Billy and Moira are coming for dinner on Sunday."

"Eh lass - yer fret ter much. What if I take Rosie on a ramble tomorrow?"

"A ramble? You haven't been for a walk for ages."

"Aye, don't I know it. I'll be in me grave afore long. I reckon I need to start using me legs agin afore I lose 'em. Anyhow it's about time Rosie were introduced ter the great outdoors. Town's no place fer a lively lass like her."

"Where you thinking of taking her?"

"Kinder Scout."

"What on earth's put that idea in your head?"

"The *Manchester Evening News*. Ewan MacColl died the other day and nobody bothered ter tell me!"

❦❦❦

Rosie *was* up bright and early the next morning, not least because her grandfather had promised her a treat. Now, after having enjoyed a good breakfast of bacon, eggs and tomatoes, and having donned her outdoor clothes, stout shoes, a woolly pom-pom hat, and having carefully wound her long soft gaudily striped scarf around her neck - for her elder mentor had assured her it was cold where they were headed - she was ready and they were closing the front door behind them.

"Where we going Granddad?"

"Fert bus lass."

"I guessed that. But where we going?"

She looked up in to her grandfather's smiling bright blue eyes, a paler version of her own, as they walked briskly down the street of red-brick terraced houses, holding hands.

"We're goin' where the wind blows fresh and the curlew cries. A place where I won this stout stick that I use to prop meseln up with now I'm an auld man."

"You're not *that old* Granddad," Rosie responded, gripping his hand tight. "I can hardly keep up with you."

"We can't hang about lass. There's only a bus once every hour. We mustn't miss it!"

"But where are we going?"

"I've told you. A wild moorland place. One of the largest areas of wild upland country, not crossed by a tarmac road, left in the whole of England."

Before Rosie could ask another question, she was hanging on to her granddad's hand as he began to run. They arrived at the bus-stop as the last passenger was scrambling aboard. They followed, but not before the young girl had read the destination board on the bus's front. Granddad paid the fare, confirming their destination, and she was leading him up the stairs to the upper deck and a front seat on the left.

"Hayfield. That sounds nice Granddad."

"Aye. It's a lovely village. Or at least it were last time I were there."

"Tell me how you won the walking stick."

"Well - It might be a shock to you young Rosie, but..."

He hesitated. Rosie had the idea he was reluctant to tell her for some strange reason.

"Come on Granddad. You always tell me we mustn't have secrets from each other."

"Well, yer see lass, I kinda nicked it."

"Nicked it! You mean you stole it?"

Rosie sounded shocked. She looked at her beloved grandfather in disbelief. She couldn't imagine him stealing anything.

"Yes, I have ter admit it. I stole it. But it were in a good cause, Rosie. I took it off a gamekeeper. He was about to hit my darling sweetheart - your poor dead grandmother - across the head with it. It were at the Battle of Kinder Scout."

"The battle of Kinder Scout. Was that in the War?"

"Aye lass, but not the war you're thinking of."

He shook his head - a gleam in his eye and a smile on his lips.

"It were a battle in a war that's gone on almost since the beginning of time, and is still going on terday if the truth be known. The war against the biggest set of rogues humanity has ever produced."

"Who are they Granddad?"

"Land thieves, Rosie my love. They call themselves gentlemen, aristocrats and country-landowners, here in England, but they operate in other countries under other guises and other names!"

"*Land thieves!*" Rosie was all ears. Granddad was always full of surprises and the best story-teller she'd ever come across. She just wished her English teacher could meet him. She might learn a thing or two - and not just how to keep her pupils' wayward attentions either.

The bus wended on its way, leaving Stockport behind. Soon they were passing the Rising Sun in Hazel Grove, following the sign for Buxton up the busy A6. Rosie remained silent as the road began to climb through the Cheshire countryside, past the occasional cottage and ancient farmhouse. Then they were through the village of High Lane and entering Disley. Increasingly Cheshire red-brick gave way to brownish golden gritstone as the main building material and barbed wire fences gave way to drystone walls.

"What's a curlew Granddad?"

The old man laughed.

"I thought you'd gone to sleep. It's the most wonderful bird in the world, Rosie - at least that's what I think. I've never forgotten the first time I heard its burbling cry and whenever I've heard it since, I know

I'm in the right place at the right time."

"What does it sound like?"

"Be patient Rosie. You'll know soon enough with a lisle bit of luck. There's a chance there might be at least one curlew in the air when we get to Kinder, assuming they haven't packed up and fled ter the coast fert winter."

He frowned, realising it was probably far too late for curlew, but he didn't enlighten his granddaughter.

"Kinder? Do you mean you're taking me to the battle-field?"

"Aye me love, and a wild, lonely and lovely place it be."

Rosie glanced out of the window, having left Disley far behind. Slightly below her, running parallel to the road they were travelling on and cut in to the hillside, ran a canal, its banks populated with trees and bushes, most of them bare of leaves, it being the last Saturday in October. The hills across the wide deep valley were becoming more prominent and the overall aspect growing wilder. Then they were turning left off the main road, descending steeply, past Newtown station on the right, in to the mill-town of New Mills. They'd left Cheshire behind and were now in Derbyshire, Granddad informed her.

"Not far now Rosie. We'll soon be there. Look out for the Waltzing Weasel."

"The Waltzing Weasel? What on earth's that?"

"Rosie - you know what a weasel is, don't you?"

"Some kind of wild beast?"

"Yes - a rather small brown and white wild beast - and you know what a waltz is don't you?"

"It's a dance."

"Exactly. So when you see a dancing weasel, let me know."

Rosie shook her head. Granddad could be exasperating at times. Still, she kept her eyes peeled, constantly scanning the side of the road as they headed uphill out of the town. Suddenly something higher than the flagged pavement that had momentarily replaced the thin strip of rough grass on the roadside verge attracted her bright eye's attention. A brightly coloured painted sign, swinging above a door in the breeze.

"Oh! I might have known. It's a pub."

"Good lass, Rosie! We're almost there. Come on. Time to get ready to disembark. We don't want to end up back in Stockport."

"Don't forget your stick Granddad. There might be a gamekeeper waiting to pounce on you!"

"Ah - but a keeper wouldn't stand a chance would he, Rosie my little love? Not with my secret weapon by me side."

"Secret weapon?"

She looked up at him quizzically.

"I mean you, yer daft ha'p'orth. One look and you'd charm anyone in to submission. Now come on. We've some tramping to do!"

Chapter Two

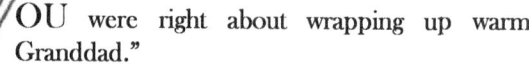OU were right about wrapping up warm Granddad."

"Just wait 'till we get a bit higher Rosie. You always need to be prepared for the worse on Kinder, whatever time of year you come."

They were walking up the narrow tree-lined lane called, rather inappropriately, Kinder Road, for it was barely wide enough for two motor vehicles.

They'd just passed the Sportsman pub, where Granddad had promised to treat Rosie to "a slap-up meal." On their right was a campsite, empty apart from two lone tents side by side, as if huddled together for warmth. The sight of them had triggered the youngster's imagination.

"Have you got a tent Granddad?"

"Aye lass. Why do you ask?"

"I was just thinking it would be nice to camp up here."

"It's a bit too cold for that at this time of year, my love."

"But we could come in the spring, couldn't we? It would be wonderful. We could come up on a Friday night and spend all weekend exploring and having all kinds of adventures!"

"Would you like that Rosie?"

"Yes - I really would Granddad."

She tightened her grip on the old man's hand momentarily and looked up at him, a mischievous smile on her face. "Providing you were with me. I know I'm safe with you Granddad and I love your stories. You bring everything to life."

He chuckled at the idea, but his old eyes were watering and it wasn't down to the cold stiff breeze; a south-westerly and blowing on their backs. He looked up to the towering mass that was the southwest flank of Kinder. His mind went back in time to his own youth - to the time when he too had first discovered the magic of this place - the day he'd met Josie; the girl who was to become his sweetheart, his lover, his wife and the mother of their two children.

She'd had the same rich dark brown hair, almost black, as young Rosie had now, and the same eyes - the sharp clear blue of a blackbird's egg-shell. They seemed to have spent a greater proportion of their leisure time, what little they had that is, up here and over the other side of Kinder in Edale, than they'd spent back home.

Over the years they'd explored the surrounding areas of the Dark Peak, and sometimes the limestone areas of the White Peak. They'd done it on a shoestring budget, because they never had any money in quantity, but who needs money when you have the power of your own legs, a canvas shelter, good sleeping bags, stout boots and warm clothing, with some of the most inspiring countryside in Britain on your doorstep and the determination to enjoy it?

There are pleasures in life no amounts of money can buy, and all too often such simple delights remain hidden from those with too much wealth. When Bill had been born and, two years later, Alice, Rosie's mum, they'd had to make adjustments, but not too many. The kids had accompanied them long before they could walk, and they'd thrived as a result...

"Granddad."

Rosie's treble voice broke in to his reverie.

"Yes my love."

"Is it far to the battle-ground?"

"Not really. It's just up William Clough, but I've somethin' else ter show you first."

They'd now left the lower cultivated land behind. The green close-cropped grass grazed by the ever-present and ever-bleating sheep had given way to coarse tussock grass, with patches of heather and ling. The old man stopped in his tracks.

"Here Rosie. Let me lift yers up onto the wall."

He bent down, placing his gnarled old hands beneath her armpits and lifted her bodily, swinging her legs over the drystone wall, and then perching her atop, with a grunt as he exhaled breath. She leant back against him, feeling the need for security as the large stone slab she found herself perched on rocked slightly beneath her. He pointed straight ahead to the eastern end of the soaring mass of greeny-brown hillside soaring up to the jagged gritstone edge with its black rugged wind and rain sculptured, ice shattered rocks, silhouetted dark and glowering against the grey October morning sky.

"That's Kinder Low End. Kinder Low's the highest point for miles around. Two-thousand-and-seventy-seven feet above sea level at its peak," Granddad announced.

She gazed in wonder across the wild landscape, conscious of the silence broken only by the brown peat-stained waters of the fast rushing gurgling stream, known as the River Sett, which lay immediately below her at this point, and the soft sough of the late autumn wind with its chilly promise of approaching winter.

"Why's it called a Low, Granddad, when it's so high up? It doesn't make sense."

"I think it's a Norse word Rosie, meaning a burial place. Some long-forgotten chieftain was probably buried there. Just on the other side of the Low and below it there's an old pack-horse road that connects Hayfield to Edale. There's an old stone cross marking the boundary. Edale Cross it's called. That's where I first set eyes on yer Grandma."

"Oh! Can we go there?"

"Not today Rosie. We won't have time. But we could go next weekend if yer mam'll let us."

"I'm sure she will, Granddad. Maybe we can get her to come."

"See if yer can. She spends too much time in the house, frettin' over stuff that's of no real importance. It'll do her good!"

"She's been moping about ever since Dad were killed. I'm always trying to cheer her up Granddad."

"I know love. She's taken it hard, but that's why we need to get her out of the house. Give her a new perspective on life. She used to love coming up here. Anyway, let's get you off that wall afore you become part of it. We'll soon be where the trespass began."

No sooner said than done. With the old man's help to turn herself on the wall without falling in to the river below, Rosie was back on terra-firma and walking up the lane. The tarmac ran out and the lane became a rough track. Here they turned left in to the entrance of an old abandoned quarry, its sheer gritstone walls forming an amphitheatre cut in to the hill-side.

"This is where we started from. See that big rock Rosie?"

He pointed and she nodded.

"That's where Benny Rothman made a short speech explaining the route we should take. There were over four-hundred of us. Lads and lasses from the engineering and textile towns of Manchester, Salford and

Stockport; many of 'em unemployed, with little prospect of work. It were 1932 - a lean year amongst starvation years fer workin' folk. They call 'em the hungry thirties now. Anyhow, work or no work, we were all united in a common cause - the fight for the freedom to roam. To force our right to at least be able to enjoy the delights that Nature provides free of charge - fresh air and blue sky, wind and rain - instead of the muck, grime and filthy smoke we had to cope with in the towns."

Rosie remained quiet, taking in her surroundings, overawed by the mass of moorland sweeping upwards above the quarry. The old man had also gone quiet, his mind travelling back in time to Sunday, April the 24th, almost fifty-eight years before, when he was a mere lad of nineteen summers. A pair of chattering jackdaws high up on the gritstone rock-face to their right interrupted both their thoughts.

"Aye Rosie. Such a simple demand - the freedom to roam. Little did we know the real extent of the forces ranged against us. Come on lass. Let me show you what we were after."

She took his hand in hers.

"I'm glad you brought me Granddad. It's such a wonderful place."

"There's lots more yet, lass."

They resumed their way up the rutted track to a point where it split in two. Granddad branched left and they began to climb, a large patch of shimmering water - a small lake - on their right-hand side.

"That's Kinder reservoir, Rosie. Built to provide clean pure water to the people of Stockport way back in 1899 by Stockport Borough Corporation. It took nine years to build. Manchester Corporation built its first reservoir not too far away from here in the Longdendale valley in the 1850s. Ted Heath handed 'em over to a regional water-board in the 1970's and that she-wolf Thatcher 'privatised' 'em this year. So we have 'water thieves' ter contend with as well as 'land thieves!'"

"Granddad. It's not good to get angry at your age. At least that's what Mam says."

"Anger's a perfectly natural emotion when injustice takes place, Rosie. Trouble with your mam is she bottles it up!"

He looked down at the girl and then laughed.

"I do get a bit excited don't I lass. But the fact is, the system stinks. If they could bottle up the very air we breathe they would and then they'd force us ter buy it off 'em and that's a fact. They're nowt but thieves and money-grubbers!"

NO MAN HAS A RIGHT TO OWN MOUNTAINS

BENNY ROTHMAN ADDRESSING THE TRESPASSERS IN 1932

Chapter Three

"WOW Granddad. This is getting better and better."

Rosie was looking straight ahead and upwards. They'd left the reservoir behind and were climbing up a narrow defile, a steep-sided little valley, cut by the fast running stream rushing down slightly below the narrow foot-path.

"This is William Clough, Rosie."

"You mean it was named after William Clough?"

Granddad chuckled.

"Well, it were certainly named after someone called William, but Clough weren't his name. If me memory serves me reet he were a blacksmith and cutler. A clough's a mountain stream, although folk often use it ter name a steep-sided valley like this."

"How do you know all this Granddad?"

"Well I used to come up here most weekends and every single bank holiday. Yer grandma were from Little Hayfield and she were a real fount of knowledge."

"You must miss her Granddad."

"Aye. I do lass, but..."

"But what Granddad?"

"Well. I've never told you this, but yer Grandma died the same night you were born. So thee see lass, although I was broken-hearted at the time, at least I've got thee to comfort me."

He speeded up, leaving Rosie in his wake, as if to prevent her responding. And then they were on a patch of almost level ground. He pointed upwards with his walking stick.

"There were about eight men strung along the hillside there Rosie; all of 'em armed with sticks like this'n. They were gamekeepers, sent by Duke o' Devonshire himself to stop us getting up on to the Scout."

"What happened next Granddad? Were you frightened?"

"Nay lass. Thing is we hadn't taken trouble to come all the way from Manchester to be halted by a few troublemaking gamekeepers, even if they were the serfs and lackeys of a nobleman. It would have been like going to Blackpool and not seeing the ocean. Young Benny Rothman blew his whistle and off we set, determined to get onto the top and enjoy the gradely view.

WILLIAM CLOUGH

"We had 'em outnumbered fifty to one, but the silly sods still tried to stop some of us, wielding thur sticks like demons. There were a bit of a fight, although not many of us were involved, and only one keeper were hurt. Daft sod tripped up, sprained his ankle and knocked himself out. A lone rambler who wasn't with us and had stuck to the public path, was arrested for it, and found guilty, although he had nowt ter do with it. Most of the women and girls had stayed behind when they saw the keepers, but yer grandma decided to cleave to me. That's how she almost got her head broke and I got this here stick!"

"It must have been awful Granddad."

"It were unnecessary. They should never have tried to stop us. Unluckily for us, the police had more sense than the keepers."

"What do you mean Granddad?"

"First things first young Rosie. I'll tell yer in due course. Now, see that knobbly bit left up yonder." He pointed upwards with his stick once more. "That's Ashop Head. That's where we got up to and that's where Benny Rothman made another speech, congratulating us on our success. And then, after contemplating the view and hugging each other and singing The *Red Flag* and the communist *International*, we came back down, feeling as though we'd been on top of the world and overjoyed it had all been so easy."

"I wish I'd been there. It sounds so exciting Granddad!"

"It were lass. But it were more than that. Because of what happened after that it changed the course of British history, and fer once it were changed fer the better. And it was all down to a few hundred working-class lads and lasses. Ordinary common folk, just like thee and me."

"Not *like* you Granddad. You were one of the heroes. Now, can we get to the top?"

"I don't think we should Rosie. Look over there. Them black clouds mean rain and Kinder's not the place to be in a storm. Let's get back to the pub and some warm grub before they stop serving meals. I promise I'll take you up there soon. Maybe in the winter when the ground's hard with frost."

"What about Christmas Granddad. That would be the best present ever."

"Christmas! It's not even November yet Rosie. Anyway, come on. I'll race you to the bottom."

"Granddad!"

Rosie was going to say he shouldn't be running at his age, but he was already off, waving his walking stick in the air, as if he'd been possessed by the demonic gamekeeper he'd nicked it off.

She began to run after him, but he didn't get far. Down he went in the tussock grass by the side of the path, and when she reached him he was holding his ankle, in obvious pain.

"Granddad. What have you done now? I wish you could be sensible for once in a while!"

He looked up at her ruefully.

"You're beginning to sound like yer mother, and yer nobbut a scrap of a lass, not yet twelve. In fact yer beginning to sound like *my* mother!"

"Never mind that Granddad. What have you done? Does it hurt?"

"I've twisted me ankle. I went down that hole."
"I'd better go and get help."
"Let me get me breath back. I'm sure I'll be able to walk."
Unfortunately, when he tried, he soon sat back down again. Rosie decided he needed help, no matter how much he pretended otherwise. Storm-clouds were gathering and the wind was getting up.

This time she started down-hill, only stopping to shout over her shoulder, "I'll be back with the first person I find! Don't you dare run away!"

Despite attempting to tell Granddad he shouldn't run, Rosie ignored her own advice and sped down-hill like a young gazelle. Just past the reservoir she spotted a lad sat on the drystone wall, laughing at a terrier stood on its hind-legs and jumping up as if attempting to join him on his perch.

"Help!" she called. "Please help me!"
He looked up and scrambled down as she approached.
"What's matter?"
"My grandfather's twisted his ankle. He can't walk."
"Townie, is he?" he asked, somewhat scornfully.
She ignored him.
"Please help us!"
"Don't worry lass. How far away is he?"
"Just above William Clough."
She was already turning back, the dog yelping at her heels. The lad soon caught up.
"Don't panic lass. He won't come to any harm."
"The weather's turning. I don't want him getting drenched. He's an old man!"
"We'll soon have him safe and sound. Where you from?"
"Levenshulme in Manchester, but we live in Stockport now. Granddad was married to a woman from Little Hayfield."
"Oh Aye. What were her name?"
"Josie."
"Naw. I mean her second name afore she were wed."
"I've no idea. What does it matter? It's Granddad that's in trouble!"
"There's no need to get ratty. Eh, is that him by side o' path?"
"Yes. Granddad! Granddad!"
He looked up, a grin on his face, waving his stick.

"Are you all right Granddad?"
"Yes - I'm fine Rosie. I've just been contemplating the view."
"Can you use that stick to begin to lift yourself a little?" the lad interrupted. "Then I can get me arm under you. Once you're upright you can lean on me shoulder. Between your stick and me as a crutch we'll soon have you in the Sportsman."
"Yes. I reckon I can do that. Thanks fer yer help son."
"Least I can do. That's it. Now let me get... Right, now lean on me. I can take your weight, no fear."
"I'm all right. As long as I don't put weight on me foot."
"Okay. Let's be off, afore it starts raining."
Rosie was about to add, "Hop to it!" but something told her not to.

"What would you like to drink Granddad?"
The old man looked up from the menu he was perusing.
"Whose beer is it love?"
"Thwaite's."
"Then I'll have a pint of best bitter. What are you having lad?"
"I'd have same, but me Dad might come in. I'm only fifteen. He wouldn't be best pleased and I'm already in enough trouble. I'd best stick to lemonade."
Rosie left them whilst she placed the order.
"Are you comfortable? We should get a doctor to see that ankle Mr..."
"O'Donnell. Jack O'Donnell. What's your name lad?"
"Gartside. Ralph Gartside."
"Do you live in Hayfield?"
"Naw. Me Dad has a farm about a mile from here."
"Well Ralph. That's a name I won't forget in a hurry. Thanks fer all yer help. I'm really grateful and I'm sure our Rosie is too."
"She's a spirited young lass. She had me under orders from the word go."
"Aye. Our Rosie is a bit special. She's..."
"Here you are Granddad. Now what are we going to have to eat?"
Rosie placed the tray of drinks on the table top, and then bent down to fondle the terrier that had followed her to and from the bar.

No Man Has A Right To Own Mountains

"What's your name, little one?" she asked, fondling his ears as the dog looked up to her with its dark brown liquid eyes.

"He's called Titch, Rosie," Ralph responded. "He were the runt o' the litter."

"He's a lovely dog. I've always liked black and tan."

Titch wagged his tail, as if he understood every word.

"He seems to have taken to you, Rosie. Perhaps he recognises a fellow Manchester terrier?"

"What's *your* name?" she asked.

Before he had chance to answer, a noisy group of men in working clothes appeared through the pub entrance. One of them, a dark-haired sullen-looking man, spotted the young lad.

"What are you doin' in 'ere Ralph. Not cadgin' off tourists I hope! It's about time yer wur off home!"

All three looked across in surprise, but Rosie was the first to break the silence.

"I don't know who *you* are, but I'd have you know Ralph's rescued my Granddad from half-way up Kinder!"

"Well young Miss. I'm the lad's father an' I'll thank thee ter keep thee nose out of my business!"

"Mr Gartside," the old man intervened. "I don't want to come between father and son, but your Ralph has done me a great service and I've already invited him to dine with us. I trust you won't rob an old man of the pleasure of returning a kindness."

"Ne'er mind a kind..." He got no further. One of his younger companions took him firmly by the shoulder.

"Come an' sit thee seln down yer silly old so-and-so! Yer forever showin' us up Faither."

He dragged the scowling parent in to a side room, giving a wink over his shoulder to his younger brother as he did so.

"I'm so sorry..." Ralph started to say, but Granddad cut him short.

"Yer've nowt to apologise fer lad. We can't choose our relatives, but we can choose our friends. And you've been a friend to me and Rosie."

Rosie smiled and looked across at her new friend, rather shyly. Titch thumped his tail. Granddad passed the menu over.

"Now, Ralph, what do you recommend we order?"

Ashop Head

Chapter Four

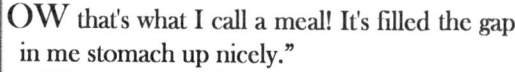

"NOW that's what I call a meal! It's filled the gap in me stomach up nicely."

"How's your ankle Mr O'Donnell?"

"I'm not goin' to be able ter get me boot back on. It's swollen up like a balloon. Anyhow lad, I'll survive, but let's have a bit less of the mister. Me name's Jack to me friends."

"But how are you going to get back home?"

"Is there a taxi service?"

"Aye. Old Ellis Broadbottom. Shall I ring him for you?"

"It would be helpful."

He glanced at the clock. It was coming up to three.

"Ask him if he can pick us up about six-thirty. I'm comfortable here and maybe Rosie would like to have a look round the village?"

Rosie looked up, still fondling Titch's ears.

"I'm fine Granddad. I need to keep you out of trouble. Anyway you haven't finished telling me about the trespass. Who's Benny Rothman and how does the Duke of thingymabob come in to it?"

"Devonshire, Rosie. The Duke of Devonshire. He owns most of the land hereabouts and the way he got it is an interesting tale in itself."

"Well - go on Granddad. We've only got three-and-a-half hours!"

"Patience is a virtue Rosie my love. Now to cut a long story short we have to go back to 1066."

"1066! What's that got to do with anything?"

The old man chuckled.

"That were the year England began to really become a nation. William of Normandy, the descendant of Norseman who'd settled in part of what is now France invaded our island and defeated Harold Godwin who claimed to be the lawful king. William changed the pattern of land-ownership for ever. He took all the land in to his own hands and then parcelled bits of it out to all the barons who'd helped him defeat Harold and to the Saxon Earls who collaborated with him. He introduced the feudal system and that's how England's system of private land-ownership began. William was the 'land-thief in chief' - he took the lot and gave it out to his favourite lackeys and Saxon traitors!"

"Oh! So that's how the Duke of thingymabob ended up owning Kinder?"

"No, at least not directly."

Rosie frowned.

"William kept a lot of the land out of private ownership. It was known as 'king's land,' or 'waste,' or 'forest,' or 'common land', depending on the part of the country it was in, or the use it was to be put to. Some of it was reserved for hunting and the keeping of game. On some of it people had the right to graze cattle, horses or sheep. In other parts people had the right to dig turf for their fires, to collect firewood, or to allow their pigs to forage for acorns. Most upland country, like Kinder was 'king's land,' and so it remained for seven hundred years, until the 18th century."

"What happened then?"

"The Enclosure Acts Rosie. Kinder were one of the prime examples, although it was rather late being enclosed."

"Why was it a prime example?"

"It were enclosed after 1830. Up to that point no individual owned it. It's wild land up there Rosie. Over 2,000 acres of it, mainly blanket bog, fit for nothing agricultural, but sheep grazing. Before it were enclosed people had the right to traverse it at will. There were innumerable tracks and old drove roads, some of them going back to Roman times. Over forty acres in two areas, one known as 'Poor Man's Piece' and the other as 'Poor Man's Wood,' were reserved for the use of the poor of Hayfield. Other hamlets and settlements dotted around Kinder had similar allotments.

"But from 1830 on all that changed. The land was surveyed and portions of it parcelled out to land-owners in the surrounding area. And what they did was to allot the biggest portions to the largest landowners. In other words to the rich, according to their riches, two-thousand acres were parcelled out, and to the poor, according to their poverty, no land was given, and the forty-acres they already had allocated for their use was taken away. You will find no mention of 'Poor Man's Piece' or 'Poor Man's Wood' on any modern map!"

"That's not fair!"

"There's nothing fair in a country like ours, run by rogues and villains, Rosie, except the weather, and that's only fair sometimes! Anyhow, I'm sure if you spoke to the local vicar he'd tell you it were all in line with the Bible's teachings."

"How can it be?"

The old man chuckled, picked up a paper napkin, folded it and tucked it under his shirt collar, like a clerical dog-collar. Then, in a deep voice he stated gravely - "'For whosoever hath, to him shall be given, and he shall have more abundance: but whosoever hath not, from him shall be taken away even that he hath.' Matthew, chapter 13, verse 12, the King James version of the Bible approved by both Church and State!"

He looked across the table at his granddaughter once more.

"So, you see young Rosie, because the Duke of Devonshire were the biggest landowner in the area, he got most of Kinder Scout! Mind you - there were another Christian cleric way back in the fourteenth century, John Ball be name, a follower of Saint Francis, a friar, who was one of the leaders of the landless English peasants in what was known as the Peasant's Revolt. He challenged the established church and the landed gentry using the teachings of the Bible as his weapon. He asked the question - 'When Adam delved and Eve span, who then was the Gentleman?' He argued that God had given the land to Adam and Eve and *all* their successors - not to a few noblemen!"

Ralph laughed.

"You and my old man have something in common at least. The two of yers would get on like house on fire, Mr O'Donnell! He's no so fond of the Devonshires."

"Why not lad?"

"He's a tenant farmer and they're his landlord."

"No wonder he's such a bad-tempered old so-and-so!"

Ralph laughed again.

"He's not that bad. His bark's worse than his bite. Like most hill-farmers he's going through a bad time. New Zealand lamb's dirt cheap and there's no call for wool. Me mother's wanting to start doing bed and breakfast, but the old man's dead against it. He says she'll be demeaning herself."

He shook his head. "He's a proud old so-and-so, but me and me brothers are working on him. Mum's quite right. We have to live and the farm doesn't provide enough income."

CHATSWORTH HOUSE - HOME OF THE DEVONSHIRES

"But what's so important about the land if it's not fit for anything but sheep?" Rosie intervened. "Why did the Duke of thingymabob stop people walking over it?"

"Grouse!" Ralph responded.

"Grouse?"

"Yes. They're a game bird, Rosie, and every year on the 'glorious twelfth' the Duke and his cronies go up on to the moors to shoot 'em!"

"You mean that's why my Grandma was...."

Rosie got no further. She was interrupted in full-flow by the sudden appearance of Ralph's father, accompanied by two younger men.

"Are you all reet ower Ralph?"

"Aye. Of course I am. What's the..."

"Come on Faither," one of the others interjected.

The older man shuffled his feet.

"I think - Well I reckon I owe thy friends an apology," he finally said, looking very uncomfortable. "Especially you young Miss. I'm sorry for me bad behaviour earlier."

Rosie smiled her sweetest smile. Granddad laughed.

"No offence were taken, Mr Gartside. Would you like a drink?"

"That's very handsome of thee. I'd..."

"Faither, we've cows ter milk!"

Young Ralph put in his two-pennorth.

"Sit down Faither. I'll do your chores. This is Mr O'Donnell and his granddaughter Rosie. This is me faither, Jed, Mr O'Donnell."

Granddad leant across the table, holding his hand out.

"Me name's Jack. I'm sorry I can't stand to shake yer hand. I'm non-walking wounded. Here our Rosie, take this ter the bar. I'll have bitter. You get yerself whatever you want. What about you Jed?"

"I'll have the same. It's very good of you."

"Your son tells me you're not a fan of the Devonshires."

"Ower Ralph's good at understatement!"

"I'll leave you to it Faither. Will you and Rosie be coming up again Mr O'Donnell?"

"Not if you don't start calling me Jack!" He paused for a moment.

"I've promised to take Rosie up to Edale Cross next weekend, but I don't know if I can manage it with this ankle and I hate the idea of disappointing her."

"She could stay with us, couldn't she Faither? She can have Sis's room. I can show her round and she'd be company fer ower Connie."

Chapter Five

O Rosie - and that's final!"

"Aw Mam! That's just not fair!"

"There's nothing fair in this..."

"Except for the weather. I know, but you're not a tyrant or a land-thief. You're my lovely Mam and you of all people should be fair! Granddad promised to take me and now he can't and now..."

"That's quite enough young Miss. I'm not having you traipsing off on your own to stay with strangers. You're only eleven for goodness sake!"

Rosie couldn't believe her ears. She flounced out of the kitchen in a rage, ignoring her grandfather who'd buried his head in the newspaper, desperately thinking how he could act as a go-between, and not sure his diplomatic skills would be anywhere near adequate. He listened as Rosie stomped up the stairs. Then she started coming down again and her head popped around the door.

"Granddad! Tell Mam I'm going on hunger strike and I might even run away in the night when you're both asleep!"

"You should never run-away on an empty stomach Rosie. I tried it once and it's not a good idea, believe you me."

Next minute she was on the sofa next to him, fighting back her tears.

"It's just not fair Granddad. Mam's just an old meany!"

He put his arm around her and within seconds she'd buried her head in his chest, sobbing her heart out.

"Come on Rosie. It's not the end of the world. Anyway, maybe me ankle will get better by next week. You never know."

Eventually she regained control.

"Does it hurt bad, Granddad?"

"Not really," he lied.

"We had a lovely day - apart from that - and we made some new friends because of it. I think Ralph's ever so nice and Titch is a lovely dog. Even Mr Gartside ended up being very kind."

"He did, didn't he. A bit of a surprise that. I'm glad you enjoyed your day love and we'll soon be able to go back. You shouldn't blame your mam. She only worries because she loves you. She's only trying to protect you."

"Humph! She's a wicked old witch sometimes!"

"Rosie! Don't say that."

"Well she is. It took me ages to convince her I could get the bus to school on me own. And if I can get the bus to school why can't I get the bus to Hayfield? Ralph said he'd meet me at the bus stop. She just doesn't understand me!"

He gave her shoulder a squeeze.

"Don't be too hard on ..."

"But why can't she be like you Granddad? You always understand me and you care about me just as much as Mam."

Meanwhile Alice, despite being busy in the kitchen, could hear every word and her ears were burning. She decided to intervene.

"Rosie, I..."

"Before you say anything Alice, I've had an idea."

She looked at her father, a frown creasing her troubled brow.

"What is it? I hope it's not another hare-brained scheme!"

"Why don't you take a bit of time off and relax? You need a break more than any of us. You could take Rosie up there and meet the Gartsides. If you're not happy with them you can bring Rosie back. If you are, you can let her stay the weekend. And - if you agree - I'll pay for you to stay at the Sportsman. You must remember it. It's a lovely pub and they do great food."

Rosie's eyes opened wide in delight. ["Good old Granddad - get out of that one Mam!"]

"Dad! I've things to do. I can't just drop everything. And how's an old cripple like you to manage without me?"

"Less of the old, Alice! As for being a cripple I'll get a crutch and anyway by next Friday I'll no doubt be able to hobble about."

["Y-e-s-s-!!! Go on Granddad. Don't let her off the hook!"]

"Well - I'll think about it. But I'm not promising anything."

She returned to her food preparation. Rosie turned to Granddad and put her arms around his neck, hugged him tight and kissed him on the cheek.

"Brilliant! You did it. I knew you would! Mam's going to take me. I'll betcha anything you like. Tomorrow tea-time she'll tell us."

Granddad chuckled.

"Don't cross your bridges before..."

"She will - she will! Betcha anything!"

The old man picked up his paper once more.

"You never told me about Benny Rothman or what you meant about the cops being cleverer than the game-keepers."

"I never did, did I."

"No - and I can't wait to find out."

"Food's almost ready! Can you set the table for me please Rosie?"

"Looks as though you'll have to wait love," Granddad said with a grin. "I'd help you but..."

"Coming Mam!"

He opened his newspaper once more, as Rosie disappeared in to the kitchen for the knives and forks, a big smile illuminating her face

❦❦❦

"Eh lass. You've done us proud!"

"Yes - that was lovely Mam. You make the best steak-and-kidney pie in the world. Can I clear the table and wash up for you?"

Alice looked at her daughter and frowned. Rosie tended to be helpful, but this was a bit over the top.

"No - we'll do it together. But I could murder a cup of tea and I bet Granddad could as well."

"I'll make it Mam!" and off she was like a shot.

Alice caught her father's twinkling eye.

"Why the bus? Last time I went to Hayfield it were by train."

"That dates yer lass. The line to Hayfield finally closed in 1970 - thanks to that stupid old so-and-so Beeching! Now we've got lorries and cars blocking up A6, bonnet to boot, burning petrol and diesel as if it were goin' out of fashion, spilling out their poisonous fumes and slowin' alt buses up. You mark my words. We'll be crying out fer railways soon, and trams fer that matter."

"You can't keep living in the past Dad. It's progress."

"Progress! Yer've got ter be joking, Alice. Progress means going forrards not backwards. They'll be privatising 'em next. And that means another land-grab!"

"What on earth are you talking about now? What's a land-grab got to do with it?"

"British Rail doesn't just own track and rolling stock. It owns vast acres of land. Station yards, old goods yards, all the land along the edge of the railway. Beautiful country stations, magnificent and highly profitable hotels, like the North Euston in Fleetwood and the Midland in Manchester. There'll be land speculators fallin' ower themselves ter get it at a knock-down price."

He returned to his paper.

"Well, there's not much we can do about it."

The paper went down.

"Isn't there! We could use our democratic rights and ensure Thatcher don't get back in, and we could occupy any land they tried ter sell off, if worse comes tert worse, and we could..."

"Dad - calm down!"

"Well - I can't help believing folk should stand up on their hindlegs. We shouldn't allow ourselns to be robbed left right and centre. So-and-so land-thieves!"

He turned back to his paper, then had second thoughts.

"An' I'll tell thee summat else. Any Government that says governments aren't fit to run public services and companies - ain't fit ter govern owt! If they can't organise the running of a railway - what right have they to say they're fit to run a country? Answer me that! They'll have us disposing of us own sewage soon and buryin' our own refuse an' diggin' well for water!"

"There's not room for a cess-pit in the backyard Dad."

"Pity. I were thinkin' of invitin' Thatcher fer tea!"

Chapter Six

"THANKS Mam."

"It's no use thanking me. It's Granddad's daft idea."

"Don't be like that Mam. You're going to love it. Just wait till you meet Titch and Ralph."

"Ermm. I must admit he sounded very nice on the phone."

"You spoke to Titch?"

"No, Ralph you daft ha'p'orth!"

Rosie grinned. They were sat on the upper deck of the bus, stuck in the traffic on the A6 between Disley and New Mills. The date was Friday the third of November 1989. It was now gone five o'clock and the sun had set a good half-hour before.

"We might have been better leaving it until tomorrow Rosie. We are not going to see anything tonight."

"But we'll be able to get up and be out as soon as it's light Mam. We'll have two full days to enjoy ourselves. Will you take me to Edale Cross?"

"Yes. Of course. But why there in particular?"

"Granddad told me that's where he first met Grandma."

"That's right, and guess what Rosie?"

"What Mam?"

"She'd tripped when she was running and sprained her ankle!"

"You mean it runs in the family?"

"Hopefully not. I haven't done it yet."

"What was she like?"

"Oh Rosie, Mum was so beautiful. She was a lovely kind gentle unflappable patient woman. Mind you, she had to be having to cope with Dad. Your granddad's always been the same. Up to some kind of mischief or other, although there's not a bit of harm in him. They were both wonderful parents. Me and your Uncle Billy couldn't have wished for better."

"Did you spend much time in Hayfield?"

"Hayfield, Little Hayfield with Mum's mother - she were another wonderful person, though her husband was a different kettle of fish. Edale as well. In fact we walked for miles all around the area. Mam Tor, Castleton, Winnats Pass, Ladybower, Bleaklow. You name it we tramped over it."

"Why didn't Granddad move to Little Hayfield when they got married? It's far nicer in the country."

"I suppose it was his job, Rosie. Grandma was a cotton-spinner at a mill in New Mills, but she was laid off in the depression. Granddad was an apprentice tool-maker in Higher Openshaw when he first met her and was lucky to escape the dole. Tool-makers are the highest skilled manual workers in the engineering industry. He's been very lucky. He's never been out of work in all his life. It was natural for your grandma to go and live with him when they married. There was no work for tool-makers where she lived."

"I wish I'd been able to meet Grandma, but I love Granddad."

"He is very special, isn't he Rosie. He was brilliant when I was a child and he's been my rock in the last few years."

She looked out of the window, peering in to the gloom, as if trying to work out where they were.

"Do you know something Rosie. He would never, under any circumstances, work over-time, although he would have been paid a lot extra if he had. He was often asked to do so. In fact he was threatened with the sack more than once for refusing to do so, but he stuck to his guns and wouldn't do it."

"Why not?"

"Because he said every hour at work was one less hour with Mum, me and Billy, and every hour of over-time worked kept somebody else out of work. He said that was wrong and he wouldn't have any part of it. He'd seen too many workers suffer in the 'thirties and he'd seen the look of hopelessness in all too many men's eyes when they were made redundant and told they had no future. Skilled hard-working family men thrown on the scrap-heap and an uncertain future.

"One of his mates took his own life because of it and that affected your Granddad badly. That's one of the reasons why we had such a wonderful childhood. Dad took us walking and camping at every opportunity he could. He didn't just want to spend time with us. He wanted us to run wild and learn about the world we lived in, and not mope around the house or be stuck in a dirty town. That's why I'm really

pleased he's started taking you walking."
Rosie smiled. Her mother sounded quite enthusiastic.

TITCH

"I'm glad you think kids should spend as much time in the country as possible, Mam. I'm really looking forward to running wild. All those weekends and bank holidays to come, not to mention school holidays! You might have to stand in for Granddad for weeks - months even. You never know - it might be ages before he can walk properly. The doctor said old people take longer to heal, and Granddad mustn't rush the healing process, didn't he?"

Alice looked in to her daughter's eyes, a look of something like consternation on her own face.

"Rosie, I...."

"Come on Mam. We're almost there. Ralph will be waiting! Don't forget your back-pack!"

She grabbed her own ruck-sack and was already heading for the stairs before her mother had a chance to respond.

Rosie was the first off the bus and Alice wasn't too far behind. As promised, Ralph was waiting for them and he had Titch with him. After the initial introductions they began to make their way through the dark narrow streets, lights shining dully through curtains, their boots echoing on the cobbles. Somewhere a dog barked. Titch's head went up, ears erect and alert, but he remained silent. Ralph informed them that his mother had prepared a room for Alice as well as Rosie.

"But Dad's arranged for me to stay at the Sportsman."

"That was before me mother decided to sort the other room out. Didn't Mr O'Donnell tell you?"

Alice frowned. "No he didn't!"

Rosie smiled her quiet smile.

"Well I spoke to him at lunch-time and he said he'd cancel the booking. You see Mother wants to prove to Faither she can make a go of providing bed and breakfast for tourists. You and Rosie are a kind of experiment, although Faither don't know it."

"Well it's very kind of your mother, but if she's conducting an experiment we'd better pay. She can have the money I was going to pay the Sportsman."

"No you won't. Mother won't accept it."

"In that case I'll stay at the pub. If your mother's going to make a go of bed and breakfast she's going to have to charge and she might as well start straight away. That's the only way she'll conduct a successful experiment!"

"My mother can be very strong-willed. I don't think she'll accept."

"My Mam's very stubborn too," Rosie informed him. "I think we are in for an interesting weekend. What do you think Titch?"

Titch wagged his tail - vigorously.

They started up Kinder Road, eventually reaching the Sportsman. Ralph rooted in his pockets, left-hand first, and handed a torch to Alice, whilst he delved in to his right-hand pocket.

"You'll need that Mrs O'Donnell and I've got one for you Rosie. There's no lights where we're heading and there's too much cloud for the moon to be of much use."

"Thanks Ralph. But O'Donnell's my maiden name. Both Rosie and me are called Akroyd."

"I'm sorry. I never thought!"

"Why should you? It's a natural mistake."

"How far is the farm, Ralph?"

"Not far Rosie. Once we're past the campsite, Edale Road goes off to the right. The farm's just through Coldwell Clough."

"That's the beginning of the old pack-horse route to Edale isn't it?" Alice asked.

"Yes. Do you know it?"

"I certainly do. I've walked it to Edale many a time. You're lucky Rosie. It's the way to Edale Cross. I'll take you tomorrow and, if you can walk that far, we'll go to the Nag's Head in Edale itself for something to eat."

She turned to Ralph.

"Do they still have the children's bar at the back of the pub?"

"Yes - and the old-fashioned penny slot machines. I used to love them when I were a kid."

"Oh my, Rosie. It's all coming back to me. What fun we had when we used to come up here. Wait 'till you see Jacob's Ladder and Mam Tor and... Oh, there's such a lot to see and explore! You're going to love it."

Rosie smiled quietly to herself, but didn't say a word. She didn't have to. All was going to plan. Precisely as she told Granddad it would do; the only problem being that he wasn't there to enjoy it.

OLD PACK HORSE BRIDGE

Chapter Seven

"WAKEY-wakey, Mam. Here's a cup of tea!"
"Rosie! What time is it?"
"Half-past-seven Mam. Breakfast will be ready when you've had that and got dressed. Did you have a good-night's sleep?"
"I think so. I think I want to go back to sleep."
"Come on. We've things to see and things to do. We can't let the day go to waste!"
Alice struggled upright, wiping the sleep from her eyes.
"You're pinching my lines Rosie. What on earth's got in to you?"
"I've been up for ages. I've been helping Ralph milk the cows and I collected the eggs for breakfast and I'm helping Mrs Gartside prepare it."
And with that she was off, down the old uneven staircase, leaving her mother to enjoy her tea and struggle to face up to a new day in strange surroundings.
As Rosie entered the kitchen Mrs Gartside smiled.
"What shall I do next?" Rosie asked.
The farmer's wife shook her head.
"I've everythin' under control here, love. Why don't you relax. Take Titch outside if you want. He seems to have taken to you. I'll give you a shout when I'm ready to serve breakfast."
Titch was sprawled out on the multi-coloured flock mat in front of the roaring coal fire. He looked across, ears pricked on hearing his name.
"Does he need a lead?"
"No love. Titch is well-trained."
Rosie squatted down.
"Here boy."
Titch responded, tail wagging. Rosie fondled his ears.
"Take me for a walk Titch. There's a good dog."
The tail wagged faster. Mrs Gartside laughed.
"I'd swear he understands every word Rosie. Don't forget to wrap up warm. It's pretty cold out there. Stay in the yard and don't go in to the

buildings alone. Farm's are dangerous places. I'll shout you when breakfast's ready. Don't wander off."

No sooner said than done. Rosie shut the door behind her and gazed around the farmyard for a moment. The back of the farm-house faced straight on to the moor. A couple of fields gently sloping uphill were bounded by drystone walls, immediately behind which the hill swept steeply upwards, the course of a stream marked by a line of trees; a distinct tracery of gnarled twisted black trunks and leafless branches against the otherwise dark mixture of rough grasses, bracken and small clumps of stunted heather. In one of the fields, half a dozen cows grazed. In the other, sheep cropped the grass, their chorus of bleats blending with the soft sough of the wind and the sound of running water.

To the left stood a tall stone barn, forming a right angle with the farmhouse and acting as a windbreak from the westerly winds, which swept in from the Irish Sea across the Lancashire plain, Kinder being the first major land-mass in their moisture laden path. To the right a low stone building, containing the cattle-byre and a couple of old stables completed a U shape enclosing the cobbled farmyard on three sides.

An old tractor, rusting away, stood in the far left corner. It caught Rosie's eye. She walked over to it and clambered up onto the cold steel seat, shaped as if moulded by a human backside, albeit one much larger than hers, and mounted on a long curved spring. This, to Rosie's surprise and delight, gave under her weight before springing upwards once more. A see-saw designed for one! She bounced up and down, gripping its sides, whilst Titch stood on his hind-legs, his fore-paws on the tractor's massive drive-shaft cover, his alert eyes concentrating on his new friend, watching her every move.

Rosie gazed around taking in her immediate surroundings. More farm implements - an old plough and a harrow - lay next the wall, slowly oxidising a rich red brown amongst a profusion of nettles. Once more her attention was drawn upwards to the jagged gritstone edge high above and the overcast sky, the colour and texture of her old grey duffel coat, reserved for wearing to school on cold winter days. A crunch of feet on loose stones. Ralph and his father appeared around the end of the cow-byre, obviously deep in conversation and unaware of her presence. At the same time, her mother appeared at the farmhouse door, the top half of which she'd opened.

"Breakfast Rosie!"

The youngster jumped off the tractor, attracting the attention of the farmer and his son.

"Good mornin' lass," Mr Gartside greeted her with a smile.

"Morning Mr Gartside, Ralph. Breakfast's ready."

"Aye - me belly were already telling me!"

"What are your plans for the day Rosie?" Ralph asked. "Are you still going to Edale?"

"I think so."

"Ralph ud better go with thee ah reckun," the farmer responded.

"Faither - yer were just telling me..."

"That were then. This is now! I quite fergot about young Rosie an' her mother. You can be theer guide. Weather's so unpredictable at this time o' year."

Ralph shook his head, thinking the weather was far more predictable than his father, but didn't argue. Rosie smiled her sweet smile. She was fast developing a soft-spot for old Mr Gartside.

They made their way in to the kitchen-cum-dining room. Mr Gartside immediately went to the black-leaded cast iron fireplace, squatting down to give the burning coals a poke before warming his hands.

Ralph headed to the door that led to the stairs.

"I'll get our Connie. Is she awake Mother?"

"Yes, and dressed. She's playing with her crayons."

Mrs Gartside turned to Rosie.

"Sit thee seln down lass and you too Alice. Do you like porridge or cornflakes?"

"Both, but can I have porridge please?"

"I'll have the same as Rosie, but please let me help, Elsie," Alice responded.

"No. Too many cooks spoil... Anyway, you're my guest, so sit down please."

Mr Gartside joined them, whilst Mrs Gartside placed bowls of porridge and a fresh jug of milk before them. Moments later Ralph re-entered the room, a young girl, with long hair the colour of carrots and a face full of smiles, held in his arms.

"This is my sister, Connie," he announced to nobody in particular, although his eyes were on Rosie.

Mrs Gartside grabbed an old wooden chair with a curved spindle back and arm rests, placing it at the table opposite Rosie.

"Sit her here Ralph. Would you like porridge Connie love?"

"Please."

Ralph carefully seated her in the chair as his mother placed a bowl of steaming porridge in front of the girl. He took the vacant seat next to her. She picked up her spoon, but then looked up, her eyes wide and an unusual shade of green, gazing straight in to Rosie's own, as if trying to access the very depths of the other girl's soul.

"Hullo," she suddenly said breaking the momentary silence. "Do you like reading?"

Rosie, caught off balance by the unexpected question, hesitated before informing her that she did.

"Will you read to me at bed-time tonight? Ralph's bought me a new book."

"Yes. Of course I will."

Connie smiled and began to attack her breakfast.

"Would you like to walk to Edale Cross with us?" Rosie asked.

Connie shook her head.

"I can't," she said. "I can't walk anywhere. Not until I get me new leg!"

She smiled once more and returned her attention to her food.

FARM AT COLDWELL CLOUGH

Chapter Eight

"IS that it? I thought it would be massive."

"Well, it may not be very big, but it's very old and once upon a time it would have been mounted on a large stone base no doubt."

"But it's got a date, Ralph. 1810. Granddad told me it was medieval!"

"Your grandfather's quite right Rosie. The date was carved on it by three farmers. They found it buried in the peat. It's definitely much older. They carved the date on it when they erected it here in 1810, along with their initials."

"Oh."

Alice laughed.

"You don't have to sound so sceptical Rosie. Ralph's not going to misinform you any more than granddad would."

"I just expected something grander."

She rested her arms on top of the wall and gazed across the Edale valley. The old pack-horse track stretched ahead, to her left, following the contour of the hill as it rounded the great bulk of Kinder Low. She pointed, turning to Ralph as she did so.

"What's that great lump there?"

"That's Mam Tor. See how it's shaped at the top. It were home to quite a large number of people a long time ago Rosie. It were an Iron Age fort. You can still make out the defensive ditches around the summit."

"Why did people live so high up?"

"Because it was safer. The valleys were dangerous places made up of dense forest, marshy ground and populated by wild animals. People lived up on Kinder during the Neolithic age..."

"Neo what?"

"Neolithic, Rosie. Basically the stone age."

"How do you know?"

"Because archaeologists have discovered stone axes and other tools buried under the peat. Neolithic man inhabited the area, and all this high ground was heavily wooded. They cut and burned the trees down to make clearings for their settlements and for pasture. Then, over thousands of years, the weather caused erosion and the wood turned in to peat. People think this is all wild natural country, but human beings have helped shape it along with Nature."

"How do you know?" Rosie repeated.

"I was taught it in school and there's information about it in the Edale National Park Information Centre."

"Come on Rosie," Alice interrupted. "If we shape ourselves we'll have time to visit the Information Centre, then you can see for yourself."

They re-commenced their journey and for once Rosie remained quiet, seemingly content to gaze around her to take in the magnificent views stretching out before her and to her right. However, this unusual turn of events didn't last long.

"Ralph. What did Connie mean about getting a new leg?"

"She had an accident, Rosie, about four years ago. She were hit by a motor-bike and it damaged her leg. They had to amputate, just below the knee."

"That's terrible," Alice responded. "Why's she had to wait so long for an artificial leg?"

"She hasn't. It's just that she's growing fast. She were only six when the accident happened. She's ten now. The leg's been lengthened twice. Normally she would have had a replacement already, but there's been some new developments. A new kind of fitting was invented earlier this year, in America I think, and Connie will be one of the first to try it in this country. There's been a slight hold up. Trouble is her old leg's worn, the sockets damaged and it hurts her when she wears it, so she's hanging on for the new one."

"Will she be able to walk then?" Rosie asked.

"Yes. She can walk fine now. She's hoping to be able to run. The only trouble is she tends to overdo it and overtires herself. It takes a lot more energy using an artificial limb. She wants to keep up with all her friends. She's stubborn, just like Faither."

"She's such a little thing."

"Yes, she is Rosie, but don't let that kid yer. My little sister's as tough as old boots and always up ter mischief. Whatever you do, don't let her think you feel sorry for her."

"Oh dear," Alice said. "Maybe we'd best keep the two of them separated. Connie and Rosie might form a lethal combination!"

"Mam!"

Alice laughed. "I'm only joking." She smiled and winked at Ralph. "At least I think I'm only joking."

"Where's Titch?"

Ralph stopped in his tracks.

"I've no idea Rosie. Maybe he got fed up and went home."

"But, he was here a moment ago."

"I wouldn't worry Rosie. He's unlikely to get lost."

At that moment something caught his eye.

"Now Rosie," he said, gripping her shoulder momentarily. "There's something I bet you haven't seen before."

She followed his pointing finger.

"Where? I can't see anything."

"There. Just under that boulder, half-way up the slope."

"Oh - look Mam. It's a white rabbit."

"No," Ralph interjected. "It's a mountain hare, Rosie. They turn completely white in winter. In summer they're a light brown or grey with a white belly. The Dark Peak is the only place in England you find them. There's plenty in Scotland and a few in the Isle of Man."

Alice strained her eyes, but it was some time before she located the animal and then it was on the move.

"I think I'm going to have to buy some binoculars," she said. "I want to see the ring ouzels in the spring."

"Ring ouzels? What are they?"

"Mountain blackbirds," Alice and Ralph informed her in the same breath.

They rounded a bend in the track.

"Look - there's Titch!" Rosie exclaimed. "With that man."

The rather diminutive figure, sitting on a rock in the shelter of the drystone wall, was eating a sandwich, bits of which he was breaking off for the dog. He looked up as they approached, a broad smile on his face. Rosie thought he looked for all the world like a wizened old elf.

Alice suddenly asked, "Is that you Benny?" and without waiting for an answer followed up with, "It's so good to see you. What are you doing up here?"

Apparently he was who she thought he was, for he scrambled to his feet, his hand extended.

"Alice O'Donnell isn't it? This is a pleasant surprise. How's your dad?"

"Sat at home, nursing a twisted ankle." She laughed. "Is it that long since we met? I married ages ago, Benny. My name's Akroyd. This is my daughter Rosie and our friend Ralph."

He nodded and shook Ralph's hand, before turning his attention to Rosie.

"Goodness Alice. She's the spitting image of your mother!"

Rosie smiled, but something niggled at the back of her mind. There was something strangely familiar about this peculiar looking man with his impish smile and elven features, yet she knew she had never met him before.

"Are you on your way to Edale, Alice?"

"Yes. We're heading for the Nag's Head for lunch. We're staying with Ralph on his dad's farm. Ralph rescued Dad last weekend."

"Do you mind if I join you?"

"Of course not Benny. What an idea. It's our pleasure. I just wish Dad was here. He'll be kicking himself when I tell him."

"Is he keeping well - apart from his ankle?"

"He's fighting fit. He brought Rosie up here last Saturday to show her the scene of the battle. He twisted his ankle running down William Clough of all places!"

Benny chuckled.

"Silly old sod!"

Rosie smiled, awareness dawning.

"Are you Benny Rothman?" she asked, somewhat shyly.

"Yes - I plead guilty to that Rosie, although I've been called far worse."

"Granddad says you're a living legend. He says..."

"Your granddad always had a tendency to be carried away with his own words, Rosie. As you can see, I'm a perfectly ordinary bloke."

Ralph smiled to himself. He might be only fifteen, but he'd seen the photographs and the displays in the National Park Information Centre, and he'd heard his father's debates with some of his farming colleagues. There were those who loved him and those who spoke about him with scorn - but there were few who didn't respect Benny Rothman.

All four began the descent of Jacob's Ladder, Rosie carefully rehearsing the questions she wanted to put to the old man as soon as they reached the Nag's Head. Granddad had never finished his story of the Mass Trespass. She needed to know what happened after they'd descended from Ashop Moor; why Granddad said those events had changed Britain's history for the better and the role his friend Benny Rothman had played in them

BENNY ROTHMAN

Thus Rosie returned to the farm a wiser young lady than when she'd started out that morning, and both Alice and Ralph returned with more information than they'd hitherto known. Little did she know that she still had a lot more to learn and that a surprise awaited her. She was the first across the yard, apart from Titch.

She opened the door to the kitchen and stopped in her tracks. A smiling face grinned at her from across the table, through the vapour arising from a mug of tea he was about to take a sip from. What looked

like a brand new crutch leant against the back of his chair.
"Granddad! How did you get here? Guess who I've met?"

※ ※ ※

MOUNTAIN OR ARCTIC HARE

Chapter Nine

"SO, what did you learn from Benny?"

"Well, that he and five others landed in jail for a start and that you were lucky not to!"

The old man nodded his head, but didn't speak.

"He explained how a group of coppers were waiting at the bottom of William Clough, near the reservoir, and how, when they tried to make arrests, the trespassers chased them away."

Granddad laughed, but Rosie hadn't finished.

"And he told me how the Chief Constable met you on Kinder Road and suggested you followed his car down towards the railway station and the police were waiting there and arrested Benny and his friends."

The old man nodded again.

"And he said the police wanted to let them go, but the Duke of thingymabob insisted on charging them, and Benny said that were the biggest mistake he could have made because it made them notorious and everybody were up in arms and thought they were being badly treated and all kinds of people were upset by it and so it became a massive public campaigning issue."

Granddad chuckled.

"Don't rush all at once, Rosie my love. Try taking a breath now and again. But you're quite right. The Duke of Devonshire shot himself in the foot and that's how the course of English history was changed. The public outcry was taken up by politicians and eventually after the War the new Labour Government brought in the first Access to the Countryside Act and initiated the first National Park, which is where we are now - in the Peak District National Park."

"Yes Granddad. But Benny said it wasn't the first mass trespass and it wasn't the last and there's going to be even more. He said it was only one battle in a war that hasn't been won. There's still hundreds of thousands of acres of uncultivated land where it's still illegal to walk and we still have to fight for the right to have the freedom to roam in our own country, and he's promised to let me know when the next one will

49

take place. I've given him our phone number and he'll be in touch. And so you see, Granddad, I'm going to be a trespasser too!"

Mrs Gartside laughed.

"Good for you Rosie. That's the spirit."

"I think I'll be a trespasser as well!"

Up to that point Connie hadn't spoken. She sat in front of the fire, her carroty red hair gleaming dark-gold in the light from the glowing coals, stroking Titch who lay in the crook of her one good leg, although she'd been listening attentively to everything that had been said.

"Connie," Mrs Gartside responded. "Don't set yourself tasks..."

"I'm not helpless Mum. As soon as I've got me new leg I'd like to show Rosie the Mermaid's Pool."

"You'll never get up there!"

"She already has," Ralph interrupted, his voice soft. "I went with her. It was last July. Connie's much more agile than you think."

THE MERMAID'S POOL FROM KINDER

"But - why did you never tell me?"

Mrs Gartside appeared staggered by this information.

Connie shook her head sending her wavy hair sweeping in a great curve, before looking in to her mother's eyes.

"I swore Ralph to secrecy. I didn't want to worry you. Anyway, if I'd told you where we were going, you would have stopped me."

"What's the Mermaid's Pool?" Rosie wanted to know. "I thought you only got mermaids in the sea."

"There's lots of tales about it..." Ralph began, before his sister interjected.

"A beautiful water nymph with a fish's tail lives there, Rosie. And on the Eve of Easter at midnight she comes to the surface and if any man sees her she has the power to make him immortal, providing he's truly not afraid of her and treats her with courtesy. But, if she takes a dislike to him, for any reason, she will drag him down in to the cold dark depths and make him her slave and he'll never be seen again."

"It's all nonsense," Mrs Gartside interrupted. "There's another story that an old woman annoyed a few of the farmers hereabouts and they accused her of being a witch. They got the local parson involved and it was decided to put her to the test, by throwing her in the pool. Poor lass couldn't swim and so she drowned - and the parson said that proved she'd been a witch all along."

She chuckled and then added, "Some said the old woman had turned cow's milk sour and made horses lame and sheep miscarry. Others reckon she were a Roman Catholic and had annoyed the parson because she wouldn't convert. Aye - and they reckon that parson disappeared and rumour has it that he lives in a great cavern beneath the Mermaid's Pool, having to wait on the mermaid and the old woman night and day, and will only be seen again on the final Judgement Day!"

"From what I've been told, it all goes back to Celtic pagan times, long before Christianity were heard of," Ralph informed them. "The Eve of Easter is the clue. Pagans divided the year in to two - the dark half and the light half - and in Britain the light half roughly begins in April. They also believed that a pool was the entrance to another world. There's even one idea that the pool is that deep it connects with the Irish Sea and that's how the mermaid arrived here in the first place."

"It all sounds very spooky to me," Rosie said, "and the wind's getting up something fierce."

"Well, you're going to have to brave the elements, Rosie," Ralph said, "It's time we all went down to the old quarry."

"Why?"

"Because it's November the 4th and we're havin' the bonfire tonight," Connie informed her.

"Oh! I'd forgot about bonfire night, but how are you getting there?" "Same as your granddad, if he's coming. On a crutch." She shuffled her bottom across the room in to a corner by the old Welsh dresser, retrieved her emergency walking aid and Rosie watched as she used it to pull herself upright. Once having it under her armpit, she swung around triumphantly.
"You can help me Rosie, by shining a torch so neither of us trips up. Can you get me coat, hat and scarf, Ralph?"
Granddad looked on in wonder. If he'd been asked to walk down to the quarry two minutes before, he'd have made his excuses. Now, he realised he had little choice but to accompany them.

From that moment on, Connie and Rosie became virtually inseparable, at least when Rosie visited the farm and on the occasions when Connie was the guest of her mother and granddad. Rosie already had a caring instinct and a respect for her elders, not least because of the role her grandfather had played in her life, but Connie provided something to emulate - a zest for life and a determination to overcome difficulties in a way that Rosie had hitherto not encountered. Furthermore, Ralph's statement that his little sister was as tough as old boots, and was always up to some kind of mischief, was soon to be proved an understatement if ever there was one.

Quite naturally Rosie had enjoyed the bonfire and the fireworks, the hot potatoes baked in the embers at the side of the fire, the homemade parkin which seemed to have been brought to the event by every household, such was its abundance, the sticky treacle toffee, the displays of Catherine wheels and golden fountains, the Roman candles and the final barrage of rockets fired off in the general direction of the moon.

But the thing that stuck in her mind for a long time after was the pluckiness of her young female companion. At one point a group of lads were throwing rip-raps behind their elders' ankles. Connie had confronted three of them, who'd frightened a particularly frail old lady. One of them told her she was "nowt but a one-legged cripple," and to "mind thy own business."

Without a word she'd made a pretend lunge at him and, as he turned to flee, shot out her crutch, expertly tripping him up in the process and sending him flying in to the mud churned up by the congregation's boots, much to the mirth of his companions.

"I might be a one-legged cripple," she told him, "but I'm twice as fast as thee Mikey Grimsditch an' always will be!"

Chapter Eleven

WINTER had come and gone and Rosie was almost part of the Gartside's farm-house furniture, she spent so much time under their roof. Sometimes her mother accompanied her, sometimes Granddad and sometimes both, but increasingly she visited on her own.

The long Easter school holidays of 1990 were no different and on Friday the 6th of April she'd disembarked from the bus in Hayfield and was walking up the Kinder Road, eager to meet up with Connie, Titch and Ralph.

It was one of those lovely spring afternoons, with a slight westerly wind. The sky was clear and the leaves were in bud as she crunched gravel and eventually made her way on to the winding track up to Coldwell Clough. As she trudged uphill she could hear the burbling brook tumbling and falling over its rock-strewn bed below and to her right, and the bleating of sheep on the opposite hillside. The track narrowed and she was under a lace-worked canopy of trees lining both sides, the steep-sided banking in their shade a vivid azure carpet of nodding bluebells.

"Ah-ah - gotcha!"

Connie emerged from behind a tree, her face illuminated by her smile. Overcoming her initial surprise, Rosie laughed.

"How long have you been there?"

"Ages. You're late. You've been dawdling."

"How's your mother?"

"She fine, except she's fussing about like a mother hen. She's three people staying this weekend. You're going to have to share my room again."

"How awful," Rosie responded, pulling her face in mock distaste. "You'd better not put your leg under my bedclothes like you did last time."

"It's a lovely leg, Rosie. Far better than the old one. I'm practising for school sports' day. Mikey Grimsditch thinks he's still the fastest runner in our class, but he's in for a surprise this year."

As if to prove her point she set off up the road, Rosie desperately trying to keep up with her. They crested the hill by the farm-gate neck and neck. Ralph was perched atop it. Titch appeared and ran to greet them, jumping up at Rosie in delight. She knelt down to fondle his ears and he licked her face to show his appreciation.

"Did you have a good journey Rosie?"

"Yes thanks, Ralph."

She looked up at him. His face broke in to a smile and his teeth flashed white against the background of his brown face. It struck her all of a sudden he was quite a handsome lad. She returned his smile and he jumped down.

"Let me take your ruck-sack. You must be tired."

She slipped it off her shoulder and handed it to him. They were just about to make their way around the side of the cow-byre to access the yard and the kitchen door when they were attracted by the sound of nailed boots advancing towards them. Two men were coming down the track, both dressed in greeny-brown camouflage jackets and trousers. Ralph frowned and leant back, lounging against the stone-wall as they passed, deep in conversation. Then he walked out in to the lane, as if to see which way they went and then came back.

"What's the matter Ralph?" Connie asked, sensing her big brother was worried about something.

"Let's get round the back. They're both keepers and I reckon they're up to no good. I want to see where they're going."

They did as he asked, but when they reached the yard Mrs Gartside was collecting her washing off the line.

"Hiya young Rosie. How are you?"

"Great, Mrs Gartside. Can I help?"

Without waiting for an answer she began to pull a sheet off the line and the farmer's wife helped her fold it, before placing it in the wicker basket with the rest. Meanwhile Ralph and his sister were peering in to the distance, both leaning against the drystone wall.

"Thanks Rosie love. Come inside. We'll have a brew."

The woman and the girl made their way in to the kitchen. Old Mr Gartside was slumped in his favourite armchair, by the fire, a newspaper on his lap and fast asleep, judging by his intermittent soft snuffling snores. They'd already made the brew by the time Ralph and Connie entered. Ralph looked across at his father. Rosie thought he was going to

say something to him, but he hesitated and then turned away, obviously reluctant to wake him.
Eventually Mrs Gartside gave her husband a prod and summoned all to the table for their evening meal. She told them that her paying guests had only booked bed and breakfast and had informed her they'd be dining in the George in Hayfield that evening. Mr Gartside nodded and suggested he might look in to converting the barn for self-catering accommodation, pointing out another farmer in Barber Booth was doing it.
Throughout the meal, Ralph remained unusually quiet and after they'd finished he'd refused a cup of tea and seemed increasingly restive. In fact at the first opportunity he said he had someone to see, donned his jacket and was out the door before anybody could query what he was in such a hurry for. Titch seized his opportunity and followed him.

※※※

It wasn't until Rosie and Connie were alone in the bedroom, getting undressed, that the younger girl brought up the subject that had troubled Ralph earlier. By then it was raining hard, drops rattling against the window panes in noisy gusts, as if somebody was throwing small pebbles against the glass to annoy them. The wind had got up and was howling around the farm-house. The old tree at the back of the house, almost adjacent to their window, creaked ominously as it swayed under its influence.
Connie informed Rosie that a pair of peregrine falcons had returned for a second year to re-build their nest on a gritstone outcrop near the Kinder Downfall, above the Mermaid's Pool. Evidently the raptors were still fairly rare in the area, having been persecuted, along with all other falcons and hawks, since the land was enclosed. Ralph had found a dead raven near the same site only the previous Wednesday. He thought it had been poisoned, perhaps accidentally by insecticide, but when he'd seen the two keepers in camouflage and noticed they'd struck off across open land towards the Mermaid's Pool his suspicions had been aroused. Poisoning and trapping ravens and raptors was common in the areas where land was reserved for game, although the birds were supposed to be protected by the law.
"Last year, Faither found a goshawk's nest scattered round the base

of a tree. Somebody had climbed up it and taken the complete nest."
"That's terrible!" Rosie responded.
"Yes and there were three eggs, all smashed, next to it."
"So that's where Ralph was going. I thought he rushed his tea and he never said a word before he put on his jacket and left in such a hurry."
"Yes - he's gone to check on the nest."
"But why should anybody want to harm the birds?"
"Sheer ignorance and prejudice. That's what Ralph says. The keepers see the raptors as a threat to their blessed grouse. Sometimes they'll take a chick or even their eggs, but they only do it to live. They have to eat, the same as any creature. The keepers guard the grouse so that gangs of boys with sticks can beat the moor and drive them to where the gentry are waiting behind their hides to blast them out of the sky with their double-barrelled shot guns."

She smiled wryly at Rosie.
"They call it sport. Ralph calls it butchery and the people who do it spineless cowards and chinless wonders. He loves birds. In fact he loves all wild things. If he ever catches a keeper - or anybody else for that matter - harming any wild thing - well, I'd hate to be in their boots!"

"He's a really lovely boy," Rosie said as she climbed in to bed and snuggled under the blanket.

Connie gave her a knowing look, before saying "Good-night, sleep tight," as she switched off the bedside light.

"Watch the bugs don't bite!" responded Rosie.

Both girls were soon in the land of Nod, dreaming their distinctive dreams.

PEREGRINE FALCON

Rosie found herself standing in a shaft of sunlight on a jagged rock looking down at the Mermaid's Pool, its surface partially shrouded in a milky-white mist. A gigantic bird with a curved yellow beak and piercing

57

black and gold eyes suddenly appeared, flying out of the pool in a great shower of spray.

At first she thought it carried a mermaid on its back, but when she looked again she realised that what she'd assumed was a fish-tail stretched along its tail feathers was in fact a single slender leg, coated in tiny water droplets, glistening silver for all the world like shiny scales. The girl smiled at her and waved. She had distinctive green eyes and long carroty-red hair floating about her head and face in the warm fresh spring breeze, like a banner of defiance - or of revolution.

☙❦❧

Chapter Twelve

BOTH girls rose early the next morning. The wind and rain had spent their fury. Sun was shafting in to the room, through a gap in the curtains, and the air seemed alive with birdsong.

"I think we should walk over towards Mam Tor," Connie suddenly said as she donned her artificial limb with its new vacuum socket.

"We'll get onto the ridge of Rushop Edge and go over to Mam Nick."

Rosie nodded, perfectly happy to walk wherever the younger girl decided.

"Will we be able to go up to the summit and see the hill-fort?"

"Hopefully. Once we're at Mam Nick it's only a fairly short steep scramble."

"Will we need to take food?"

"No. There's usually a mobile food-stall in the car park below it, and sometimes an ice-cream van."

By the time they'd gone downstairs Mrs Gartside was dishing out bacon and eggs to Ralph. His father sat beside him, a used plate wiped clean indicating he'd already had his fill. Both were in discussion, the latter seemingly agitated about something.

"Good morning everybody," Rosie said.

"Aye - it's a lovely day lass," the old farmer responded, his mood changing in an instant. "Did thee both have a good sleep? What are thee plans fer terday ower Connie?"

"I'm taking Rosie over Mount Famine, then up Rushop Edge and on to Mam Tor."

"Eh lass. Are thee sure. It's a good walk."

"That's why we're going there. Not much point if it's not a good walk is it?"

The old man laughed.

"I wish I could keep up with thee, Connie love. I really do." He rose from his seat and left the room, emerging in moments wearing a rather ragged old coat and a battered and equally old flat cloth cap. "Reet. I'll love thee and leave thee, and mind yer remember what I said Ralph."

"Everything will be fine Faither. Stop fretting."

"Well - look on. I won't be back 'till late afternoon. I'll go an' pick old Sutcliffe's brains about his self-catering barn and then I'm off ter see our Richard and Jem in Bradwell."

"Okay Faither. I'll see to things here."

"Well - just don't ferget that ewe in't barn. I reckun she's about ter drop twins and she allus has problems droppin' more than one."

"Don't worry Faither."

"I can't help worryin' lad. I dunna know what we gonna do about cows, unless we can find somebody else ter tek milk!"

He was about to close the kitchen door behind him when he turned and grinned at Rosie.

"Have a good day lass and don't let that dowter o' mine lead yer inter mischief."

"Umph!" Connie exclaimed, turning to Ralph as soon as her father had disappeared. "I was hoping you and Titch would come with us."

"So did I," Rosie said without thinking.

Ralph gave her a bemused look and then turned to his sister, as Rosie blushed.

"It can't be helped, Connie. But take Titch. He'll keep you out of trouble."

"Fat chance! I'm always dragging him out of holes. He's never got me out of one yet!"

"Well - there's a first time for everything, our Con!"

"Can I get a word in sideways...?"

"Porridge first, please Mum," Connie responded, whilst Rosie nodded her head to second the motion.

Mrs Gartside retreated to her stove once more, wondering when her guests would appear in the front parlour.

※ ※ ※

After breakfast Ralph went in to the yard, returning moments later with a stick in his hand.

"I've made this for you Connie."

His sister bridled.

"I don't need a walking stick Ralph! I'm not an old maid!"

"Well don't take it then. There's plenty of able-bodied folk would be proud to have that. I use a stick meself when I'm climbing steep slopes." He broke in to a laugh. "I'm sorry. I suppose you're going to be sensible and take the easy way aren't you?"

"Oh no I'm not!"

She glared at him for a moment, but then put out her hand. "Let me see it."

He handed it over.

She weighed it up. The knobbly hazel shaft felt smooth to the touch. He'd obviously spent a lot of time sanding it shiny smooth before applying the varnish, but it was the top that was its crowning glory. It consisted of an intricately shaped and highly polished ram's horn. After some time of close and detailed inspection she turned her sharp green eyes on to him.

"It's beautiful Ralph," she said quietly. "It must have taken you ages. Thank you ever so much."

His eyes lit up.

"Do you really like it, Con?"

"Of course I do. In fact I might take it with me after all, just in case Rosie gets tired. It might come in handy for her!"

"I'll make one for you Rosie. I'll try and have it ready in a few weeks' time."

With that he turned on his heels and they watched him as he crossed the yard and disappeared through the small gap in the wall that led to the field where the sheep had been brought down to lamb.

"Ralph's ever so clever," Connie said.

"He's ever so lovely!" Rosie declared.

Connie gave her a look, suppressing a giggle.

"Romance is in the air. It happens every spring," she remembered her mother once saying, but she decided to keep her thoughts to herself - for the time being at least. Nonetheless, she couldn't help wondering how Ralph would react when she finally told him he had an ardent admirer who on more than one occasion had said he was, "A lovely boy!"

🐏🐏🐏

The two girls sat side by side near the trig-point on Mam Tor, enjoying the warm sun, the view over the Winnats Pass and the plateau of the White Peak. Connie had explained that the ridge of Rushop Edge and that of Mam Tor, marked the boundary of the Dark Peak, so called because the predominant rocks were comprised of millstone grit, with its limestone counterpart. Rosie had been struck by the sharp contrast between the dark drystone walls of their immediate area and the bright white walls of the latter. Furthermore, the grass and vegetation over the valley was a much brighter green, than the dark olives and browns of their immediate surroundings.

Connie had also taken the trouble to take her down on to the main road, before retracing their steps and making the final ascent of Mam Tor. She'd shown her the junction where the road swung right to access Winnats Pass and from there make its way to the village of Castleton in the Hope Valley far below. At this junction, however, she'd branched left where the old coach road had taken the shorter route snaking along the southern face of the steep-sided hill before descending steeply.

"Only walkers and cyclists can use it now," she explained. "Mam Tor is basically a massive lump of gritstone lying on top of shale, which is unstable. Large sections have slipped."

She'd shown her to the top section of what had once been the main road, now closed off to traffic. Great cracks zigzagged along the old tarmac and in more than one place large sections of the road were ten feet below what had once been their adjoining surface.

"That's why it's called the Shivering Mountain," she informed her friend. "It's always on the move."

Once having retraced their steps to Mam Nick, where the road in to Edale left the main road through a narrow valley separating Rushop Edge from Mam Tor, they'd soon accessed a footpath over a style and made it to the high-point of the latter. Here both girls had been glad to flop down on to the sheep-cropped turf to rest their weary limbs.

"Oh, my goodness. Where did he come from?"

Connie laughed at Rosie's exclamation. A young man had suddenly appeared over their immediate horizon, having soared upwards on a thermal, transported through the air by means of his hang-glider. He hovered straight in front of them, only a few yards away as if held in the air by an unseen hand, before soaring upwards once more and to their right. Rosie gazed in wondering admiration, her eyes following every graceful manoeuvre of the pilot.

"I wish I could do that," she finally ejaculated. "It must be absolutely amazing."

"So would I," her companion concurred. "He soars like a buzzard on outstretched wings."

She turned to Rosie, suddenly serious.

"That reminds me of something. When I first lost me leg, I had terrible problems, Rosie. I was so sad all the time. I thought my world had come to an end. I started having all kinds of nightmares and funny things happened when I was awake."

"How do you mean?"

"I'd suddenly get a pain in my foot, as if I had cramp in my toes or something, but it was my right foot and I didn't have a right foot. Weird things like that. Sometimes it would be a sudden stabbing pain and sometimes like an electric shock. Anyway, it went on for months. Sometimes I'd be fine for weeks at a time and then suddenly it would start all over again."

"It must have been awful."

"Yes, it was. It drove me mad. My hand would go down to the spot and there'd be nothing there, except for hard plastic and metal if I had my leg on. But then one night I went to bed early. I was really tired for some reason. It was raining and there was a wind and the old tree was creaking like anything."

"It must have been spooky!"

"No. I quite like it. It's like music. I find it soothing. I love it when the rain rattles against the window. Anyway I went off to sleep and I had the most fantastic dream. The rain had stopped. It was a starlit night and there was a full-moon. I found myself running up to the Mermaid's Pool. It was shimmering silver and I dived straight in. Next thing I realised I couldn't get out and I thought I would drown.

"It became very cold, really freezing, and then somebody had hold of me and everything went black. I woke up in a great cave and the mermaid sat next to me, except she wasn't a mermaid at all. She had legs and she was wearing a beautiful long white shimmering dress of some white silky material I'd never seen the like of. She was combing my hair and singing softly in a language I didn't understand. Then she asked in English how I'd got there with only one leg. She had a soft sing-song accent that seemed like a mixture of Welsh and Irish. I didn't know how I'd got there really. I thought I'd run there. I'd somehow forgotten I only had one leg."

"What happened then? How did you escape?"

"I didn't want to escape. It was lovely and warm and there was a kind of pale pinkish glow about everything. She was lovely and I felt safe with her. But then she said I must go and she carried me further in to the cave. There was a giant bird. It looked like a buzzard, but much bigger. She placed me on its back and told me to grip its feathers tight and then it took off, but it flew out the way we had come and dived in to the water.

"I thought I was going to drown again, but next minute we were bursting out of the pool in to bright warm sunlight and it carried me all the way home, soaring and diving on the way. I remember wondering how I could make my way across the yard on one leg, but the very next minute Ralph was waking me up to carry me downstairs for breakfast and I realised it was all a dream."

Rosie didn't say a word, remembering all too vividly her own dream just the previous night.

"The thing is Rosie. I've never really been unhappy since that moment and I've never had any phantom pains in the missing part of my leg either. It was as though I'd come to terms with the fact that the bottom half of my right leg had gone for ever."

She smiled, before continuing.

"Ralph used to tell me there's no such word as can't. Now I know what he meant, and I also realise that nothing is really impossible. All I have to do is try and I can make things happen, if I really want them to happen and work at it long enough."

"That's amazing," Rosie said quietly.

She wondered if she should relate her own dream, but decided not to. Instead, she suggested they walk down to the car-park and get an ice-cream before returning to the farm. However, before they arrived, Connie came up with another surprise.

"I've just remembered. In my dream the water nymph told me her name was Coventina. I'd never heard that name before. When I asked Ralph he told me it was the name of the Celtic water goddess."

Chapter Thirteen

"I'VE had a brilliant idea!"

Rosie looked across the bedroom. Connie sat on the side of her bed, with a triumphant look on her face, as she struggled to remove her leg.

"What is it!"

She finally got it off with a grunt, and let it slip to the floor.

"It's Easter Eve on Thursday. We could go up to the pool and see if Coventina appears at midnight."

"We've already discussed this. The grown-ups won't let us."

"They don't have to know."

"But how can we get out of the house without them knowing?"

"Simple. We borrow Ralph's tent tomorrow and pitch it in the old paddock. Then we'll camp out every night. So, you see, we won't have to leave the house to go up to the pool."

"But how do we persuade them to let us camp?"

"We'll tell them your mother's taking you camping in the summer and you need to practice."

"I can't do that. It's not true!"

"Rosie!"

Connie's tone indicated disappointment with her friend's seeming lack of spirit. Rosie laughed.

"It's Granddad that's promised to take me camping!"

"You mean you'll do it!"

"Yes - of course I will."

"Right. Last one to sleep brings me tea in bed in the morning."

"Sleep tight Connie."

"Make sure the bugs don't bite!"

Thus the initial plans were made. Little did the two girls know what they were letting themselves in for. Other spirits were planning to be out and about that auspicious night, full of meaning as it was for practising Pagans and Christians alike.

65

It had proved surprisingly easy to persuade Ralph to allow them to use his tent. To cap it all he'd volunteered his sleeping bag and insulated mat for their use and then gone in to Hayfield, bringing back another bag and mat he'd borrowed from a friend. Once they had him on side, persuading Connie's mother was an easy task. On the Tuesday night it started to rain heavily at nine-thirty and Mrs Gartside had hurried out to persuade them to spend the night indoors, but they'd assured her they'd be fine. Ralph's mountain tent was both wind and storm proof.

"We're as snug as a bug in a rug," Rosie assured her, "and we have everything we need."

On the Thursday evening, there was a full moon and a clear sky. The air was sharp and the radio had forecast frost. They'd walked up to the pool earlier in the day and selected a spot where two great wind sculpted boulders, with another balanced on top, formed a small shelter from which they had a good view of the pool, whilst remaining protected from any wind or rain, if the weather forecast proved wrong.

They were now walking away from the paddock, Connie armed with her walking stick and Rosie carrying a torch, although she didn't believe they'd need to use it. Suddenly an owl hooted, somewhere from a tree behind the farm-house. Rosie jumped and looked around, surprised by the unexpected sound.

"Tawny owl, male," Connie informed her.

Then an echoing cry from across the clough.

"Yip, yip!"

"Tawny owl, female. It's that time of year, when wild creatures are either begetting or begatting!"

Rosie laughed. Somewhere a dog barked as she adjusted the rucksack slung across her right shoulder. They listened for an answering call, but none came. Disappointed dog, Rosie decided. They continued towards their objective, the incline increasing the further they moved away from the farm. They were following a narrow sheep path, a distinct black ribbon against the rough grasses, which were beginning to turn a pale grey in the moonlight. The weather forecast seemed to be proving to be correct. Connie remained in the lead and Rosie was quite happy to follow in her footsteps.

She noticed how her companion swung her right leg in a slight outward curve as she brought it up off the ground to swing it forward for the next step, giving her a very slight rolling gait. Otherwise, she decided, nobody could possibly know it was a replacement lower limb. Then they heard somebody whistling, out of tune, followed by laughter and chattering voices.

"Doesn't sound travel at night," Connie remarked. "That's people leaving the Sportsman."

Rosie pushed up the left sleeve of her wind-proof.

"It's almost half-past-eleven by my watch," she replied quietly.

"Good, our timing's perfect," Connie said. She pointed with her stick without stopping. "There's the pool. If we follow the track to the left behind it and then scramble up there we'll be home and dry."

"As long as the mermaid doesn't pull us down in to the deep watery depths!"

Connie stopped in her tracks and turned towards her. Rosie caught the flash of green as the moonlight touched her friend's eyes. For a moment they looked just like a cat's - a wild cat!

"Coventina is not a mermaid, Rosie. She's a water goddess. That's why she can grant immortality."

Rosie smiled, but she couldn't help thinking Connie sounded serious, as though the distinction was somehow of importance. The younger girl turned away and continued upwards before she could respond to her statement. The sheep track disappeared and the grass crackled sharply beneath their feet. The frost was coming fast.

"Here we are," Connie announced.

Rosie slung her bag off her shoulder.

"Help me put this old blanket on the ground. We're going to need both."

They soon settled in their snug hideaway, one blanket protecting them from the cold ground and the other wrapped around their feet, legs and up to their chins.

"What time is it Rosie?"

"Twenty-three minutes to go."

The pool lay immediately below them, about thirty feet away, a dark shimmering patch against the grey background, its surface illuminated by the moon and rippled by a slight breeze.

They remained sat next to each other, their arms cuddling their knees, their sides meeting and their blanket clutched around them for warmth. It was becoming far colder than they'd expected. Connie pulled her woolly hat downwards over her forehead and the back of her head.

"What time is it now?"

"Fifteen minutes to go. Don't the farm-house lights look bright?"

"Yes. Dad should be home from the pub by now. Mum will be making his cocoa."

Time was dragging and Rosie became increasingly tense. The silence seemed overwhelming and the whole atmosphere somewhat spooky. Connie seemed to sense her friend's anxiety, but it was Rosie who broke the silence.

"Where did Ralph go?"

"I've no idea. Shall I tell him you fancy him tomorrow?"

"Don't you dare Connie Gartside!"

The youngster laughed.

"So you do fancy him!"

"I never said that!"

"You said he was a lovely boy. In fact you said it twice."

"I just meant..."

"Well. Go on. What did you *just* mean?"

Before Rosie could answer her annoying little friend, a man's voice floated upwards.

"Do yer 'ave ter do that?"

"Shurrup. I need a fag."

"Well, we don't need everybody knowin' we're up 'ere. Lightin' a fag is sendin' a signal fer miles."

The girls stared in to the dark, trying to discover where the voices came from.

"There they are," Connie whispered, pointing downhill to her left. "They're coming up here. They'll ruin everything!"

Rosie strained her eyes and followed Connie's pointing finger, but it was all in vain. She could see no sign of human beings. Then a flash of fire as the smoker lit his cigarette.

"Who can they be?"

"Keep your voice down, Rosie. I don't know who they are, but I do know we have to get rid of them."

"How on earth can we do that?"

"How good are you at imitating a mermaid?"

"No Connie! Don't do it."

Too late. The stone was already on its way, speeding through the cold night air to its intended target. Both men stood to the left of the pool, staring upwards and away from it, as if trying to work out the best way to get to whatever their objective was.

They turned, startled by the loud echoing plop as the stone landed exactly where Connie wanted it to go. Ripples disturbed the centre of the pool, widening out in a growing circle of ruffled water.

The thrower drew breath and began to open her mouth, intending to scream like a banshee and put the fear of the Goddess up the men, but as she began to do so one of them pointed across to the far side of the water. The alarm in his voice was clear and distinct.

"Jesus wept! It's the mermaid!"

Simultaneously they both took flight, running down the hillside as if the hounds of hell were on their heels. The two girls looked at each other in disbelief. Events were moving faster and far more dramatically than they could possibly have envisaged. Then Rosie was on her feet, thrusting the blanket aside, panic in her voice.

"Come on Connie! We've got to get out of here!"

Connie stood up, but didn't move, rooted to the spot in amazement at the sight her eyes were revealing to her confused brain. Seconds later she pulled herself together, a broad smile illuminating her face.

"No, it's all right! Don't..."

Rosie was already yards away and running fast, as if trying to outpace the men.

"Rosie! It's all right. It's Coventina. She won't hurt us! She has the old woman and the parson with her. Come back!"

Her friend was still running and continued to do so.

Connie looked across the pool. The young woman in the long white robe remained standing on the rock, her hands uplifted to the moon, her golden hair streaming down her back. An older woman and a man stood on the rough tussock grass, either side of her. Both were looking upwards and both were dressed in similar white robes.

The young lass began to walk towards them, stick in hand, absolutely calm, as if this was a regular occurrence.

Rosie suddenly felt guilty, ashamed she'd abandoned the girl who she regarded as her closest friend. She stopped and turned to see her walking around the nearside of the pool obviously intent on joining the mysterious ghostly apparitions.

"Connie! Connie! Don't go near. Don't!"

The girl either ignored or simply didn't hear her.

Rosie began to run back the way she'd come, continuing to shout. The wind rose in a sudden wailing gust carrying the sound of her voice away from her and in the wrong direction. She tried to run faster, growing desperate and in great fear for her friend's safety, but the increasing steepness of the hillside was rapidly turning her legs to lead. She looked across and saw the younger apparition embracing Connie and enfolding her in the long white robe. At that point, she tripped and fell full-length.

"Oh, Connie, poor darling Connie," she sighed in a frustrated torment of hopelessness and desperation.

Chapter Fourteen

THE inquest in to events on the land adjacent to Gartside's farm came later. Two young, rather inquisitive, and highly imaginative girls had proceeded up to the Mermaid's Pool on the night of April the twelfth, 1990. Two delighted young girls returned in the early hours of Friday the thirteenth, unlucky for some, although both had reasons to be somewhat embarrassed.

They were accompanied by two women and one man. All three of the latter were members of the Ancient Manchester Order of Druids.

On their way back to the farm, where the three pagans were paying guests - "lovely people, so quiet you wouldn't know they were there," according to Elsie - they came across Ralph, armed with a stout stick, standing over one of the men who had fled down the hill earlier. The latter looked sullen and defeated as he slumped against the drystone wall, clutching his ankle.

Connie's brother looked across to them as they approached.

"Rosie, Connie! What are you doing out at this time of night?"

"Catching game-keepers by the look of it," his sister responded.

"Aye. Two of 'em came charging down here as if there was no tomorrow. I tripped this one with me stick."

He pointed to a stout canvas bag lying nearby.

"Open that Connie, but be careful. Don't put your hand inside."

She did as he asked.

"What's in there?"

"One pigeon, dead and bloody. One plastic pigeon - a lure no doubt. One pole trap. A small bag with a draw-string top."

"Okay, Connie. That's enough."

He turned to the keeper, a grim smile on his face.

"Looks as though you're in serious trouble Colin. A pole trap to break or cut off the legs of a peregrine. A poisoned lore for a raven or any other carrion eater. A bag of strychnine no doubt and an artificial

71

lore for any raptor. You're going to jail I reckon! You've already killed a raven close to here. It's buried in our yard. It won't take long to dig it up and I bet the poison in the pigeon and in that bag are from the same source."

The keeper remained silent, but inside he too knew the game was up, and it wasn't the game he was paid to protect by his lord and master, the Duke of thingymabob, the privileged and hereditary successor to a land-thief and therefore "nobbut a knowing and known receiver of stolen goods," as Granddad pointed out to young Rosie when she finally had the chance to relate the full story to him.

"Our noble Duke is the real villain of the piece. Them two keepers are nowt but his lackeys, dependent on his largesse for their wages and the Duke hisself in his turn is but an ignorant victim of a system dedicated to the maintenance of a tiny minority comprising moneygrubbers, rich rogues, wealthy thieves and assorted vagabonds!"

Rosie continued to be a regular visitor to Gartside's farm and later that year Connie beat Mikey Grimsditch in the one-hundred yard dash and became school champion. She confessed to Rosie the same evening that she quite liked Mikey. Evidently, shortly after she'd lost her leg and on her first day back at school following the accident, he'd told her not to worry, he loved her and one day they'd marry.

"Now I've got him where I want him - chasing me. One of these days I'll surprise him again - and let him catch me!"

Connie Gartside's Triumph
A Tale of Family Values

"NOTHING in the world can take the place of persistence.
"Talent will not; nothing is more common than the unsuccessful man with talent.
"Genius will not; unrewarded genius is almost a proverb.
"Education alone will not; the world is full of educated derelicts.
"Persistence and determination alone are omnipotent."

Calvin Coolidge 1872-1933

Chapter One

AUTUMN was fast turning to winter. The curlew had already fled the High Peak moors for their annual winter holiday on the Lancashire coastal estuaries. The sheep were beginning to gradually descend from the high ground to the lower slopes. The sky was overcast and gloomy, although it had only just gone noon.

Life on the Gartside's farm, nestling below the soaring mass of Kinder Scout in the High Peak of Derbyshire, was beginning to slow down as the days grew shorter. However, the playground of nearby Birch Vale secondary school did not reflect this seasonal change. The prevailing atmosphere was one of shrieks and giggles and laughter as a horde of boisterous children participated in the variety of activities children do best when freed from study and classwork. Connie Gartside, in her second year at the school, stood out from the rest, apart from one other - a boy of her own age - with whom she was deep in conversation.

The lad was Mikey Grimsditch. He was desperate to get back in to Connie's good books. Connie was equally keen to be on good terms with him, but anybody listening to their conversation could be forgiven for believing the opposite was the case. Basically Connie was playing with Mikey's affections and enjoying every moment of the subtle torture she was subjecting him to.

Finally the young girl shook her head.

"I'm sorry Mikey. Tell your mum I'm not able to come for tea tonight. I'm meeting Rosie."

Mikey shrugged, trying to hide his disappointment. He'd pulled out all the stops persuading his mother to invite Connie to share tea with them that evening and it had all been to no avail. The sound of the bell ending the lunch break rescued him from further embarrassment.

As they began to make their way inside Connie stopped.

"You can walk home with me if you like, Mikey."

The lad's face lit up, momentarily.

"Of course I will," he responded, trying to sound matter of fact, but all too conscious he wasn't exactly succeeding.

Rosie Akroyd had a smile on her face as she climbed aboard the bus that would transport her from Stockport to Hayfield, her rucksack on her back. It was a rare event nowadays if she failed to travel straight from school on a Friday afternoon to spend the weekend with Connie, Ralph and Titch. Sometimes her grandfather travelled with her and occasionally her mother, but more often than not she travelled alone. Now approaching her fourteenth birthday, her mother had finally realised she was "extremely sensible" and quite capable of looking after herself "within limits." It was the first of November and she had a whole week with no school and bonfire night to look forward to.

She was still in her school uniform, but she'd already exchanged her shoes for walking boots and her blazer was hidden by a wind and waterproof jacket. She climbed the winding stairs. Her favourite seat at the front was taken, but its counterpart on the right was vacant. She made her way to it, slinging the rucksack from her shoulder and carefully placing it on the floor between her legs. She'd borrowed her mother's binoculars, which were safely stowed in the bag as well as their leather case. She wasn't taking any chances with them.

It almost seemed a lifetime away, but it was just two years previously that Granddad had first taken her to Hayfield to visit the scene of the Mass Trespass of Kinder Scout which he had participated in way back in 1932. Next April would be the sixtieth anniversary of that historic and ground-breaking event and she was already aware that plans were well underway to celebrate. That was one of the reasons she was travelling alone to meet her friends. Granddad was on the organising committee and had a meeting that night.

By the time they'd reached the small village of High Lane it was already dark. The A6 was full of traffic in both directions, a sluggish stream of red lights preceding the bus and a rapid white river approaching them. Rosie looked out for the familiar landmarks; the impressive gates marking the entrance to Lyme Park; the Ram's Head in the centre of Disley; then the descent in to New Mills past Newtown station; and, at long last the Waltzing Weasel.

"What time is Rosie's bus due in?"

"Mum. That's the third time you've asked me. The same time as always. Five twenty-five."

"Well – it's quarter to five. Don't you think you should be on your way?"

"Oh, my goodness. Is it that late?"

"Wrap up warm love and don't forget your torch."

"I'll come with you Connie."

Ralph was already donning his jacket and Titch was standing by the kitchen door, eager to join them.

Their timing was perfect. Forty minutes later, as they crossed the main road that sliced through the bottom remnant of the village, passengers were disembarking from the bus and Rosie, as usual, was in the lead. She hugged Connie and then squatted down to receive Titch's greeting, fondling the Manchester terrier's ears as he licked her face. Ralph looked on, an amused grin on his own face.

"Let me have your rucksack Rosie."

She rose, swinging the bag from her shoulder to hand it to him.

"How are you Ralph?"

"Fine Rosie. Let's get moving. The wind's beginning to bite!"

They made their way across the main road and in to Hayfield proper to begin their journey up to Coldwell Clough and the farm. Rosie suddenly became aware of the wind. It began to blow in noisy gusts, sending the dry leaves collected in the gutter by the old church in to a skittering rustle of a dance across the road. They passed the Three Trees café, crossing the River Sett by the narrow stone bridge and turned right to access the lane known as Kinder Road. As they did so it started to rain. Not that Rosie minded. She was used to changeable weather in this part of the world and was dressed accordingly. There was every chance the morning would bring dry weather.

Eventually they'd passed the Sportsman and reached the junction where the lane up Coldwell Clough struck off to the right over Bowden bridge. Rosie had been amazed by the number of tents pitched on the campsite, which no doubt explained why the pub had been such a beacon of light and merriment. There must have been a couple of dozen. There were no street lights now and Connie and Ralph switched on their torches to illuminate the pitch dark. The sound of running water from the brook, added to the sigh of the gusting wind and the crunch of their boots on loose gravel.

They were soon making the final climb through the dense canopy of trees immediately before the farm when the beam of headlights from a vehicle travelling towards them intermittently swept the hillside as it followed the curving lane. Then they heard the sound of its engine and found themselves blinded as it crested the hill and swept in to view. Instinctively all three moved to the right hand side of the lane, leaning against the drystone wall, turning away to protect their eyes from the glare.

The vehicle kept its lights on full-beam as it swept past them at speed. Ralph, turning as it passed, realised it was a Land Rover towing a covered trailer. He watched as it descended the hill and turned left down Kinder Road, barely slowing down to negotiate the junction.

"Maniac!" he ejaculated angrily.

"Was that Billy Cragg?" Connie asked.

"No - his Land Rover's grey, not blue. Anyway, he'd have slowed down and dipped his headlights as soon as he saw us."

They made their way through the farm gate and walked down the path and around the cattle byre to access the yard and the kitchen door. Mrs Gartside looked up as they entered.

"Did you have a good journey, Rosie?"

"Yes thanks, Mrs Gartside."

"Apart from the fact we were nearly mown down by a road-hog!" Connie added.

The expression on Mrs Gartside's face immediately changed to one of concern.

"Road-hog!"

"A Land Rover and trailer," Ralph explained. "Under the trees where the lane narrows. He shot through as though the Devil was on his wheels."

Elsie blanched. This was the spot where the motor-cyclist had hit Connie and where her daughter had lost the bottom half of her right leg.

Connie, sensing her mother's alarm, reacted accordingly.

"Don't be upset Mum. As you can see we are all safe and sound."

COLDWELL CLOUGH

Chapter Two

"WHAT do you fancy doing today?"
Rosie laughed as she snuggled under the warm duvet.
"I don't want to think about it. I'm happy doing what I'm doing. Absolutely nothing! I'm as snug as a bug in a rug."
"Oh, come on lazy-bones. You can't waste the day."
"I don't intend to waste the day. I intend to stay warm and re-charge my batteries."
"Please yourself, but you'll be going hungry."
Connie gave a final grunt as she fitted the stump of her leg in to the socket of her artificial limb. Pulling her cord trousers on she left the bedroom, but not before she'd drawn the curtains to let the early morning daylight weakly illuminate the room and then, as a parting shot to her friend, sent a pillow flying through the air, grinning gleefully as it found its target. She left the bedroom door open behind her, for strategic reasons, resolving to do the same with the door at the bottom of the stairs which accessed the kitchen.
Rosie's determination to have a lie-in began to evaporate at roughly the same rate as the scent of cooking breakfast wafted up the stairs from the kitchen. Before she knew it she was climbing out of bed and putting on her clothes, ready to do battle with a new day. A glance out of the window told her the morning was dry, although how long it would remain so was another matter. She retrieved her watch from the bedside table. Seven forty-five she noted.
As she entered the kitchen Ralph and his father were about to leave.
"Ah, there you are young Rosie," Mr Gartside beamed. "Connie said thee were stayin' in bed."
Rosie smiled.
"I had second thoughts. I realised I'd be needed to keep her out of mischief."
The farmer chuckled.
"Fat chance, but I wish thee luck lass."

With that he made for the door, followed by Ralph.

"See you later, Rosie," the latter said, as he shut the door behind him.

She gazed out of the window as he crossed the yard, wishing he'd stayed long enough for a chat, although she knew if he had she would most probably have found herself tongue-tied. Ralph was now seventeen and seemed hopelessly out of her reach, but a girl could dream.

"Would you like mushrooms, Rosie?"

She turned with a start.

"Yes please. Can I help you?"

"No. Everything's under control. Connie's just gone to get some eggs from the cellar, but you could put some more coal on the fire."

Rosie turned to do as bid. Titch, sprawled out on the flock mat warming his belly, looked up at her with his dark brown liquid eyes and wagged his tail as she approached.

She fondled his ears before picking up the ornate iron claws to pick a lump of coal out of the bucket and place it carefully on the burning embers.

"What are your plans for the day Rosie?"

"I'm not sure. Connie will no doubt decide. She usually does and I'm happy to go along with whatever she wants to do."

Mrs Gartside laughed.

"You've transformed her life Rosie. It's good for her to have a friend of more or less her own age. It's not easy for a young girl in a house full of males."

"I thought she had a sister."

"She has, but we didn't plan it very well. Her sister's the eldest of five children. She was married by the time Connie was six."

Before Rosie could respond the cellar door opened and Connie entered the room.

"Fancy meeting you here," she said with a grin. "I thought you'd decided to stay in bed!"

Rosie ignored her.

"Pity you missed Ralph."

"I didn't. He hadn't left when I got up."

"Have you told him yet?"

Mrs Gartside looked up from her frying pan.

"Told him what?"

"Rosie's madly in love!" Connie responded.
Rosie blushed, feeling as though her face was burning.
"Connie!"
Mrs Gartside laughed.
"Leave the lass alone Connie. Affairs of the heart are not to be belittled."
Rosie didn't know where to put herself.
"Come on Rosie love. Take no notice of Connie. I hear she's fallen for Mikey Grimsditch, although what she sees in that young scoundrel I'll never know."
"Mikey is not a scoundrel," Connie responded sharply, "and, anyway, he's just a friend."
"Have it your way Connie dear. Sit down Rosie. Your breakfast's ready. Help me dish it out Connie and then I'll poach your eggs."
At that point the phone rang.
"Can you answer it Connie? I'll sort Rosie's breakfast."
Rosie immediately went to assist as Connie did as she was asked.
"Gartside's farm. Good morning."
A pause.
"Yes, I think so. Just a moment. Let me check. Mum. Can you manage a room for two tonight? Bed and breakfast?"
"Yes, love."
"Yes, we can manage that. Can you let me have your name please? Yes. No problem Mr Gore-Booth. About eight-thirty. Yes, the first farm on the left as you breast the top of the first rise of Coldwell Clough, just after the tunnel of trees crossing the lane. Yes. You can park your car anywhere on the track through the farm gate. Fine. I'll let Mum know. Thank you."
She turned to her mother.
"He sounds a bit posh Mum. Your fame must be spreading."
"It takes all sorts to make a world Connie. As long as they behave themselves I don't mind."

With breakfast over Connie suggested they should walk up to the top of the Kinder Downfall, but before Rosie could respond her mother intervened.
"I need you to go in to Hayfield first. We're going to need more

bacon and a fresh supply of tomatoes for tomorrow. I didn't expect guests tonight."

"Okay Mum. We've got plenty of time to go up to the Downfall later."

"Well, just be careful on the road."

"Mum. I'm the last person you need to tell that!"

"Yes. You're right love. But I can't help worrying."

"You used to tell me that worrying never buttered parsnips."

Mrs Gartside laughed.

"Did I?"

"Yes Mum. Now is there anything else you need?"

"A large loaf. White unsliced. There's some money in my purse. Make sure you take enough. You can buy Rosie and yourself a treat."

"Thanks, Mum. We won't be long. Are you ready Rosie? Don't forget Titch."

The last remark was superfluous. Titch was already at the door; ears erect and tail wagging in anticipation.

"Right, that's sorted. Now, what shall we have for a treat?"

"How about a lemonade at the café?"

"We could buy sweets."

"I'd rather sit in the café."

"Okay. The Three Trees it is."

They were soon sat down at a table by the window, Titch making himself comfortable on the floor between their legs. The café was full of people who, judging by their bags, had been shopping like themselves.

A waitress approached, notepad in hand.

"I think I'll have tea," Connie informed Rosie. "It's too cold for lemonade."

Rosie nodded.

"I'll have the same."

"Pot of tea for two, please," Connie said to the waitress, sounding all grown-up.

"Would you like anything else?"

"Not for the moment, thank you," Rosie responded, putting on what she thought was a rather middle-class accent.

Both girls giggled as the waitress turned away.

Then Rosie was pointing out the window.
"Oh look. There's Mikey Grimsditch."
Connie was out of her seat in a flash and exiting the café door almost before Rosie realised what was going on. Next moment he was crossing the road accompanied by another lad. They both entered following in Connie's wake.
"Hallo Rosie," Mikey said as he took a seat.
She returned his smile and said, "Hiya."
The other lad sat down without saying anything.
"So, what have you been up to Mikey?" Connie asked.
"Not a lot. Hayfield's dead."
Rosie looked at him for a moment before asking, "What makes you say that?"
"Nothing exciting ever happens here. I wish I lived in Manchester."
"Well. I'm from Manchester and I now live in Stockport, but I think there's far more excitement out here."
"Umph! Hayfield's a dump. I can't wait to leave school and get away from here."
Connie frowned, but didn't say anything.
"Don't you enjoy school?"
"Why should I? I'm not learning anything. The teachers are boring. It's all a waste of time, Rosie."
"But what will you do? What kind of work can you get if you give up on school?"
"I'll do anything. I just want to get away from here."
"But this is such a beautiful area," Rosie responded, somewhat taken aback by his negative attitude. "You're in the midst of wonderful countryside. There's so much to do and you have family and good friends here."
Mikey stood up shaking his head.
"I have no real family," he said making for the door. He turned towards them, but looked straight at Connie. "And I have no real friends here either."
His companion stood up, shrugged his shoulders and followed him, remaining silent as he had done throughout.
Connie watched, a crest-fallen expression on her face, as he walked over the bridge and turned right, ignoring his companion who was hurrying to catch him up.

"What did he mean when he said he had no real family?" Rosie asked.

"His father left his mother in the lurch. As soon as he found out he'd put her in the family way he left Hayfield and he's never been seen since."

"That's terrible. Poor Mikey!"

"Never mind poor Mikey. What about his mother. She's the one who has been hit the hardest!"

HAYFIELD CHURCH

Chapter Three

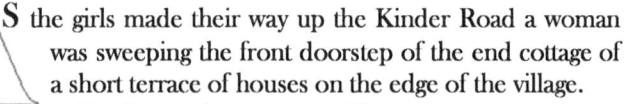

As the girls made their way up the Kinder Road a woman was sweeping the front doorstep of the end cottage of a short terrace of houses on the edge of the village.

"Hello Pearl. Is Mikey in?"

The woman ceased her work.

"Hello Connie love. Yes. He's slumped in front of the telly and he's in a foul mood."

"Can I see him?"

"Of course you can. You might cheer him up. Go straight in. Let me finish this and I'll make a brew. I've just baked some scones."

"Oh. This is my friend Rosie."

Pearl laughed.

"I know, but I'm very pleased to meet you Rosie."

Her careworn face lit up in a smile which Rosie returned. Both girls made their way in to the cottage's small living room, preceded by Titch. As his mother had predicted Mikey was slumped in front of the television, looking dejected. The terrier approached him, his tail wagging, no doubt expecting to be petted. Mikey studiously ignored him.

"What are you doing here?" he asked without getting up.

"We are going up on to Kinder when we've taken this shopping back to Mum. I thought you might like to come with us."

He stared at Connie for a moment, obviously undecided. Eventually he made his mind up.

"No!" he said sharply. "I'm happy where I am."

"Mikey. Don't be like that."

"Like what? Just leave me alone Connie Gartside. I don't want to spend time with you!"

"Okay. If that's how you feel. We'll leave you to it."

With that Connie left, followed by a bemused Rosie.

"That was quick," Pearl said.

Connie shrugged.

"Mikey wants to be on his own. I'll see you later Pearl."

"Yes. See you soon Connie and you Rosie."

She watched them make their way up the lane, a frown on her brow, before returning to her sweeping.

"Mikey really is in a bad mood," Rosie observed quietly.

"Yes, and yesterday he was pleading with me to have tea with him and his mother."

Rosie looked at her in astonishment.

"And you refused! Playing hard to get as usual I suppose!"

Rosie sounded angry. Connie looked uncomfortable.

"I had to meet you!" she protested. "And anyway, I did let him walk me home from school!"

"Oh Connie. No wonder he's upset. You could have had tea with him. Ralph was meeting me and we could have met up later. You know very well Mikey's mad about you."

The younger girl remained silent. For once she didn't have a smart answer. Her friend was right. Maybe she'd played with Mikey's emotions once too often.

They continued walking up the lane in silence - a silence not broken until they were approaching the farm.

"I think you've got to find a way of letting Mikey know you care about him, Connie."

"Who says I care about him?"

"You have, and you know you do. You told me last year and it's obvious you're feeling guilty now. You've been as quiet as a mouse for ages."

Connie kicked a loose stone across the road, disconsolately.

"But how do I tell him?"

Rosie shook her head.

"I'm not sure, but there must be a way."

"Well. Maybe, but I don't know what to do."

"Perhaps we'll think of something when we're up on Kinder."

"Do you still want to go?"

"Of course I do. I haven't travelled all the way here to mope about indoors. I can do that in Stockport."

༄༅༄

"Mikey."

"Yes Mam."

"What did Connie want?"

"They were going up on to Kinder."

"Well - why didn't you go with them?"
"I didn't want to."
Pearl Grimsditch shook her head. Mikey was going through a bad patch.
"I'll tell you what. Make me a cup of tea and we'll have some scones. That might cheer you up."
"Do I have to?"
"Mikey - what's got in to you? You're not normally like this."
He shrugged, but rose from the sofa anyway and made his way in to their small back kitchen to put the kettle on.

"Can you put the bacon and tomatoes in the fridge for me please Connie?"
"I've already done it Mum. Your change is on the table."
"Good girl. I don't know what I'd do without you sometimes."
"Can I make you a cup of tea Mrs Gartside?"
"Oh Rosie love. That would be perfect, but I thought you were going for a walk."
"We are. But we're not in a rush Mum," Connie responded.
Rosie was already filling the kettle. Elsie finished her task of placing damp clothes on the rack over the fireplace and hoisted it up to the ceiling.
"There. That's another job done. I can take the weight off me feet for a minute."
She made her way to the large white deal table and sat down. Connie joined her.
"Was the village busy?"
"The Three Trees was heaving and there were quite a few walkers about."
"First weekend of the school holidays. It always makes a difference."
"Ermm. Yes."
Elsie sensed her daughter was distracted.
"We met Mikey Grimsditch," Rosie intervened.
"That's nice." She glanced at her daughter. "He's not a bad lad really. A bit harum scarum, but he was very good when Connie lost her leg. We couldn't have kept him away from the farm if we'd wanted to."
Connie remained silent, her eyes focussed on the tabletop.

"It must have been a horrible time for you."

"It was Rosie. But Mikey Grimsditch was like a ray of sunshine in a gloomy overcast world. There was nothing he wouldn't do to help and he was but a little mite. Six years of age and acting like a grown up. He doted on our Connie even then."

"I need a pee," Connie said and with no more ado left the kitchen for the outside toilet in the yard.

"Why's Connie so quiet Rosie?"

"She's worried she's upset Mikey."

"Why on earth should she think that?"

"He asked her to tea yesterday and she wouldn't go. When we talked to him today he was obviously down in the dumps. He said he wanted to get away from Hayfield. That he had no real family and no real friends here."

"That's not right. Mikey's a bit of a loner, but there's plenty of people who like him. Me for one. And as for family, his mother's a wonderful young woman, no matter what some narrow minds might say."

"But you said he was a bit of a scoundrel earlier."

Elsie frowned then chuckled.

"That was more of a playful dig at Connie. I just meant he was in to mischief. There's no harm in the lad and a great deal of good."

"Are there any other family members in his life?"

Elsie's eyes narrowed.

"His grandmother in Little Hayfield, but I don't think they have any contact." Anticipating Rosie's next question she added, "His grandfather died not long ago, but he'd thrown Pearl - that's Mikey's mother's name - out of the house when he discovered she was pregnant. Strait-laced narrow-minded church people the elder Grimsditches, with no understanding of the role of love, compassion or charity, let alone simple Christian duty. I doubt if there's been any contact between them since."

"How old was Mikey's mother at the time?"

"Sixteen I think. Yes, she must have been. She'd just started work at the co-op."

"Sixteen! That's terrible. How can parents be so mean? She was only two years older than I am now."

"I thought you were thirteen Rosie."

"It's my birthday at the end of the month."
"Oh - we'll have to celebrate. Anyhow most people rallied round young Pearl and luckily her manager had a much better attitude than her parents. He didn't sack her and he found her somewhere to live. Once she had Mikey he even kept her job open for her until she was able to return to work. Not many employers would have done that."

At that point Connie came back in to the kitchen.

"Are you coming or not Rosie?"

"Of course I am. I've been waiting for you."

"Well - I've been waiting for you!"

Elsie laughed.

"Don't you two start arguing. It's bad enough that you've upset young Mikey, Connie. I think you should apologise to him as soon as possible and tell him how you really feel about him."

Connie glared at her mother, then gave Rosie a withering look and with no more ado stomped out of the house, slamming the door behind her with a resounding bang.

"Did I say something?" Elsie asked.

"I'd better go after her," Rosie responded.

"Don't forget your binoculars love."

Chapter Four

"**CONNIE! Wait for me.**"

The younger girl ignored her. She'd already squeezed through the narrow gap in the drystone wall and was marching resolutely in a diagonal across the field, Titch running ahead of her. Rosie began to run to catch up.

Her friend was no slouch when it came to speed walking, despite her artificial leg. Connie was about to squeeze through the gap in the next wall before she finally caught her.

"I thought we were going for a walk together," Rosie said after she'd caught her breath.

"Some friend you've turned out to be!"

"What on earth do you mean?"

"Telling Mum about Mikey Grimsditch!"

"You're being silly."

"No I'm not. You didn't have to tell Mum I fancy him."

"You're quite right. I didn't have to tell her. She already knew!"

Connie didn't look convinced, although she knew it was true. She set off once more. Rosie followed, wondering how she could placate her friend. They'd already reached the Mermaid's Pool before she broke the silence.

"Perhaps we should ask Coventina what to do about Mikey?"

Connie stopped abruptly and turned to face her friend.

"There's no need to make fun of me!"

Rosie shook her head.

"You really are in a tantrum aren't you?"

"No I'm not."

"Well, why do you assume I'm ribbing you?"

"Because of what happened last Easter Eve."

"But it was very exciting Connie, and Ralph caught the game-keepers and they're in jail where they belong, and it was all because of you insisting we came up here to see the Water Goddess at midnight."

Connie's green eyes narrowed, cat-like. She turned and continued her up-hill march. Rosie watched her for a moment and then looked upwards to the jagged dark gritstone outcrops marking the boundary between moor and sky before following in her friend's tracks. They were climbing up a steep barely defined track to the right hand side of Red Brook. Despite the previous night's rain the water coming over the Downfall was a mere trickle of silver. The sky remained grey and overcast, and there was little breeze. Both girls remained silent. At the best of times this was a place to save breath, such was the incline they were making their way up. Not for the first time Rosie marvelled at Connie's tenacity and determination. This was a test for the fittest human being, let alone for one reliant on an artificial limb.

Eventually they were making their way on to the plateau, threading their way through overhanging rocks of millstone grit, oxidised black. Rosie had the sudden idea they were about to enter in to a prehistoric world. Once on the top, Connie flopped to the ground, her back against a massive wind, rain and ice sculptured rock, whose smooth rounded and intricate shape reminded Rosie of a photograph Granddad had shown her of a bronze sculpture by somebody called Henry Moore.

Rosie stood by the side of her friend for a moment, leaning against the rock. She unfastened the leather case hanging round her neck and took out the binoculars to contemplate the panorama lay out before her.

"Magic!" she said out loud before taking her seat next to her companion and replacing the glasses in their case.

Connie began to remove her right-hand trouser leg from her long woollen sock and then to roll it above her knee.

"Is it hurting?" Rosie asked as she watched.

"Not really. I just want to give my stump some fresh air."

Titch appeared and took a seat leaning against her left leg.

"Do you remember when you told me about the phantom pains you used to have long after you'd lost it and how long it was before you finally came to terms with the fact that you had lost it?"

Connie glanced across at her, as she fondled Titch's velvety ear.

"Yes."

"Well, when my Dad was killed something similar happened to me. It was maybe a year later. I was walking along Castle Street in Edgeley near where we live. I spotted a man on the other side of the road, ahead of us and walking in the same direction. 'Look,' I said to Granddad, 'there's Dad' and I began to drag Granddad across the road. I really thought it was him. Granddad had to restrain me and to remind me my Dad was dead and I would never see him again."

"I didn't know your dad had been killed. I just thought you didn't have a dad."

"Everybody must have had a dad at some point Connie. Maybe Mikey's having similar problems."

"Mikey never met his dad."

"Yes, but he knows he has one somewhere. There could be all kinds of things going through his head. Do any of the other kids tease him because he's illegitimate?"

"There was one lad used to call him 'bastard', but Mikey soon sorted him out. I don't think anybody else has said anything. Most kids who know him like Mikey and they couldn't care less about his parentage."

"Do you mind if I talk to him Connie? I might be able to help and if he knows I lost my Dad that might help to build a bridge between us."

Connie shrugged. "I suppose so, but it might be easier if I just do what Mum said."

"Well I think that's right, but it might help if I speak to him first as well. It could make it easier for you."

"It might, but let me think about it Rosie."

"Okay. But does that mean we are friends again?"

Connie laughed.

"I didn't know we'd stopped being friends!"

Rosie shook her head and then rooted in her pocket, retrieving a brown paper package which she quickly unwrapped revealing a slice of parkin which she then broke in two.

"Here you are Connie. Your mam gave me this before we left. I'd forgotten about it."

"Good old Mum. She'll have made loads for bonfire night."

"What night's the bonfire?"

"Tuesday. In the old quarry again."

❦❦❦

"Come on Rosie. It's getting cold."

Having replaced her leg Connie was eager to be on the move. "We'll walk along the edge towards Ashop Head and go down by

William Clough."

Rosie nodded assent and they were soon over the stream that fed the Downfall, Titch once more taking the lead, darting forwards, occasionally snuffling between the rocks as if searching for a scent and then running back towards them, as if to ensure they were following him.

"You can see Stockport from here on a clear day," Connie pointed out.

"Not much chance today," Rosie replied.

"With a bit of luck we'll have snow soon. Ralph's building a sledge. It'll be fine. He's learnt how to braze at night-school and he's making it with metal runners and a metal frame. He says it'll be super fast."

"You need to be careful Connie."

"Umph. I might be a one-legged cripple but it's no more dangerous for me than anybody else!"

"You're right there, but I wasn't thinking of you. I was thinking of those who might just happen to be in your way!"

"You can be very provocative Rosie Akroyd."

"I wonder where I caught it from?"

"Hang on a minute." Connie stopped in her tracks. "What's happening down there?"

"Where?"

She pointed.

"There in the quarry."

Rosie screwed up her eyes. The quarry was a long way off.

"It's just three men loading sheep in to a trailer."

"Yes. A trailer towed by a blue Land Rover. I bet that's the one that came at us last night."

Rosie had the binoculars out in a flash.

"Well, it is blue, but that doesn't mean..."

Before she could finish Connie was turning off the main path.

"We can take a short cut here down across Blackshawe. We might just get to the quarry before they've finished loading."

Without waiting for a response she was scrambling down a narrow track, little more than a sheep path, between the rocks on the edge, to begin the steep descent towards Kinder Head. Rosie followed in her wake, stuffing the glasses back in to the case, not without difficulty. Unfortunately, by the time they'd got onto Blackshawe the men were lifting the trailer's tail gate, fastening it in to position. Moments later they were driving towards Hayfield.

"Umph," Connie ejaculated. "Too late, but I think we'd better tell Ralph. I'm sure none of the local farmers will be moving sheep at this time of day. The markets are held on Saturday morning and Wednesdays. We'll cut across to the farm from here instead of going to the quarry."

ROCK FORMATION, KINDER EDGE

Chapter Five

"IS Ralph back yet Mum?"

"Good grief Connie love. Can't you enter the house in less of a rush? You're enough to give a body heart failure."

"It's important Mum."

"No. Not yet." She looked up at the old grandfather clock in the corner. "I doubt if they'll be back for at least another half-hour. What's got in to you?"

"Nothing!"

"Nothing? One minute it's important and next it's nothing!"

"No Mum. I mean it's important but nothing's got in to me."

"Okay. Let's start again. What is so important Connie my love?"

Rosie turned away, attempting to suppress a laugh and having to turn it in to a cough. As she did so she noticed the headline on the front page of the *Farmer's Weekly* resting on the cushion of Mr Gartside's favourite armchair by the fire.

"Look at this!" she said, grabbing the paper.

She placed it on the table between Connie and Elsie.

The headline read, "*Sheep Thieves in Longdendale.*"

"Isn't that just the other side of Glossop?"

"Yes Rosie, but what's this got to do with us?"

Connie gripped her mother's arm.

"That's what I'm trying to tell you Mum. There was a Land Rover and trailer in the old quarry and men were loading sheep in to it. It was the same colour as the Land Rover and trailer that nearly hit us yesterday."

"Right Connie. Why didn't you say that at first? I'll phone around and see if any of our neighbours were moving sheep. When was this?"

"Only about half-an-hour ago. That's why I was suspicious. It was too late for today's market and far too early for Wednesday's."

"I'll put the kettle on," Rosie said marching over to the sink.

"Good idea," Elsie responded as she picked up the phone and began to dial. "I could murder a brew."

"Can I make some sandwiches Mum? I'm starving and I bet Rosie is too."

"Yes. There's some cold beef in the fridge and a jar of pickle in the larder. Hallo, could I speak to your mother Louise? Tell her it's urgent."

♥♥♥

They'd just finished their impromptu brew and snack when Ralph and his father returned. Elsie informed them what was going on.

"None of our neighbours have been moving sheep. I've phoned every one. I've also phoned the police and given them a description of the Land Rover and trailer."

"They could have crammed at least a dozen in to that trailer," Ralph pointed out.

"Aye and a few more if they were determined," Mr Gartside added. "Did either of you notice whose sheep they were?"

Connie shook her head.

"We were too far away to see the markings, Faither."

"What markings?" Rosie asked, puzzled.

"All the sheep have painted marks on them Rosie," Ralph responded. "Each farmer has a particular colour so they can sort them out when they're brought off the hill."

"There were some with blue and some with a dark red."

"Blast! The red uns art owers," Mr Gartside exclaimed. "How many lass?"

"I'm not sure. By the time I had my binoculars out they'd almost finished loading them. At least three I think."

"We'll be lucky to get away with three, Faither," Ralph responded.

"Aye lad. And we Gartside's aren't famous fer ower luck are we?"

"Is the glass half-full or half-empty?" Elsie responded.

Ralph grinned, putting his arm around Connie's shoulder.

"Aye. Don't be daft faither. Your glass is more than half-full. We've got my little sister haven't we and we could have so easily lost her six-year back."

Rosie gazed at him in admiration.

"What a lovely lad you are Ralph Gartside," she said to herself, and not for the first time either.

"Anyhow," Elsie said. "There's not much we can do tonight but we can keep our eyes skinned from now on. We can make our own luck. If they were here yesterday and today, chances are they'll be back soon. We'd best spread word around the village and Little Hayfield, Edale and Rowarth, Birch Vale and Chinley. In the meantime I'll get tea on. Once we've had hot meal I can prepare for our guests. What time did they say they'd arrive Connie?"

"Eight-thirty Mum. It's on the notepad by the phone."

At that point the phone rang. Elsie sped across the room and lifted it to her ear.

"Oh. It's you Jack. No, don't be daft. There's always space for one more. No. I won't hear of it. Come over now. You can eat with us. I'm just about to prepare the food. Never mind the Sportsman! They can't match mine!"

She replaced the receiver, a beaming smile on her face.

"We've got a surprise visitor. Your granddad young Rosie. You'd best go meet him and take extra torch. He's down in the village. It's pitch-black out there."

"I'll come with you Rosie," Ralph volunteered.

"And me," said Connie.

Rosie looked at her. Connie frowned. Rosie didn't look happy. Elsie intervened.

"I need you here Connie. You can help me prepare the meal young miss."

Rosie went to retrieve her jacket, woolly hat and scarf, a big grin illuminating her face. Ralph opened the door to allow Rosie out when Connie called after them.

"Are you going to tell him Rosie?"

If looks could kill Connie would have died on the spot. As it happened she merely returned Rosie's glare with a mischievous and defiant laugh. Elsie chuckled and then turned away. Ralph looked nonplussed.

"What did Connie mean?" he asked as they made their way across the yard.

Rosie looked up at him with her bright blue eyes.

"I haven't got a clue," she lied.

They were soon through the gate and walking down Coldwell Clough.

"What have you been up to today, Rosie, apart from tracking down sheep rustlers?"

"Trying to sort out your sister's love life and walking on Kinder."

"Connie's love life? She hasn't been falling out with poor Mikey again as she?"

"I think she's played hard to get once too often. Mikey was obviously feeling pretty miserable when we met him in the village this morning."

"She's always winding the poor lad up. What she doesn't realise is that Mikey's a very sensitive soul."

"Well, at least I think she's learnt her lesson. We called in to see him and Connie asked him to come walking with us. Trouble is he turned her down point blank and said he didn't want to spend time with her."

"Good for him! Let's hope you're right and she has learnt her lesson."

Rosie looked up at him once more, although he was concentrating on the crumbling road surface and didn't notice. She finally plucked up her courage.

"Have you got a girl-friend Ralph?"

He shook his head.

"There's a girl I like a lot, but who'd fancy a farmer's lad like me? Anyway she's too young for me. She won't be fourteen until the end of this month."

"You're only seventeen. When you're twenty she'll be seventeen and when you're thirty she'll be twenty-seven. That's not a big difference. My Dad was seven years older than Mam."

"I never thought of it like that." He looked down at her and smiled. "Maybe I'll ask her for a date on her birthday."

He seemed to speed up, as though the idea had put a spring in his step. Rosie was not happy. She wondered who the lucky girl could be!

HAYFIELD

Chapter Six

"IT'S good to see you again Mr O'Donnell."

"And you too Ralph, but how many times do I have ter ask you ter call me Jack?"

Rosie smiled. "It *is* good to see you Granddad. How's Mam?"

"I'm afraid she wasn't in a good mood when I left Rosie love. In fact she wasn't in a good mood when I got home from my meeting last night."

"Oh no! How did you upset her? Did you get home late?"

"No. *I* haven't upset her. It's that dastardly blue blot on the landscape!"

"What do you mean?"

"Not what. *Who,* Rosie."

Rosie shook her head. Granddad could be exasperating when he wanted to be.

"Who then?"

"That circus clown - John Major."

"Why's *he* upset Mam?"

"Evidently, whilst I was out last neet, he was slagging off single parents on the television. Going on about so-called family values. Saying single mothers were a major British problem and breeders of future generations of thieves, scoundrels and malcontents. Every news bulletin on the radio today repeated the message."

"No wonder Mam's angry. I'll ask Mrs Gartside if I can phone her when I get back."

"Good fer you Rosie. Anyway, I'm sure she'll sort her head out. I'm looking forward ter a quiet break. Thank goodness I can relax here."

"Are you sure Granddad?"

"Why shouldn't I be?"

"I might be planning a series of burglaries or muggings or something. I'm the daughter of a single mother aren't I?"

"I've a feeling yer more likely ter channel any errant feelings inter more useful and positive outlets young Rosie."

"No doubt about that," Ralph agreed. "Rosie's a girl of many talents."

"Oh aye. What's she been up ter now?"

"Granddad!" Rosie protested.

Ralph laughed.

"She's taken on the role of advisor and peace-maker to love-lorn couples. Our Connie's upset Mikey Grimsditch - again!"

The youngster stopped in her tracks.

"Goodness. I wonder if that's what really upset Mikey?" she said thoughtfully.

"What do you mean Rosie?"

"John Major! Mikey's mother is single too. What if Mikey heard the speech? He might think he has no chance in life; that he's destined to be a delinquent. What if his mam heard the news? My mother's a single parent because she's a widow, Ralph. If she's so upset just think of the effect on Mikey's mam. She didn't choose to be a single parent. She could be horribly upset as well and Mikey might be blaming himself for being the cause of all her problems!"

"Have you ever thought of becoming a social worker, Rosie?" Granddad asked.

"No. Of course not! I want to change things, not mess about with the symptoms. I'm going to be a political campaigner when I grow up. I'm going to sort out the land thieves and money grubbers and stick up for ordinary common people like us and Mikey's mam!"

"You've got my vote," Ralph retorted.

Granddad chuckled.

"I don't know where she gets her ideas from! Mind you, Rosie, yer could be a social worker *and* a political campaigner."

"And you have got to stop telling fibs, Granddad. You know very well where I get most of my ideas from!"

Granddad chuckled again.

"Chip off the old block," Ralph interjected.

"Less of the old!" Granddad responded.

"Typical!" Rosie said shaking her head.

Ralph and granddad looked at her.

"What do you mean?" Ralph finally asked.

"Both of you assumed I was referring to Granddad's ideas. But I wasn't. Well - not entirely."

"So - who exactly did you mean?"

"The other Communist in my life! My friend and mass trespasser Benny Rothman!"

❦❦❦

"Good girl Connie. That's all sorted. Let's have a break. Jed, how about putting the kettle on!"

Connie laughed.

"Faither's fast asleep."

"Typical man. Go and give him a prod Connie. Tell him he either makes us a brew or we're going on strike. Tell him we're joining the Wages for Housework campaign."

Before Connie could make a move Mr Gartside gave out a final explosive snore and looked across at them, his face a portrait of innocence.

"Would you like a brew Elsie?"

"Oh! That's so very thoughtful of you dear."

He hauled himself out of his more than comfortable armchair with a grunt.

"Put kettle on Connie, love. I'll get cups."

Connie looked at her mother, a frown on her brow. Mrs Gartside laughed.

At that point the telephone rang. Connie was across the room before her parents had time to react.

"Looks as though you're putting kettle on after all Jed," Elsie instructed.

"Gartside Farm. Yes. Oh dear. No don't worry. I'm sure that will be fine Mrs Gore-Booth. Yes. Just leave your car on the track once you are through the farm gate. Then walk round the back and through the yard. Yes. See you in about half-an-hour then. Bye."

"What's going on Connie?"

"Your paying guests have had a change of heart, Mum. Seems they were going to eat at the Sportsman. Evidently they now prefer to eat here."

"You have to be joking!"

"No, I'm not. Shall I go and give the fire a poke in the front room?"

"Yes love. Now what am I going to do about food?"

"You'll have to give them ours I expect."

"This is the last thing I need."

"Don't worry Mum. We'll manage. There's plenty of cold roast beef and roast ham. We've home-made cheese. We're not going to go short."

Mrs Gartside shook her head and then smiled. Connie could always find the bright side of any cloud.

"Right. You go and get that fire roaring. At least they can eat their humble fare in a warm and pleasant room. They probably won't want to eat with us."

"I could always eat in the Sportsman Elsie."

"That's ever so thoughtful, Jed. But there's plenty for you here."

"Are you sure lass? I dunna mind."

"Well I do! Now go and make that brew afore I think of something else for you to do."

♥♥♥

"Wow! What make of car's that Granddad?"

"Looks like a Bentley, love."

"Somebody with brass slumming it in the Sportsman no doubt," Ralph added.

At that point a middle-aged well-dressed couple emerged from the pub.

"Of all the places to bring me, Robert!" the woman exclaimed. "Full of working class riff-raff with their walking boots and their sweat!"

"Never mind my dear. We'll soon be at the farm."

He strode across the road and opened the passenger door for her. She took her seat with a swish of nylon and a flash of thigh as she tucked her legs in to place. Having closed the door carefully, the gentleman looked up at the sky for a moment as if for inspiration, or patience perhaps. The sound of approaching boots attracted his attention. He turned to them.

"Excuse me," he asked in a Home Counties drawl. "Could you be so kind as to direct me to Coldwell Clough? I'm heading for Gartside's Farm."

"That's where we're heading," Rosie responded.

Granddad noticed she seemed to emphasise her Manchester accent, almost as if she was drawing attention to her working class roots. He intervened.

"If yer continue in the direction yer car's facing and tek the first right immediately after the camp site, yer on the right road. Eventually the lane ull begin to climb fairly steeply and yer'll find yerseln travelling beneath a tunnel of trees. Immediately after yer'll see a tall stone barn and the farm house adjoining it. Immediately after turn left and stop. The farm gate ull be closed. Once you're through it yer can park anywhere but my advice is ter keep to the left. They may need ter use tractor in the morning."

"Thank you my man. That was extremely clear."

With that he turned on his heel, walked in front of the car and accessed the driving seat. The well-appointed car moved on its way with a purr.

"He could have offered us a lift," Rosie observed.

"He could have refrained from calling me 'his man!' I'm me own man and a citizen of the world."

"We could be in for an interesting weekend," Ralph responded. "But I'm sure I've seen that face before."

"He didn't sound local," Rosie pointed out.

"The nobs have their own particular and peculiar accent, Rosie, irrespective of which part of the country they're from. In the main they go to the same public schools."

They continued on their way, Ralph wondering how his parents would react to their guests.

VIEW FROM BRIDLEWAY

Chapter Seven

BY the time they walked through the kitchen door Jed was dozing off in front of the fire and there was no sign of the strangers, Connie or Elsie. Ralph immediately busied himself putting the kettle on. Rosie collected the tea pot and generally made herself helpful. Granddad sat down at the table, reluctant to disturb Jed.

Titch knew his place and accordingly made himself comfortable on the mat in front of the fire. Elsie entered the room.

"There you are! How are you Jack? It's good to see you."

"I'm fine Elsie. You are looking well."

"Do you want a brew mother?"

"Yes please, Ralph. I'm afraid I'm a bit harassed." She smiled at Jack. "Unexpected guests. Said they wanted bed and breakfast and then decided they wanted an evening meal as well."

"Ermm. We met them outside the Sportsman. Evidently they weren't enamoured by the riff-raff that frequent the place."

"I'm not sure they're too impressed with us either. Connie's showing them their room now. Mind you. I won't be too disappointed if they go. They haven't paid a deposit so if they dunna like us, they know what they can do! She's more stuck up than ower Jersey cow!"

The door from the front room opened and Connie entered the room.

"Shush Mum! They're coming downstairs. They'd like a cup of tea."

"I've just brewed, Connie."

"Great, Ralph. They'll think we're super efficient. Can you make another brew in a small stainless tea-pot please? Then I can take that in to them afterwards and really impress them."

She selected two of their best china cups and saucers from the Welsh dresser, placing them on a tray with a small jug of milk, a bowl of sugar and two silver Apostle tea-spoons. Then she carefully poured the tea, without adding milk, lifted the tray and departed the kitchen.

"Here we are," they heard her say. "Please help yourselves to milk and sugar. I'll bring you a top-up soon."

With that she returned to the kitchen, closing the door carefully behind her, a big grin on her face.

Rosie noted there had been no sign of any thanks from the guests.

"They would like to start with soup Mum."

"Soup! How on earth am I going to make soup in time?"

Connie laughed.

"Easy. I explained we hadn't planned for evening guests, but I could provide leek and potato with Stilton cheese."

"Very clever. But leek and potato isn't instantaneous either and we haven't got any leeks."

Connie left the kitchen through the door to the cellar, returning with a family size can of leek and potato soup and a large lump of Stilton.

"We can't use canned soup!"

"It's an emergency Mum. Once the Stilton's melted in to it they won't have a clue."

Elsie shook her head, gazed at her daughter for a moment, and then laughed.

"You are a star my darling Connie! You really are."

She hugged her daughter close and then frowned.

"What about the main course?"

"There's that shoulder of lamb an' a leg as well in deep freeze," Jed pointed out.

"Typical," Elsie retorted. "It'll take all night to defrost. Anyway, that's for tomorrow's dinner."

"Mum," Connie intervened, "I've told them they have a choice. Home made Lancashire hot pot made to my great great grandmother's secret recipe..."

"Or!"

"I told them they could have it with home made pickled red cabbage or home grown and home boiled sliced beetroot in best wine vinegar, or both!"

"Are they happy with that?"

"He was. M'Lady seemed a bit unsure, but didn't argue, especially when I told her I could rustle up frozen fish fingers at a pinch."

"We haven't got any fish fingers!"

"I know Mum!"

She took the proffered tea pot from Ralph and returned to their guests without more ado.

Jed put his knife and fork down on his carefully mopped up plate.
"That were gradely lass. Yer've done us proud again."
"You certainly have Elsie and I for one would like to show my appreciation."
Elsie looked at Jack O'Donnell quizzically.
"How about you, Jed and me nip down to the Sportsman? There's a good hour left before they call time."
"That would be a real treat Jack, but I have guests to look after."
"Not 'til tomorrow Mum," Connie informed her. "They've gone to bed and they don't want breakfast 'til nine-thirty tomorrow."
"Nine-thirty? What a waste of daylight hours."
"You should be pleased," Ralph pointed out. "Anyway, me and the girls can look after things here. Go and enjoy yourself for once in a while Mother. You really deserve it."
Elsie shook her head, but her face sported a smile.
"Okay. Why not? I'd be a fool to refuse. Me an' you have a date Jack. Are you sure you want ower Jed to accompany us?"
"Suit yerselns," her husband retorted. "But I'm havin' a pint or two at the Sportsman whatever you two decide."

It wasn't long after the grown-ups had left, and they'd finished the washing up and had the cutlery and plates neatly stacked on the draining board, that Ralph put his hand on Rosie's shoulder to attract her attention. He nodded in the general direction of the fire. Connie was fast asleep, curled up on her father's armchair. Her artificial leg lay on the floor by the side of the chair, evidently superfluous to requirements.

At that point Titch rose, walked over to the kitchen door and began to scratch it with an uplifted front paw. Ralph stood up and let him out in to the yard.

"It's begun to snow Rosie," he said softly.

She joined him and sure enough, it was snowing, albeit thin wispy flakes. She looked higher up the moor.

"Wow. The hill's already turning white on the top."

Titch returned, having completed his business. They closed the door and returned to their seats at the kitchen table.

"Connie told me you were making a sledge."
"It's finished apart from the varnishing."
"Does it need to be varnished?"
"Only the wooden seat slats."
"What a shame. We won't be able to test it tomorrow."
"Course we can. I can always varnish it later."
Rosie's eyes lit up.
"Can I see it?"
"Yes. Get your jacket and scarf. It's in my workshop. It'll be freezing in there."

Having followed his advice, the girl followed Ralph outside, closing the door carefully so has not to wake Connie. He walked over to the building housing the cattle byre and opened the first door. Rosie entered as Ralph switched on the light. She found herself in a square white-washed room with an ancient work-bench along the opposite wall under a small barred window.

Mounted on the wall to the left of the window was a board to which were clipped a variety of metal-cutting files and other hand tools. A large engineer's vice was mounted on the left-hand end of the bench. A sledge, manufactured from tubular steel, stood upright against the left-hand wall. Two large cylinders, complete with pressure gauges, which Rosie knew contained oxygen and acetylene respectively, were mounted in a trolley next to it.

"Oh, this is marvellous Ralph. Why have you kept it a secret from me? Will you teach me how to braze and do bronze-welding? Can you silver-solder?"

He looked at her, obviously surprised.

"Are you sure?"

"Of course I'm sure. I don't want to be a social worker. I want to be an engineer like Granddad. I've wanted to be one ever since I can remember!"

She began to examine the sledge in great detail, running her fingers around the brazed joints as if looking for flaws. At last she turned to him.

"It's brilliant Ralph. You obviously take pride in your work."

"If a job's worth doing..."

"It's worth doing well!" she completed the statement for him.

He laughed.

"You're full of surprises, Rosie Akroyd."
"You're not bad yourself, Ralph Gartside - for a boy that is!"
He smiled.
"We'd better get back in case Connie wakes up."
"Okay, but Ralph..."
"What Rosie?"
"You will teach me won't you?"
"Of course I will."
"That's brilliant! If we make some more we might be able to sell them."
He gazed at her for a moment.
"I never thought of making things for sale."
"Why not? You told me it's hard making the farm pay. Surely every little bit helps?"
"Do you really think we could sell them Rosie?"
"Why not? Especially if we have a good hard winter. It's only the first week in November. January and February are the coldest months. Anyway if we build two more and can't sell them we can still make good use of them."
"Right. But we'd better give this a thorough test tomorrow to make sure I've got the design right."
"I've thought of that. We need a dare-devil test pilot."
Ralph's eyes narrowed and a frown crossed his brow. Rosie's face broke in to a smile.
"Don't look so serious. I've already thought of just the person for the job."
"Who?"
"Your Connie!"
He laughed.
"Rosie Akroyd! I could kiss you!"
"Do you want to switch the light off first?"
The lad blushed and shook his head.

KINDER ROAD WITH KINDER LOW IN BACKGROUND

Chapter Eight

ELSIE looked up, as Ralph entered the warm kitchen.
"Would you like a cup of tea, Mother?"
"I'll make it. You get in front of the fire. You look frozen."
She retreated to the sink and began filling the kettle.
"I thought you were with Rosie and Connie."
"They've monopolised the sledge. They won't let me have a turn so I thought I'd leave them to it."
"Are you sure Connie will be safe? I can't bear to think of her damaging herself."
"Mother! You should know by now that Connie's a risk-taker, but she does think carefully about her options. She might be crazy but she's not daft. Anyway, I've learnt that the more I try and restrain her, the more likely she is to do it."

Once the tea was brewed Ralph joined his mother at the table.
"Have they gone?" he asked glancing upwards in the general direction of the main bedroom reserved for guests.
"Have they heck. They're still in bed!"
"They must be worn out," he returned with a wry smile.

They'd disturbed his sleep with their antics more than once the previous night. He stirred the pot and then poured the tea. Elsie helped herself to milk and then passed the jug to him.
"Where's Faither?"
"He went out with Jack as soon as they'd had breakfast. I thought they were going to join you and the girls."

Ralph shook his head and took a sip of tea, looking at his mother through the vapour rising from his cup.
"You're looking tired Mother."
Her eyes met his and she smiled.
"No. I'm fine Ralph."
She frowned and looked thoughtful for a moment. Ralph had the idea she was about to impart some important information. He was right.
"Ralph. I need to say something."

"What Mother?"

"I... Well, I just want you to know you're very special to me. You've been wonderful with our Connie over the years..."

"Mother! You're embarrassing me. There's no need."

"There's every need. Things could have turned out quite differently. You encouraged Connie from the moment she lost her leg. You gave her hope and encouraged her to think the unthinkable. You gave her the will to strive and overcome her difficulties. You..."

"Stop it Mother. Connie's very special. She did it all by herself."

"Have it your own way, Son. But she's not the only one you think is special, is she?"

He put his cup down.

"What do you mean?"

"Rosie Akroyd. You think she's special too, don't you?"

He felt the colour rise from his neck upwards. Eventually he responded.

"She's full of surprises. She wants to be an engineer. She wants me to show her how to braze and bronze-weld. She reckons we should make sledges for sale."

Elsie smiled.

"I know I should be, but for some reason I'm not surprised. Will you do it?"

"Yes."

"Do you know she has a crush on you?"

"Mother..."

"Never mind mother! She does and I've a feeling it's not a one-way street."

He remained silent.

"I'm not saying it's wrong Ralph. Rosie's a wonderful lass, but she's young and could be vulnerable. You're seventeen. Look after her Son. Don't rush things and don't do anything you might come to regret. Do you understand?"

He looked in to her eyes once more and then nodded.

"Yes, Mother. I promise."

"Right. We'll leave it at that. I know I can trust you Ralph. Do you think I should wake them two up?"

"No Mother. Leave them to it. You put your feet up while you have the chance."

Inwardly he breathed a sigh of relief. Later he would realise his developing relationship with Rosie had just received his mother's seal of approval.

"You'd have ter go a long way ter get a view as good as that."

"Aye, yer reet Jack and the snow meks it look quite new and clean and pure."

Jack O'Donnell and Jed Gartside were leaning against the dry-stone wall next to the Edale cross, having visited a farmer in the tiny hamlet of Barber Booth.

"Anyway. We'd best get movin'. Elsie'll be wond'rin' where we've getten to."

Jack took one last look at the distinctive breast-shaped summit of Mam Tor across the Edale valley. Then he looked down at the old medieval cross for a moment, remembering the young girl he'd first met there when he was a teenager - the young girl who was to become his wife and the mother of Billy, their son, and Alice, their daughter. After a brief moment he nodded to his companion and the two men continued on their way.

The sky was overcast and grey, but there was little wind. A couple of inches of soft snow covered the ancient bridle-path beneath their feet. They kept to the central stony ridge. The snow hid ice in the track's depressions which the day before had been small puddles of water. Neither man was a youngster any more and they knew better than court a slip on the treacherous surface.

Jed was just about to inform Jack he reckoned the snow would have melted away by the following morning when he stopped in his tracks.

"Eh, that looks like young Mikey Grimsditch."

They'd reached a junction. The left hand branch climbed up to Southhead, near the source of the River Sett, at a right angle, whilst the main track carried straight on before curving to the right. Here they would enter the steep sided Coldwell Clough, cut by the same swift flowing Sett, which would take them back to the farm. A dark figure, oblivious to their approach sat on the bank with his back to the drystone wall, his head in his hands.

"Hey Mikey! What ails thee lad?"

The youngster looked up, obviously surprised at their presence. He looked dismayed, as though he'd been caught in the act of doing something he shouldn't be doing.

"Hello Mr Gartside," he finally said, standing. "I was just thinking." His cheeks were damp and his eyes red. He'd obviously been crying.

Jed shook his head.

"Yer look frozzen son. Come along with us," he said in a tone so soft and gentle, that it took Jack by surprise. "Thes a cheerin' fire, good friends an' hot cocoa where we're goin' to."

The lad remained silent, seemingly unsure.

"This is me mate Jack O'Donnell. You know young Rosie that visits us. Jack's her grandfaither."

The lad and Jack exchanged nods in way of greeting and Mikey managed to return the old man's smile.

"Now, come on lad. It's too cald ter be hangin' about in this spot. Me auld eyes are waterin' and thine are almost as bad as mine."

He had his arm gently around the lad's shoulder before he had chance to decline the offer and the three commenced walking homeward together.

Eventually Jed broke the silence again.

"Young Mikey's a rare talented lad," he informed Jack. "I met his mother on Kinder Road a couple of weeks ago." He looked down at the youngster, giving his shoulder a slight squeeze. "She told me about the reading lamp you'd made fer her birthday, young un. I asked if I could see it."

Mikey glanced upwards for a moment, but his face remained expressionless.

"Eh, it were a work of art in varnished oak, Jack, with a wonderfully carved ornate base. Young Mikey ull mek a real craftsman if he sticks to his last."

Jack noticed the lad's countenance seemed to lighten and his back straightened slightly.

"Being able to manufacture things with yer own two hands is a source of great satisfaction," Jack responded.

"Aye. I reckun so, although my auld hands are only fit for sheep shearing' an' sheep washin'!"

They reached the farm and Jed began to open the gate.

The Bentley had disappeared.

"I'll be off then Mr Gartside."

"Nay lad. Thee mother ud never forgive me if I let thee walk home without hot drink in thee. Come on and dunna bother arguin' coz yer'd be wastin' yer breath. Anyway ower Elsie ull want ter say hallo to yers."

The lad didn't bother arguing, although he'd rather have carried on. He half-hoped Connie wasn't in and half-hoped she was.

MOUNT FAMINE

Chapter Nine

ROSIE and Connie sat at the kitchen table, engrossed in a game of draughts, when the two men and the boy entered the kitchen.

Connie's face lit up in a smile on seeing Mikey, as if the sun had suddenly emerged from behind a particularly thick dark cloud.

"Mikey Grimsditch! You look as frozen as an icicle," Elsie exclaimed. "Come here lad and get yourself by this fire."

She gave a final poke to the coals and stood up.

"What on earth have you been up to? You're shivering and turning blue."

"I'm okay Mrs Gartside. I..."

"Never mind you're okay. Just do as you're told for once!"

The lad sank down on his knees, holding his hands out towards the flames now leaping halfway up the chimney. Titch rose from his own comfortable position on the flock mat and licked the lad's cheek in greeting.

"Get off yer daft dog," Mikey retorted, although there was now a sparkle in his eyes, a sparkle moreover that was not the result of the bright fire or recent tears.

Jed already had the kettle on and Jack was adding tea to the large teapot. Elsie busied herself digging out crockery from the dresser.

"Would you like some parkin, Mikey?" she asked.

"I'll get it Mum!"

Connie swung around on her chair and leapt in to action. At least that was her intention. Instead, much to everybody's surprise, she took a dive and ended up full length on the floor, on her side. Mikey was across to her and kneeling down besides her before anybody else had recovered, apart from Titch who was marginally ahead.

"Are you alright Con?"

She gazed up at him, a frown on her brow.

"I think so," she said quietly, obviously subdued by the unexpected accident.

"Let me help you sit up."

117

He put an arm around her neck, somewhat gingerly.
She nodded and smiled and then placed both arms around his neck in turn, pulling with her full weight as if attempting to lift herself. Caught off balance, Mikey fell on top of her, all in a heap.
"My hero," Connie laughed, kissing the end of his nose.
Eventually they both sat up, but not until the young girl had followed up her advantage by kissing the lad once more - this time full on the mouth. She emerged from the tangle with a big grin on her impish little face. Mikey's visage, in its turn, had turned as bright red as Connie's carroty hair.
The girl looked around at their rather amazed audience.
"I've never done that before," she announced. "I forgot I'd taken my leg off."
"Lucky Mikey!" Rosie said out loud, much to everybody's amusement.

"Hello Pearl. We've got your Mikey with us. Is it alright if he stays for a meal? No, don't be daft we've plenty. We always leave the main meal 'til late on a Sunday. No. Of course it's no trouble. I'll make sure he gets home safe. Okay Pearl. Are you working tomorrow as usual? Okay. I'll call in and see you. Okay love. Bye."
Elsie replaced the phone and turned, a smile on her face.
"Right. That's all arranged. Now why don't you kids go outside? It'll be dark soon, so make the most of it. I reckon the snow will have melted by tomorrow."
She began to turn away and changed her mind.
"Fix Mikey up with a pair of gloves, a hat and a scarf, Connie. We don't want him getting hypothermia."
"You can have first go on the sledge Mikey," Ralph informed him.
"No Ralph," Connie said firmly, passing gloves, woolly hat and scarf to the lad. "He can sit behind me the first time. I don't want him getting hurt!"
"You must be joking, Connie Gartside!" Mikey exclaimed. "I'll take my chances on my own thank you very much!"
"Very sensible!" Rosie agreed.
The phone rang and Jed answered it.
"Gartside Farm. Jed speaking. Yes, of course. Just let me check."

He put his hand over the receiver.

"The Gore-Booths. Can yer do bed and breakfast again Elsie?"

"Yes. I suppose so, but tell them I can't manage an evening meal apart from a snack for supper."

"There. Now we need some small pieces of coal for the eyes and mouth, and a carrot for the nose"

Rosie had just placed the twelve-inch diameter snowball on top of the two much larger ones, thus completing the main structure of the snowman she and the two boys had carefully constructed.

"I'll sort it," Ralph said, turning towards the gap in the drystone wall which would take him in to the adjoining field and from there in to the farm yard.

"Whee-e-e-e!!!"

He turned at the sound of Connie's long drawn-out delighted squeal just in time to see her hurtling down the hillside, leaning back on the sledge, her feet braced against the front bar, normally for use when the sledger lay on his or her stomach. She was heading straight for the newly constructed figure at great speed.

"No Connie!" he shouted in serious alarm, knowing that the large compressed snowball he and Mikey had carefully rolled was fairly solid and would in effect be an immoveable object.

To his amazement, Connie evidently had grasped this scientific truth too, because, just as the sledge was about to hit, she rolled off the fast moving chariot in to the soft snow lying thick in the field as expertly as if she'd been doing it all her life. The sledge, however, hit the intended target with great force and, much to Rosie's annoyance, the whole structure shuddered and the head fell off.

She turned to give her friend a piece of her mind, only to discover that the younger girl remained sat in the snow, her clothes covered in the white stuff from top to toe, laughing uncontrollably.

Ralph ran over, looking down at his youngest and favourite sister, shaking his head, partly in disbelief, partly in fear she'd hurt herself and partly in sheer astonishment at her audacity. He leant forward, holding his hands out to help her stand.

"You're so crazy, Connie, it's unbelievable."

She took his hands in hers and swung herself upright.

"It's all your fault, Ralph," she retorted gleefully. "You always insisted there was nothing I couldn't do if I put my mind to it."

Meanwhile, both Rosie and Mikey were each rolling a snowball ready to ambush their friends. However, before they could do so two more snowballs came whizzing through the air, one landing at their feet and the other hitting Ralph on the back. All four teenagers turned to see who their mysterious assailants were. There was no sign of a soul in sight.

"Must be kids hiding behind the wall," Connie said, bending down for a supply of snow.

Ralph followed her lead and then all four were charging down the hill towards the field below, Titch yelping at their heels, as excited as they were. Granddad and Jed suddenly appeared from behind the wall, armed with a fresh supply and the kids found themselves being bombarded once more, but this time the two adults had six snowballs each.

Undaunted, the children instinctively fanned out and, realising they'd been out-manoeuvred, the two men fled towards the farmhouse and safety. The kids finally caught them in the yard and, before Jed and Jack could open the kitchen door, four snowballs hit home. The snowball battle now began in earnest and only ended when the two adults held their hands up in abject surrender.

Elsie looked round in surprise as two allegedly sensible adults, four fun-loving youngsters and a Manchester terrier invaded her domain, all laughing fit to burst, with the sole exception of Titch who yelped and leapt up at them all in obvious delight.

BRIDLEWAY FROM EDALE

Chapter Ten

RATHER luckily, perhaps, the Gore-Booths returned to the farm they had decided to make their rural retreat, shortly after the Gartsides and their friends had finished their dinner.

Mr Gore-Booth knocked on the kitchen door and Ralph bid them enter.

"Would you like a cup of tea?" he asked. "I'm just about to put the kettle on."

"That's a very welcome offer," Mr Gore-Booth retorted. "Yes, we would. Thank you for asking."

Jack stood up, pulling out the vacant chair from under the table, next to his own.

"Would yer like ter tek a seat, Mrs Gore-Booth?" he asked with a smile.

"No thank you," the lady responded rather haughtily. "I will take tea in the living room. Will you join me Robert?"

Rosie thought the latter remark sounded more like a command than a question.

"I'll be along shortly, my dear."

His partner in crime departed. Connie followed. The fire would need a poke and a fresh supply of coal.

"Sit down, Mr Gore-Booth," Ralph stated. "You might as well rest your legs whilst I make the brew."

The gentleman smiled, removed his fawn coloured overcoat and draped it over the back of the chair Jack was still standing by.

"Let me introduce yers, Mr Gore-Booth," Jack said. "Mrs Gartside yer've already met. This is our host, Mr Gartside, this is my granddaughter, Rosie Akroyd, this is young Mikey Grimsditch, a very talented young wood-worker, Ralph's meking yer tea and I'm Jack O'Donnell."

The gentleman nodded to each in turn.

"I'm pleased to meet you all," he said rather grandly, taking the proffered seat.

Silence reigned for a moment, everybody seemingly lost for words.

Then young Mikey suddenly came to life. He produced a small rectangular thin wooden box out of his pocket.

"Have you got a Thatcher?" he asked Mr Gore-Booth.

The gentleman's eyes narrowed as a frown crossed his brow. Elsie, Jack and Jed looked equally surprised. Ralph, waiting by the sink for the kettle to boil, smiled to himself. Rosie looked on in anticipation.

"A Thatcher?"

"He means a pound coin," Rosie informed him.

"Yes. I believe I have."

He pulled a small purse out of his jacket inside pocket and retrieved a coin.

"Would you like me to change it for you?"

"In which way?"

"This box is magic," he informed their guest. "It has the power to change pound coins in to smaller more convenient denominations, which I find very handy when shop-keepers are short of change."

Now the youngster had his audience hooked. All, including Ralph, gazed at him wondering what he meant. All except Rosie that is. Mr Gore-Booth was no exception. He extended the hand holding out the coin across the table towards the youngster. Mikey in his turn pulled out a drawer in the box and extended his hand, the box in its palm, towards the other.

"Place the Thatcher in to the round slot, please," he instructed.

The gentlemen did so and Mikey slowly pushed the drawer back in to the box.

"Now," he said softly, passing the palm of his hand over the top of his other and the box it held. "We have successfully made the Thatcher disappear."

He smiled, removed his top hand sideways to reveal the box again, which he then held out towards Mr Gore-Booth once more. He slowly pulled out the drawer.

"Please extend your hand, palm up, Mr Gore-Booth."

Again the gentleman obeyed and the lad slowly tilted the box towards the awaiting palm revealing a new coin in the slot previously occupied by the Thatcher. It dropped in to Mr Gore-Booth's hand - a shiny copper coloured new penny.

The adult laughed out loud.

"How did you do that?" he asked, showing the coin to everybody.

"Like I said it's a magic box!"
"But where's the rest of my change?"
Mikey laughed in his turn.
"There isn't any. Like I said it changes a Thatcher in to a lower denomination. It's a magic box, not an automatic safe full of loads of coins."
"But, you said you found it very convenient when shop-keepers had no change."
"Yes, I did and I do," Mikey informed him triumphantly. "I offer to change their pound coins and transform each one they give me in to a penny!" He looked his victim in the eye. "Trouble is, I rarely get away with it more than once."
"Good lad Mikey. A perfect example of laissez-faire capitalism!" Jack O'Donnell pointed out. "An enterprising twist on the old entrepreneur's adage, 'Buy cheap and sell dear!'"
Mr Gore-Booth, realising he'd been had, gazed at the youngster for a long moment, seemingly non-plussed and lost for words.
"Why did you call the pound coin a Thatcher?" he asked eventually.
"Because it's hard and brassy and thinks it's a sovereign!" Rosie exclaimed triumphantly.
The door to the living room opened and Connie emerged. A shrill voice followed in her wake.
"Robert! Are you avoiding me?"
"Just a moment dear."
He rolled his eyes and stood up.
"Here's your pound back," Mikey said, his hand held out.
Mr Gore-Booth smiled and shook his head.
"You keep it Mikey, my boy. You deserve it. That was a revelation, in more ways than one. Very entertaining. Yes indeed. Good evening all."
He made a bow and left the kitchen. Ralph followed with a tray of tea things and a steaming pot. Rosie, no longer able to contain her mirth, burst in to a fit of giggles.
Connie sat down next to Mikey, looking at Rosie as she did so.
"What's got in to you, Rosie?"
Rosie looked at Mikey and burst in to another giggling fit. Ralph returned.

"Can I see your box?" he asked the younger boy.

Mikey handed it over and Ralph examined it closely, turning it this way and that and finally removing the drawer, which he then slid back inside.

"Where did you get it from Mikey?"

"They sell similar ones, made in China I think, at the Outdoor Gear shop in Hathersage. My mate's got one, but I made that myself after I'd figured out how his worked. They're really made to make a coin disappear and then appear again. I kind of adapted the idea."

"You made it?" Ralph's face expressed his surprise. "It's a work of art Mikey. I've never seen such fine joints."

Jack took it out of Ralph's hand, examined it carefully and then passed it onto Jed, obviously impressed. Jed in turn passed it onto Elsie, whispering something in to her ear. Rosie, who had examined it earlier, smiled and looked across to Ralph.

"We'll need a good woodworker if we are going to have a successful sledge-making business, and, with three of us involved, we can form a workers' co-operative."

"Hang on. What about me?" Connie interjected.

Rosie shook her head.

"Sorry Connie. We can only involve skilled workers, plus, we need people we know can work as part of a creative team."

Connie frowned. Rosie had the sudden feeling her friend's temperature was rising rapidly and she was about to raise a head of steam and thus blow her top. Ralph no doubt felt the same.

"We could take on an apprentice, perhaps?" he interjected.

"They're the ones that spend the first five years watching the others, fetching and carrying, holding their tools and stuff, and brewing up aren't they?" Mikey asked.

Rosie laughed.

"Umph! See if I care. I'll start my own worker's thingamejig!" Connie retorted sharply.

Mikey found Rosie's laughter infectious and joined in, but then he glanced up at the grandfather clock.

"I'd better be off," he said. "It's getting late."

"Okay Mikey," Elsie smiled. "But come back soon. Ralph will walk home with you."

"And me," Connie interjected.

"And me," Rosie added.

Titch was already waiting by the door.

"Take those gloves and the hat and scarf, they're yours now," Elsie instructed, "And take care on the road. It will be icy no doubt."

As it happened, the thaw had already begun.

※ ※ ※

"Well. That's sorted your dilemma out," Rosie said to Connie as they left the Grimsditches and began their return up Kinder Road.

"What do you mean?"

"Your fantastic dive. It solved the problem of telling Mikey how much you love him."

Connie smiled, threaded her arm through Rosie's and hugged it close to her side. Then she frowned and stopped in her tracks.

"I didn't do it on purpose. It was an accident!"

Rosie chuckled.

"I'm sure it was. Even you are not that talented, and you wouldn't choose a bare stone floor to do it on anyway. But you seized your opportunity didn't you? I saw you kiss him!"

"Well, you're only jealous. You've yet to sort Ralph out."

Rosie didn't rise to the bait, determined to keep Ralph's kiss in the workshop a secret. Instead she said, "I think with your talents you should seriously consider going in to films when you leave school."

"Films? I don't think I'd make a very glamorous actress."

"Don't put yourself down Connie Gartside. I think you're quite beautiful, but I really meant as a stunt-woman!"

"Come on you two, don't dawdle."

Ralph was a good ten yards in front of them. They hurried to catch him up, giggling as they went.

"There won't be any snow left by morning at this rate. Just listen to the drips from the trees. It's melting fast."

"That means the Downfall could be quite spectacular tomorrow," Connie said.

"Especially if we get a strong south-westerly wind," Ralph concurred.

"Why?" Rosie asked, somewhat puzzled.

"Four different streams come together at the top of the Downfall, Rosie, all collecting water from different areas of the Scout. The melting snow will give the Downfall real force, but when you have a strong southwesterly it creates an up-draft and blows the waterfall back high in to the air in a fine spray. It then falls back onto the Scout and finds its way in to the streams again to feed the waterfall once more."

"Oh!" Rosie said. "So it keeps feeding itself in a continuous cycle?"

"Yes. More or less."

"Wow! I'd like to see that!"

STREAM ON KINDER

Chapter Eleven

"COME on Rosie. Time to get dressed."

Rosie peeked from underneath her duvet. Connie was already dressed, leaning on the sill, peering out of the bedroom window intently. The wind was whistling in the eaves and the old tree outside their bedroom window was creaking as if ready to break. The snow had completely disappeared.

"No. I'm on holiday and I'm staying put."

She turned over, wrapping her duvet firmly around her body in the process, seeking to make herself immune from any invasion her friend might be planning.

"Please yourself. But you're missing the Downfall uprising!"

Rosie unravelled herself from her warm soft body armour and was out of bed like a shot. Much to her astonishment a great spray of what looked like water vapour was rising in a massive cloud high in the air above the gritstone edge of the Scout. But what really grabbed her attention was the fact that the lower point of this moving tower of spume began round about half-way down the waterfall's sixty-yard drop.

"Wow! How amazing. I wonder if Granddad's seen it?"

"He must have, the number of years he's been coming to Kinder," Connie pointed out. "Anyway, get dressed and you'll soon find out. He's probably tucking in to breakfast right now."

With that she made her way out of the room and down the stairs.

Rosie continued to gaze out of the window taking in the spectacle the natural phenomena provided, as it unfolded in front of her eyes. A yelp from Titch attracted her attention and then Ralph was walking across the yard. He opened the door to his workshop and disappeared inside. The girl smiled to herself and resolved to get dressed and join the family below.

By the time she emerged in to the kitchen Connie was helping her mother prepare breakfast, having assured her that Rosie would be hungry. This was to be expected, but the male figure sat at the kitchen table, reading the *Farmer's Weekly* and sipping a cup of tea was a surprise. Evidently Mr Gore-Booth had decided to slum it.

"Morning!" Rosie said to nobody in particular.

The greeting was returned by the other three occupants of the room. In particular the gentleman looked up from the paper and said, "And how are you young lady this blustery morning?"

Rosie smiled her sweetest smile.

"Fine Mr Gore-Booth. Have you seen the Downfall?"

He looked at her, somewhat puzzled by the question.

"The Downfall?"

"Oh, I forgot. Your bedroom looks over the Clough. You must see it. The waterfall's blowing back upwards. It's quite a sight. Come in to the yard."

Overcome by her enthusiasm he followed in her wake and made his way to the drystone wall.

"Isn't it wonderful? Have you ever seen anything like that before?"

She looked up at him, her long dark hair blowing wildly in the wind, her bright blue eyes shining beneath thick black eyebrows. He remained silent for a moment looking upwards to Kinder. Finally he turned to her and smiled.

"Quite remarkable. I've never seen anything quite so wild and beautiful in my life."

"I love it up here," Rosie responded. "Nature always has some surprise in store whatever the season. I wish Mam could be here."

"Where is she?"

"Back in Stockport at work, winning wages so she and I can live. She's a single parent." She looked at him once more. "Did you hear the Prime Minister's speech on Friday? Evidently I'm one of those feral children destined to become a scrounger and a leach on society at best." She shook her head and laughed. "And I thought I was going to be an engineer!"

※ ※ ※

"Are we going to make a start on a new sledge today?"

Ralph looked up through the steaming vapour of his cup of tea at Rosie and shook his head.

"I need more materials. There's an engineers' supplies warehouse on the edge of New Mills that has all kinds of odds and ends, but I need more cash. Anyway we need to collect wood for the bonfire tomorrow."

Granddad looked at his granddaughter.

"What's this about Rosie?"

"Didn't I tell you Granddad? Ralph and me, and hopefully Mikey, are going to manufacture sledges and maybe other stuff. Trouble is we need some thingymabob - oh you know - whatderyercallit Granddad?"

Jack O'Donnell seemed completely mystified.

"Working capital - that's it!" Rosie exclaimed, remembering her lessons in basic capitalist economy. "We need working capital to get us off the ground. I'm going to have to save up all my pocket money. Without raw materials we can't make anything."

"I've got seventy-six pence," Connie divulged somewhat hopefully, remembering the rebuff she'd received the night before.

Granddad's eyes narrowed and he looked thoughtful.

"Where yer going ter carry out this work?"

"Ralph's got a wonderful workshop. Do you want to see it?"

Granddad grunted and began to rise from his seat at the table.

"Why not, lass?"

"Put your coat on. It's not over-warm out there."

"I'll come with you," Ralph said.

"Me too!" Connie added, determined not to be left out, whatever the others might think.

Once suitably clothed, they trooped out of the kitchen and Ralph opened the door to his workshop, leant around the door jamb and switched on the light.

"After you, Mr O'Donnell!"

Jack entered the brightly illuminated room. Rosie joined him as he took in the neat layout of the workshop and its contents.

"This really does have possibilities. Very impressive Ralph."

"Where's the sledge?"

Rosie's tone of voice signalled her alarm.

"We left it behind above the field last night," Connie pointed out. "I'll go and get it," she volunteered, eager to be useful and thereby gain a foothold and hopefully become part of 'the creative team' her friend evidently envisaged.

She set off outdoors, Rosie following her, along with an excited Titch.

Jack O'Donnell continued to examine the workshop. He went over to the oxy-acetylene equipment, inspecting the pressure gauges, the blow-back arresters on the twin hoses and the brazing torch minutely, before returning to the work-bench. He picked up a metal fabrication consisting of two pieces of tubular steel, brazed together in the form of a tee. One of Ralph's test pieces he supposed.

Ralph remained silent watching the way Jack minutely inspected the bronze-welded joint. The older man looked up at the board on which Ralph had mounted his tools. He selected a small square and placed it against the tee-piece, holding it up to the light from the small window.

"Ermm."

He returned the square to its place on the board.

"How did you mitre the tube?" he finally asked the lad.

"By hand, with a one inch half-round file."

"How did you ensure its accuracy? You need a tight fit for a good joint."

"My eye and daylight, in the same way you checked whether it was a right angle or not."

Jack smiled.

"What's the tolerance for a good brazed joint?"

"Three thousandths of an inch, but, if you hold the component parts to the light, even a one thou gap will allow light through and you can see the gap quite clearly."

Jack nodded, his mind going back to the days when he was a tool-maker's apprentice and had first learnt the skill of low-temperature brazing, or silver-soldering as it is more commonly known, although it is not really soldering in the accepted sense.

"Where does Rosie come in to this?"

"She wants me to teach her to braze and bronze-weld. She's told me she can silver-solder and mitre joints. She says she wants to be an engineer. It was her idea to start a business."

Jack nodded.

"Yes," he said quietly. "She's wanted to be an engineer ever since she was knee-high to a grasshopper."

He put his hand on Ralph's shoulder, gripping it slightly for a brief moment.

"I'll tell thee somethin' else, Ralph. One way or the other, ower Rosie will become an engineer. Yer can bet yer life on that. She can be as determined as that little sister of yours when she sets her mind on summat."

He chuckled, before adding, "And I reckon you're the one to teach her the art of brazin'. I'm gettin' too old fert job!"

At that point they heard the giggle of girls and the sound of metal sliding and scraping over gravel and gritstone flags. They left the workshop to see the two youngsters dragging the sledge across the yard.

"Look at the bronze-welding on this, Granddad!" Rosie enthused.

"I've seen enough, lass!"

Much to her astonishment and profound disappointment he headed towards the kitchen door and then disappeared inside without another word.

"Umph!" Rosie managed to get out. "Have you upset him Ralph?"

Ralph laughed. "I don't think so."

※※※

After breakfast Mikey Grimsditch joined the other children and they spent the rest of the day scouring the farm and the countryside round about for anything that would burn, dragging it in great bundles down the lane to the old quarry; the only break in their activity being a short respite for a quick lunch. A horde of kids and a few adults from the immediate area were doing the same, and thus, by that evening, a sizeable bonfire had been erected ready for the festivities the following night.

Elsie Gartside had visited Pearl Grimsditch that morning as she'd promised. Mikey's mother now worked in the accounts department of the local co-operative society. As a consequence of their conversation over a cup of tea, Elsie had invited Pearl to share their evening meal and to assist her in making treacle toffee and more parkin for November the Fifth, an invite the younger woman had accepted with enthusiasm.

Mr Robert Gore-Booth had finally persuaded his partner to go for a drive in the White Peak, promising his lover a visit to Chatsworth on the way back. This decision hadn't been easy. He knew the Duke and Duchess of Devonshire personally and it would be rather inconvenient if they met. Nonetheless, his lady love had set her mind on visiting and he'd finally decided there was little chance of meeting the landowner - he being unlikely to frequent Chatsworth's cafeteria. Having no great love of the countryside, she'd been slightly upset when he'd informed her he'd extended their stay at the farm for another three days. He finally persuaded her by means of a bribe or two - a day out on a shopping expedition in Manchester city centre and a trip to fashionable Knutsford and Tatton Park in Cheshire.

She claimed to be a woman with simple needs. Robert knew better. Florence had many appetites, some of which could not be discussed in polite company and were confined to the boudoir, in the main. She had a penchant for fashionable clothes, expensive lingerie and underwear, combined with a burning desire for Government office.

※※※※※

KINDER DOWNFALL

Chapter Twelve

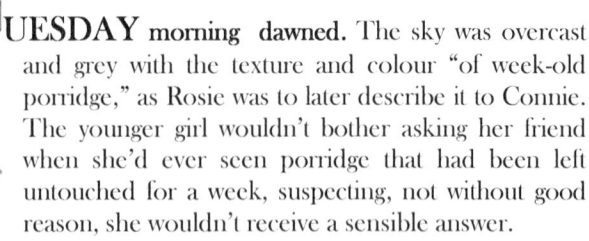

TUESDAY morning dawned. The sky was overcast and grey with the texture and colour "of week-old porridge," as Rosie was to later describe it to Connie. The younger girl wouldn't bother asking her friend when she'd ever seen porridge that had been left untouched for a week, suspecting, not without good reason, she wouldn't receive a sensible answer.

For once Rosie was out of bed and dressed first. Her spirits were buoyant; so much so that she'd escaped downstairs without the other girl's knowledge and careful to keep it that way. Eventually she re-entered the room, two steaming cups of tea in her hands. Connie remained fast asleep, her carroty red hair spread over her pillow in a fan of gleaming bright red-gold.

"Wakey-wakey! Here's a brew."

She placed her friend's drink on the bedside table, careful not to knock over the artificial limb stood upright next it, and then shook her exposed shoulder gently with her freed hand.

Connie gave out a soft groan and turned, blinking her green feline eyes in the early morning daylight.

"There's a cup of tea for you."

Rosie sat down on her own bed, watching her best friend slowly coming back to life.

"Thanks," she eventually sighed. "I'll let it cool down for a moment."

༺༻

Jack O'Donnell emerged from Ralph's workshop with a list in his hand and retreated in to the farmhouse. Elsie informed him there was tea in the pot. He nodded but didn't speak. He sat down at the kitchen table with her and perused his list thoughtfully, before extracting a pen from his inside pocket and adding to it. He looked up at last, obviously satisfied with his work.

"May I use yer phone, Elsie?"

She nodded her agreement and he rose and walked across the room to make his call, looking at the old grandfather clock as he did so. It was coming up to ten past eight.

🐏🐏🐏

At two o'clock that afternoon Rosie Akroyd, Connie and Ralph Gartside and Mikey Grimsditch left the farm and began a short walk down Coldwell Clough accompanied by Jack O'Donnell and Titch. Granddad had informed Rosie and the others they were going to the Sportsman to meet a friend of his, who would no doubt prove helpful to them.

Approaching the pub Rosie's eyes lit up. She ran forward, Titch at her heels. A tandem leant against the pub wall, with bulging pannier bags, front and rear. A collection of aluminium cooking equipment, a small kettle and a zig bottle for paraffin hung from the rear panniers. A green bag, which she knew contained a mountain tent, together with two rolled Karrimats, were strapped across the top of the bags.

The others soon joined her. Ralph began to examine the tandem frame in detail. It was stove enamelled a plain black, but the lugs were fancy with diamond cut outs and ornate delicately filed fleur de lys picked out in gold. The head badge comprised a white oval with a narrow red border outlined in black. This outer oval sported gold letters, proclaiming "HANDBUILT FRAMESETS MANCHESTER" The centre of the badge portrayed the black silhouette of a swift soaring on outstretched wings, with the maker's signature, *Malc Cowle*, above it and the slogan, "*Swift & True*" beneath it.

"Is Tom with Malc, Granddad?"

"I expect so. Where else would he be."

"Who's Tom?" Connie asked.

Rosie smiled. "He's about ten and he's another feral child doomed to become a villain like your Mikey and me! His dad's a bicycle frame builder and another single parent. We used to live near them in Levenshulme."

She led the way in to the pub, looking round for her friends. They were nowhere to be seen. She turned to tell her grandfather, puzzled, only to discover he had remained outside with the others.

"Hiya Rosie."

She swung round and laughed.

"Trust you to be hiding in an alcove near the door, Tom. Ready for a quick getaway no doubt!"

The boy and his dad laughed. The latter stood up.

"Where's your granddad, Rosie? Do you want something to drink?"

"He's with my friends admiring your tandem. Could I have orange squash please with tap water, no ice?"

At that point the rest entered the pub and Rosie went to grab a seat next to Tom.

"Long time, no see, little one," she said.

Tom smiled. It was a long time since Rosie had called him "little one." She used to babysit him.

"How are you Rosie?"

"Great," she responded. "Oh, this is my friend Connie and her boyfriend, Mikey."

Connie grinned and Mikey blushed.

"Come on you two. Sit down. This is my friend Tom. He won't bite."

"Is it hard?" Connie asked, looking in to the young boy's hazel eyes as she sat opposite him.

"What?" he asked, looking puzzled.

"Pedalling the tandem?"

He leant forward as if to let her in to a confidence.

"Don't tell me Dad, will you Connie? I just sit there in the toe-clips and let my feet go round, giving out a few grunts when we're struggling uphill. Dad does all the work!"

Rosie laughed.

"Don't be a fibber Tom Cowle!"

"Do you think I could have a go?"

"Ask me Dad. I'm sure he'll take you for a spin, Connie."

He looked across to the bar. Mr O'Donnell, a youth and his father seemed deep in conversation, whilst they waited to be served.

"Best leave it 'till tomorrow. He'll soon be on his second pint. It takes a great deal of skill to steer the bike from the back when he's had a skin full. I've been on that tandem since my fourth birthday and I'm only just getting the hang of it!"

Connie grinned. She was beginning to like this youngster.

"What brought you up here, Tom?" Rosie suddenly asked.

"Your granddad. He phoned Dad this morning. We're going to camp over the road."

"No, you mustn't," Connie intervened. "You can camp in our paddock free of charge and then you can eat with us as well."

❦❦❦

Initially, Tom had been a little miffed when his father had said they were riding out to Hayfield and would be camping for a few days. Not that he wasn't used to camping in cold weather or disliked riding on the tandem. Far from it. He loved cycling and camping. The fly in the ointment was the fact that Manchester City Council had organised a bonfire and firework spectacular in a local park that self-same evening, and he'd been looking forward to it for weeks. Now, however, he was glad they had come.

Rosie's friends were brilliant company and made a great deal of fuss over him, not least because he was the youngest, as had Mr and Mrs Gartside. The fact they were camping on the farm was an added bonus. Mrs Gartside had refused his father's offer of payment and wouldn't be contradicted.

His father was always a bit strapped for cash, but Tom knew that any cut in camping fees would give him the opportunity to insist on his fair share of the money saved. And, to add icing to the cake, the bonfire and fireworks in the quarry proved to be brilliant. Moreover he was convinced the proceedings were far superior to that enjoyed by his schoolmates back in Burnage, where he now lived.

He snuggled up in his sleeping bag that night a happy and contented lad, wondering what delights the next day would bring. Perhaps Dad would take him to Edale. They camped there at least once a year and he had friends in the village his own age.

❦❦❦

"What do you think of young Tom?"

Connie looked across to her friend, who was already tucked up beneath her duvet. She finally had her leg off and placed it by the bedside cabinet. She swung the stump and her left leg onto the bed, pulling the duvet over her body in the process.

"He's really nice. He's got an amazing sense of humour."
Rosie laughed.
"He has to have to cope with his dad, I expect."
Connie frowned.
"What's wrong with his dad?"
"Nothing, but he's not your average kind of man."
"How do you mean?"
"Well, he's brought Tom up more or less on his own since the lad was twenty-two months old. And he's brought him up on the back of a bike. First in a child-seat on a normal race bike and then, when Tom was coming up to four, he built the tandem. When Tom was five they cycled from Manchester to the Isle of Skye and back in the school holidays, camping on the way."
"The Isle of Skye? That's Scotland isn't it?"
"Yes, off the west coast and way beyond Glasgow. I'll show you on the map tomorrow. It's miles and miles away. They've cycled all over the place. They spent the last summer holidays cycling round Ireland for five weeks."
"His dad's taking me to New Mills on it tomorrow."
"New Mills?"
"Yes. Your granddad's asked him to pick up the tubing for another two sledges, and when I asked if I could have a go on the tandem he said I could go with him. I know where the warehouse is."
"Did you tell him about your leg?"
"No, but what's my leg to do with it?"
"Have you ever ridden a bike?"
"No. Ralph's got an old one in the barn but it's too big for me."
"I think you'd better tell Malc. Cycling's quite different from walking. Your leg's moving with a circular motion when you're cycling."
"But the top half of my leg and my knee joint are completely normal."
"But your foot and your ankle aren't! You need to tell him."
Connie frowned.
"Alright, but I'm sure it will be fine."
She leant over to switch off the table lamp.
"Sleep tight!"
"Watch the bugs don't bite!"

THE SPORTSMAN WITH KINDER LOW IN BACKGROUND

Chapter Thirteen

JUST let me move the tandem away from the wall, Connie, and then you can get on. I need to make sure the saddle height is right for you."

Connie placed her left leg in the toe-clip on the left-hand pedal and swung her right leg over the saddle and sat down. She attempted to place her right shoe in the right-hand toe-clip, but was having trouble.

The pedal kept rotating as soon as the shoe made contact. Malc took hold of the back of what he presumed was her ankle to assist her. He looked up at her in surprise.

"You've an artificial leg!"

"Yes. I meant to tell you."

She gazed at him with her bright green eyes, afraid he'd refuse to take her. However, although he shook his head, he placed her shoe in the toe-clip and tightened the strap slightly.

"Is the ankle articulated?"

"Yes, and it's spring-loaded."

He nodded his understanding.

"The question is, is it articulated enough? Pedal backwards Connie, but do it slowly. Stop if you feel any problem."

He watched carefully as she did as he asked, completing two revolutions.

"Okay. That seems fine. Can you dismount safely? I need to take the saddle up slightly."

She was off the bike quick as a flash and watched him release the saddle clamp, raise the saddle post a quarter of an inch, and then re-clamp it.

"That should do it Connie. We'll give it a try round the yard and then we'll be off, but if you feel the slightest discomfort you must tell me."

She smiled.

"I will. I promise."

All this time he'd been holding the bike upright by holding his saddle with his right hand, leaving his left hand free to assist her. He now grasped it with his left hand, facing forwards. Much to Connie's surprise he suddenly lifted his left leg and swung it over the handlebars lifting the limb as high as any showgirl on the stage. Now straddling the tandem's top tube, with his hands firmly on the handlebars, he placed his left foot in the toe-clip, pressed forward on the crank, simultaneously lifting his body to sit on the saddle. His right foot found its place in the toe-clip, as they began to move forward.

She squealed as they circled the yard, but before she knew it he'd made his way round the cow-byre and came to a halt by the gate next to the Bentley.

"Oh. I forgot to tell you Connie. It's your job to open and close gates."

She laughed as she dismounted, feeling more excited than she'd felt in a long time.

※※※

"What do you want to do Tom, now you've been dispossessed of transport?"

"I was hoping to go to Edale. I don't know now."

"We could walk there."

"Walk!"

Rosie laughed.

"You've got a good pair of legs. You can't have forgotten how to use them."

"But it's miles to Edale."

"Don't be daft. It's not that far. We can go over by Edale Cross."

He looked across the table at her for quite a long moment.

"Do you know the way?" he finally asked.

"Of course. I've walked there many times."

Another long silence.

"Okay. But don't walk too fast."

"Right. Go and get your windproof and I'll let Mrs Gartside know where we are off to."

※※※

"This is wonderful!"

"What did you say Connie?"

"This is wonderful!" she repeated, raising her voice. "How fast are we going?"

"Not fast. Almost twenty miles an hour."

They were speeding down Kinder Road towards the village, seemingly without any effort. They seemed to have been free-wheeling for ages.

As soon as they entered the village Malc slowed the tandem down to negotiate the narrow streets. They were soon at the junction with the main road to Glossop.

"Turn right and then left," Connie informed him.

Malc shook his head.

"No, I need to do some shopping for food first. I'll head towards Newtown and turn right in to the main shopping street in New Mills. Then we'll come back on the top road after we've picked up the tubing."

Connie realised it made sense and quickly agreed.

At first their route was fairly flat, but they soon built up speed again, the sheer momentum of the tandem taking them over the small rises they came across. Malc informed her they were cruising at twenty-two miles an hour. Eventually they reached the long straight downhill stretch that led them in to New Mills and Connie began to understand just how fast a tandem could move. By the time they were nearing the valley bottom they were travelling at over forty-five miles an hour and much to Connie's joy had overtaken two cars.

Then the brakes were being applied, Malc looked quickly over his shoulder to check the road behind was clear, signalled right with his arm outstretched, and moved to the centre of the road, before stopping at the tee junction. A couple of cars passed, then the road was clear and soon they were climbing the hill to the right, eventually coming to a halt outside the co-op.

"You get off first Connie and then I'll shove it against the wall."

She did as asked and then volunteered to guard it whilst he did his shopping.

"What do you think so far Connie?"

"Brilliant. It really is. I want a bike of my own now!"

He smiled, obviously pleased with her reaction.

"I won't be long. See you in a couple of minutes."

He disappeared in to the store. The girl didn't have to wait too long before he emerged with a carrier bag of food.

"Is there anything you need whilst we're here Connie?"
"No. I just want to get back on the tandem."
He stuffed the food in to the left hand pannier bag, asking, "Have you ever cycled before?" as he did so.
"No."
"Well. You must be a natural. You make a good tandem stoker. I could really feel the difference when we were riding up the hill."
She remained silent, but his praise had found its mark. She felt a warm glow inside.
"Right, I'll get on first this time. Then you climb aboard, but I'm not going too far. I'm in need of a cup of coffee."
"There's a nice café up the road at the junction with the road to Marple."
"Good choice, Connie. I know it well."

"How's your mam, Tom."
"She's okay. She's got a new job working for the Victorian Society, but she was really upset when Dad dropped me off on Friday night."
"Why?"
"Bloody John Major!"
"Tom! You shouldn't swear."
"Dad says John Major's enough to make a parson swear!"
Rosie laughed in response, but then looked thoughtful.
"My Mam was upset by what he said as well. Trouble is Major thinks everybody has the chance to live in some kind of ideal family. He hasn't a clue how people really live and how they cope to survive."
He looked at her for a moment, knowing only too well the terrible circumstances that had deprived Rosie of her father.
"I'm lucky," he said. "I know Mum and Dad love me. The fact they can't live together's a shame, but they've never let it affect me. I've got friends who live in so-called 'normal' families and their parents are constantly rowing. I couldn't stand that. I've never known my parents argue."
Rosie looked at him in surprise.
"I've heard your Dad argue!"
Tom laughed.
"Only about religion or politics. I meant I've never known Mam and

Dad have an argument about me, and they've never been nasty to each other."

"Granddad says your Dad loves an argument. He reckons he could start a row in an empty paper bag!"

Tom laughed again. They were sat on a grassy bank above a stream near the old packhorse bridge at the bottom of Jacob's ladder. Eventually, Rosie stood up.

"We'd better make a move. By the time we get to Edale it will be time to go home."

Tom nodded his agreement.

"Once we're through Barber Booth we can walk up the road to Edale village."

"Isn't there a footpath, Rosie?"

"Yes, but the road will be easier and quicker."

🐾🐾🐾

"How did you lose your leg, Connie?"

There it was. The inevitable question she didn't like being asked.

"A motor cyclist hit me, but it wasn't really his fault. He spotted me on the road and put his brakes on to slow down, but he skidded on loose gravel and went over on his side. His front wheel just slid in to my leg and took a big lump out of it."

She looked him in the eye, steeling herself against the look of pity she hated so much. Instead, much to her surprise, he just shrugged.

"Life's a struggle and then we die," he said with a wry smile. "The important thing is to make sure we make the best of it whilst we can."

"Exactly! That's what Ralph always said. Pick yourself up..."

"Dust yourself down..."

"And start all over again!"

"Good for you Connie. Come on, we've work to do and miles to ride."

"Malc..."

"Yes."

"Do you know why Ralph and Rosie want this stuff we're picking up?"

"Yes, to make sledges. Ralph showed me his workshop last night."

"Are you going to help them?"

"They seem to know what they're doing without my help. Ralph's obviously good at brazing and he's got tube bending equipment and all the other tools he needs."

"But there's not much of a future in building sledges is there? It's a very brief season for snow."

"Well... Yes, you're right, but he can use the same skills and equipment to manufacture all kinds of things."

"Like bike frames? Is that what you mean?"

"Well. Yes. That's a possibility."

"Would you be willing to teach him..." She interrupted herself. "No. I don't mean that. What I mean is would you be willing to teach ME?"

Her new found friend frowned, obviously caught off balance. He took a long sip of coffee.

"Why do you want to learn?" he eventually asked.

"I want to be useful. I want to be part of their team and I want to build myself a bike."

"It's not easy work, Connie. Mitring bike tubing cuts your hands to ribbons."

He showed her his fingers and the palms of his hands. His right palm in particular was a mass of fine cuts and scars.

"It's dirty work. You get covered in carbon from the oxy-acetylene and filings from the steel. It gets in your hair and on your clothes, and up your nose and in your mouth unless you wear a mask."

"I don't mind hard work and I don't mind muck. I'm a farmer's daughter. We delve in muck day in and day out."

He smiled, realising from the vehemence of her tone she was serious.

"Okay." He finally said. "If you are willing to work at it, I'll give you all the help I can."

She nodded.

"I'm deadly serious. I HAVE to prove I can do it!"

♥♥♥

"So. How was your day?"

"Just let me get me leg off and I'll tell you."

Rosie sat up in bed, her back propped up by a pile of pillows.

"There," Connie grinned, making her own way under her duvet.

She gazed across at her friend.

"It was the best day ever. Malc's really nice. He talks to you as if you were an equal and insists you call him by his first name. After we brought the tubing back we went for a ride. We went to Whaley Bridge and then to Chapel en le Frith and climbed up Rushop Edge. We whizzed down Winnats Pass to Castleton and then went to Hope and up through Edale and over Mam Nick and then we whizzed down Rushop Edge and overtook three cars. You should have seen the drivers' faces! He told me I'm a really good tandem stoker. But best of all he's going to teach me the art of building bike frames. In fact he's going to teach me how to measure people up and build frames tailored to their particular size and their individual requirements, like making a made to measure suit. I'm going to build myself a bike. He's going to provide me with some Reynolds 531 tubing and it'll be so light I'll be able to lift the frame with one finger."

She finally paused for breath. Rosie stared in disbelief, her dark brown eyes open wide.

"You don't have to look like that Rosie Akroyd. If you and Ralph are lucky I might be able to provide you with work when your customers for sledges melt away with the spring sunshine!"

RIVER GOYT AT NEW MILLS

Chapter Fourteen

WHEN the two girls entered the kitchen for breakfast the next morning they were not surprised to find Malc and Tom at the table along with Ralph, Granddad and Elsie. They were surprised to discover that Mikey was with them.

Granddad looked up.

"Ah. There you are. We've been waiting for you two."

"What's going on?" Rosie asked.

"Has something exciting happened?" Connie echoed.

"As your financial backer I've decided to call a business meeting."

The two girls exchanged glances and took their places at the table. At that point Mr Gore-Booth entered.

"Morning everybody," he greeted them. "Is there any chance of a cup tea?"

"I'll make it," Rosie volunteered.

"We were just about ter begin a business meeting," Granddad said, rather pointedly.

"A business meeting?"

"Yes. These children and Ralph are embarking on a business venture."

"Surely they are rather young to commence a business?"

Granddad shook his head.

"Although young Rosie, Connie and Mikey here are still at school it's important they think of their future. The days are long gone when a youngster could leave school and walk in to a job. Thanks to Thatcherism and the disastrous neo-liberal idea that the country can rely on banking, the financial and service sectors to pay its way, the engineering industries and manufacturing generally have collapsed. Industrial capitalism isn't working is it Mr Gore-Booth? What are today's unemployment figures?"

"Two and a half million officially," Malc intervened sharply. "Probably nearer three in reality and still growing."

"Aye, the Tories are good at fiddlin' the books."

Mr Gore-Booth did not rise to the bait, but he did ask if he could observe the proceedings and it was agreed, in the form of a round of nods, that he could.

Rosie produced his tea and took her seat next to him.

"Now then, to sum up where we stand. Ower Rosie wants to be an engineer an' has done so fer a long time. Ralph has already learnt how ter braze and bronze-weld and, having had some experience in that field myself, I can assure you he's good at it. He's attending a night-school course in mechanical engineering. He has a workshop and the tools he requires and has already made a prototype sledge which, I understand, young Connie has subjected to a number of severe tests, although she's failed to damage it. Mikey is a keen and I must say highly skilled woodworker. Rosie and Ralph want to start a business making sledges and they want Mikey to work with them. Is that what you want Mikey?"

"Yes."

"Right. Now, I've put up the cash for enough materials for two more sledges. Once you've sold them you're on your own. You'll have to buy more materials with whatever money you make. Work at it when you can, make a success of it and none of you will have to search for work when you finish school. Do you understand?"

Ralph, Rosie and Mikey nodded. Connie remained noticeably silent. Ralph looked across at her. She returned his look, but still remained silent. Her face was a mask, giving no hint of her feelings at being left out of Jack's final summing up. Ralph frowned, wondering what was going on in her mind. Normally her face was as expressive as a book.

Finally he said, "I think we should involve Connie."

Her face broke in to a smile at long last, much to Ralph's relief. Unfortunately, Connie soon wiped the smile off his face.

"I may not be available. I've arranged a course of instruction," she pronounced gravely, looking at Malc for a brief moment, as a result of which he gave her a quick smile of encouragement. "A course of instruction in the art and science of bicycle frame design and construction. Once I am qualified I may be able to sub-contract the brazing work to you, providing your work is up to my exacting standards."

Everybody, with the sole exception of the frame builder, looked at her in astonishment, including Rosie who had been given a prior warning, but hadn't taken it seriously.

"Umph. I never thought you'd turn out to be a selfish capitalist," Rosie responded. "Fancy you wanting to exploit other people's labour."

"That's a bit unfair, Rosie," her grandfather intervened. "Isn't your business going to be a capitalist enterprise?"

"No, it is not! And you of all people know it's not. We've agreed to form a worker's co-operative. We'll employ ourselves using our own capital and we'll all share equally in the results of our own labour."

Granddad smiled. Ralph backed Rosie up.

"Yes. We've agreed our enterprise will be under democratic management and control. If you want to be involved, you can be little sister, but we are not sub-contracting our labour to you or anybody else. Our workshop will be a capitalist-free zone. We are all free labourers. We have no intention of becoming anybody's wage slaves."

"Does that mean you'll take turns brewing up and doing all the basic work like keeping the place clean, the fetching and carrying and labouring generally?"

"Of course. And we'll train each other to do each other's jobs, so if somebody's ill or on holiday or something, there will always be one of us to fill in for them."

"And will you consider making other things besides sledges?"

"Of course. We're not daft. We've already agreed to make walking sticks like the ones I made for you and Rosie. Mikey will be really good at that and there's a big market for them."

"Right," Connie said with a grin. "I will consider your offer and let you know my decision when I've had chance to consult my business advisor!"

"Would you like to go for a ride this morning, Connie?" Male asked. "I fancy visiting Buxton."

Tom looked at his dad in disgust. He hadn't bargained on a walking holiday. Mr Gore-Booth sipped his tea, quietly and somewhat thoughtfully.

"What are your thoughts on the meeting you've just witnessed, Mr Gore-Booth?" Elsie asked.

The children and Ralph had left the kitchen for the workshop, leaving the adults alone.

"Quite remarkable," the gentleman responded. "I've never come across a set of children quite like them. So self confident, and each and everyone so polite and well behaved and yet full of fun and all so lively. I had a chance to talk to that young lad Tom this morning. I was admiring the tandem. He told me, with great pride, that you'd made it Mr Cowle, and he related some of the adventures you've shared. It's hard to believe he's only just turned ten years of age. He has a remarkable vocabulary for one so young."

Malc remained silent.

"Can I ask how you became a bicycle frame builder? It's an unusual occupation."

Malc shook his head, with a wry smile.

"Necessity is the mother of invention!"

The gentleman seemed to be puzzled, but before he could pursue the question further Jack intervened.

"I know Malc well. He served his time as an engineering apprentice. He completed his time as a draughtsman, a creative job he loved. He was an active trade unionist and eventually became interested in politics. He joined the Communist Party. A lethal combination. From that point on he was a marked man. He found himself blacklisted by the Engineering Employers' Federation and the Shipbuilders and Repairers' National Association, simply because he had the temerity to help to defend and advance the conditions of his fellows. Unable to obtain work in the trade he took great pride in, unwilling to accept a future of life on the dole, and with young Tom about to appear on the scene, he re-invented himself as a frame builder."

"Me and thousands more over the decades," Malc pointed out. "Good job we live in a free country."

The gentleman, whose father was a captain of industry, was about to respond when Elsie decided to put in her two-penn'orth.

"I'm no expert on politics, but I don't think any of the children are particularly remarkable at all, Mr Gore-Booth. They are perfectly normal children. They all come from different backgrounds, but they do have important things in common."

Her guest looked at her, somewhat surprised. Elsie smiled once more.

"Rosie, Tom and Mikey are all being brought up by a single parent. None of their parents planned to be single parents, but that is the way things have turned out. None of the parents have had an easy time, but they all got on with it. More importantly all the children, just like our Ralph and Connie, know they are loved and have stability in their lives. It is my belief that love and stability are probably the two most important factors children need if they are to flourish, and I've yet to find a single person who can prove otherwise. The four family units are quite different from each other, but they are all focussed on the well-being of the kids. They and I know the children are our future. They and thousands like them are this country's future. They and their parents, single or otherwise, deserve better than the cheap hypocritical jibes and threats the present Government are trumpeting."

Male smiled.

"I agree with Elsie," he stated quietly. "You can take that message back to your friend John Major, Mr... err, Blackwell, isn't it? Mr Blackwell, MP? Tell him to forget Victorian family values. Victorian family life was no picnic. Any student of the Industrial Revolution knows that for working people in our part of the world it was virtually impossible to have any family life. Husbands, wives and children had to work in the mill twelve hours a day, six days a week for a subsistence wage.

"As for the middle and upper classes, their family life wasn't up to much either was it? Childcare was never an upper class forte. Didn't the mothers put their children's breastfeeding out to a wet-nurse and their childcare in the hands of maids and governesses? As soon as the boys were seven didn't they send them away to preparatory school and then to public school? In fact, isn't that what happened to you in the 20th century? The wives and daughters were their husband's and father's chattels. The former were often seduced by their husband's business competitors and the daughters were all too often bartered in marriage in order to cement business, financial and political alliances. Love and marriage were two quite different concepts weren't they? In short many examples of middle-class and upper-class marriage were little more than a form of enforced prostitution.

"You need to remind Major it is not the role of Government to dictate family structures or lecture parents on a subject he clearly has no knowledge of. It's the Government's job to assist the development of economic and social conditions in which children can thrive and be encouraged to play a positive role in the society his predecessor, the sainted Margaret, had the temerity to deny even existed.

"They need to know they have the right to work when they leave school and that their parents have the right to leisure and be enabled to spend time with their children, instead of working all the hours God sends in order to eke out a living."

At this point the Right Honourable Robert Blackwell, Member of Parliament and junior minister in the John Major Government had had enough. He sported a face resembling that of a little boy caught with his hand in the jar of barley-sugars. He realised he had to inform his lady friend and fellow MP, Florence Clutterbuck, that they had been rumbled. He wondered if he should phone his wife and advise Florence to contact her spouse. Would the story be given to the press? He made his excuses and left the room.

"I've a feeling I've lost two paying guests," Elsie said with a grin.

"How on earth did you know who he was?" Jack O'Donnell asked Malc.

"Well. I recognised him for a start, but only after I'd been told his name. I debated with him once at a public meeting when I worked in London for the Communist Party as National Election Agent, although it must have been over fifteen years ago. He's changed a lot since then - his hair's disappeared and his paunch has grown. No doubt I've changed too. He obviously didn't remember me."

"So, who told you his name?"

"Young Connie. She and Elsie were changing the sheets. He'd left a letter from one of his constituents on the table next to the bed. Connie noticed the name."

"That's right," Elsie smiled. "And M'Lady's not his wife either. Now we know just exactly what the Tories mean by a return to Victorian Family Values! You should have seen the lingerie she'd left all over the floor. Talk about a strumpet and in my best bedroom too!"

"Ah well", Malc said. "There's one law for the rich and quite another for the labouring poor, as Disraeli pointed out many decades ago when Victoria was but a young Queen and he was a bit of a radical."

Postscript to Connie Gartside's Triumph

WHEN I commenced writing this short story I didn't know where the characters were going to lead me. I never do. However the year I set the tale in naturally took me back to my own situation at the time. Like Pearl Grimsditch and Rosie's mother, Alice Akroyd, I too was a single parent in November 1991.

My son Tom, around whom my life inevitably revolved, had just turned ten. And like Pearl and Alice I found the message of the then Tory Government with regard to the need for a return to Victorian family values both offensive and hypocritical, not least because in the case of divorced parents like myself it tended to create unnecessary divisions between the parent with day to day care and the so-called "absent" parent. In 1993 Major compounded his error with his "Back to Basics" campaign.

We have yet to see how the lives of Rosie and Mikey pan out, but I am pleased to report that my son, now aged thirty at the time of writing, is a highly successful website designer and plays a positive role in the society to which he belongs. The fact he has achieved this, despite my rather eccentric methods of childcare and nurture, is in itself proof of the resilience of children, and, without doubt, the positive role in his life played by the "absent" parent, namely his mother.

During the same period John Major was of course recovering from his four-year dalliance with Edwina Currie. As for the blessed Margaret, she remains, as far as I know, the only British Prime Minister to have reared a son who is a convicted international terrorist. So much for Victorian family values. I think I'll stick with my own!

Malc Cowle
Manchester, 2012

NOTE

The bus from Stockport to Hayfield now forsakes the busy A6 to travel via Offerton, Marple, Strines, Hague Bar and New Mills. From there the journey is as described in the book. On reaching the Waltzing Weasel in Birch Vale you are within two stops of your destination.

THE AUTHOR AND FRIEND KAREN SUTTON
CYCLING IN THE PEAK DISTRICT, CIRCA 2000.

The Bicycle Frame Builder's Apprentice

A Tale of Job Creation

BOOK AND BIKE FRAME BUILT BY MALC COWLE

THE BICYCLE is just as good company as most husbands and, when it gets old and shabby, a woman can dispose of it and get a new one without shocking the entire community. -

Ann Strong

The bicycle is the most civilized conveyance known to man. Other forms of transport grow daily more nightmarish. Only the bicycle remains pure in heart. -

Iris Murdoch, *The Red and the Green*

When man invented the bicycle he reached the peak of his attainments. Here was a machine of precision and balance for the convenience of man. And (unlike subsequent inventions for man's convenience) the more he used it, the fitter his body became. Here, for once, was a product of man's brain that was entirely beneficial to those who used it, and of no harm or irritation to others. Progress should have stopped when man invented the bicycle. -

Elizabeth West, *Hovel in the Hills*

For instance, the bicycle is the most efficient machine ever created: Converting calories in to gas, a bicycle gets the equivalent of three thousand miles per gallon. -

Bill Strickland, *The Quotable Cyclist*

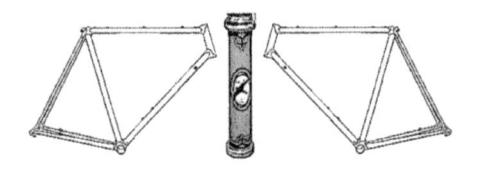

Chapter One

AS the sun sank towards the horizon, the sky to the west of Manchester turned a spectacular deep ruby red tinged with yellow gold. Rosie Akroyd, was about to change out of her school uniform and make herself ready to meet her friend Connie.

Attracted by the sheer beauty of the moment she gazed out of her bedroom window in wonder. Such sunsets were not uncommon - the pollution produced by the urban conurbation in which she resided virtually guaranteed them, given the right weather.

In this case a cold snap following a mild winter spell had provided the necessary atmospheric conditions. Moreover, the small terraced house she shared with Granddad and Alice, her mother, perched high on top of the hill in Edgeley, Stockport, overlooking the Mersey valley from what had been its Cheshire bank to the neighbouring old county of Lancashire, provided a perfect view. At last she turned away. She needed to get ready and then organise Granddad. The bus from Hayfield would arrive about five o'clock.

It was Boxing Day, 1991, and Connie had arranged to stay with her friends in Stockport - an unusual occurrence. Although Rosie was looking forward to the visit, she didn't understand why her friend had been so insistent on staying at her home. As a townie she much preferred the Gartside's farm in Hayfield. What she didn't realise was that Connie had ulterior motives, let alone that Granddad enjoyed her friend's confidence.

"Now, are you sure you have everything you need?"
"Of course, Ralph. Stop fussing!"
"Have you packed all the Christmas presents safely?"
"Ralph! Stop treating me as though I'm daft."
Connie bent down to fondle Titch's ears for one more time.
"Look after my big brother whilst I'm away, please Titch," she said softly.

157

The Manchester terrier wagged his tail vigorously, as if understanding every word. She turned back to her brother with a big smile on her face.

"Look after Mum and Faither, Ralph, and stop worrying about me. I'll phone you when I arrive and then you can speak to Rosie."

She gave him a final hug and climbed aboard the bus. Her timing was perfect. As soon as she'd handed over the fare and made her way towards the stairs to the upper deck the vehicle was on its way.

Ralph watched the bus depart and then turned on his heel.

"Come on Titch. Let's go and see how Mikey's getting on."

Connie gazed out of the window, as the bus made its way through Birch Vale towards the neighbouring town of New Mills. To any who happened to lay eyes on her she appeared to be a perfectly normal and calm young girl; a teenager without a care in the world. Internally her mind was a turmoil of hope and anticipation, tinged with more than a touch of excitement, not quite sure if the task she had set herself would be attainable.

With the encouragement of Rosie's grandfather, whose socialist ideas had their roots in the 19th century working class concepts of self-help and co-operation, Rosie's, Ralph's and Mikey's plans to form a producer co-operative, with the long-term aim of providing themselves with full-time employment, were now well advanced. In a situation of continuing economic crisis and deepening recession, which was also having its negative effects on already struggling hill-farmers, Connie's immediate family had not been slow in providing quiet support for the children's long-term plans.

Unfortunately for Connie her brother and friends had refused to involve her in their enterprise. To make matters worse, Rosie's insistence they would only involve individuals with appropriate skills and whom they were convinced could work as part of a creative team, remained fresh in her memory - the implication being that she was neither skilled nor likely to have the capacity for team-work.

Connie had the sense to realise she was extremely competitive, and sometimes this led to unnecessary friction, no matter how unintentional. But she also reasoned, and not without justification, that circumstances had forced her to be competitive. She remained convinced being so was not a bar to being creative, or to working with others to achieve a common end.

As a result she had determined to prove that she not only had the capacity to learn a useful skill, but could be as creative as any of them, and possibly more creative than most. Moreover, the one person she believed could assist her in achieving her objectives was a resident of Manchester. She'd arranged to meet him and this was the primary reason for her intended stay in Stockport.

"Come on Granddad. We mustn't be late!"

"Stop frettin' lass. It's downhill all the way ter the bus station."

"Yes. And last time you rushed down a hill you sprained your ankle. It was half-way down Kinder Scout if I remember right!"

"And if I hadn't yer wouldn't have met Ralph or Connie, so count yer blessings."

Rosie shook her head. Granddad always seemed to have the perfect response, although she knew instinctively the response this time was far from perfect. One part of her wanted to run and thus make sure she was in plenty of time to meet Connie. The other insisted she stayed with Granddad. He was now in his eightieth year and, despite all his protestations to the contrary, nowhere near as nimble as he used to be.

As it happened she needn't have worried. They arrived at the bus station adjacent to Mersey Square a good three minutes before the bus arrived. As usual Connie was the first to disembark, a rucksack on her back, a large canvas bag in her hand and a big grin on her face.

"Hiya Rosie. Hiya, Mr O'Donnell. Happy Christmas."

"Happy Boxing Day," Rosie responded with a smile. "Let me take your bag."

They set off to climb the steep hill, the two girls chattering like a pair of magpies, whilst Granddad brought up the rear, breathing heavily, his lungs wheezing like a worn-out old steam engine. Twenty minutes later, during which time the old man had stopped to catch his breath at least four times, Rosie had opened the front door and her mother was fussing over Connie like a mother hen.

More or less at the same time, about three miles away in the Manchester suburb of Burnage, Malc Cowle was relaxing in his favourite armchair, listening to the radio and wondering if he should make an effort and go down to the pub later. The Christmas holiday was not the best of times for him. For once the family home was quiet. Tom, his ten year old son, always spent Christmas with Clare and she was visiting her sisters in London. They wouldn't be back until New Year's Eve.

At least the holiday would soon be over. He had work to do in the morning, although customers were thin on the ground. Rising unemployment not only prevented those directly affected from spending; it also made those still in work more cautious in their budgeting. Nonetheless, he'd agreed to train a youngster eager to learn the craft of building bike frames, although she was still at school and would be for another three years. He had the feeling Connie might test his patience. He smiled to himself, remembering his first encounter with the young lass who had accompanied him on the tandem to pick up the steel tubing for her brother's sledges the previous November. No doubt she'd be with Rosie, Alice and Jack right now.

He wondered how much she'd learnt from the book on bicycle frameset design and construction he'd lent her. There was a slim chance it would have put her off the idea of building a bicycle frame for herself, but somehow he doubted it. He hadn't known her long, but he'd been more than impressed by her spirit and tenacity, not least because of the way she'd taken to riding his tandem, despite her artificial leg. He'd since learnt from Jack O'Donnell that once she put her mind to a task it was extremely unlikely that Connie would be deflected from her intended purpose, and certainly not without a determined fight.

At last he made his mind up. He'd go for a drink, but not at his local. He decided to visit the house in Edgeley, say hallo to Alice and the girls and take Jack for a pint. He looked at his watch - five forty-five. There was plenty of time yet. He decided to listen to the six o'clock news and then the Archers, before having a shave. If he cycled over to Edgeley he'd arrive shortly after eight o'clock. By that time they would no doubt have finished their evening meal and Jack would be ready for a pint not too long after.

✧

Alice returned to the living room with a big smile on her face.
"A visitor for you Connie."
The thirteen year old rose from her seat, looking puzzled. Alice had returned from answering the front door bell unaccompanied.

"Where?"

"He'll be in the back entry. Go and open the backyard gate. He's on his bike."

The lass shook her head of carroty red hair. Her green feline eyes flashed, as illumination dawned.

"Is it Malc?"

"That's for me to know and you to find out. The sooner you open the gate the sooner you'll know."

Rosie looked at Granddad. He returned her gaze, but his face gave nothing away.

"Did you arrange this?"

He didn't answer, but before she had chance to follow up her question Connie conducted Malc in to the room.

"Hallo everybody," he said. "I thought we might go for a pint later Jack. Do you fancy one Alice?"

"Not tonight. I'm working tomorrow, worse luck, and I need to keep my eye on the girls." She smiled. "Have you had a good Christmas Malc?"

"Nice and quiet. I treated myself to a lie in on Christmas day and enjoyed a roast pork sandwich complete with stuffing. I'd made it the night before and put it under my pillow along with my present from Tom."

"Pull the other one!" Alice responded with a chuckle.

"What did Tom give you?"

"A kiss Rosie. He gives me a kiss every year and I give him one back!" He smiled and then asked, "What about you? Did you get plenty of presents?"

"Loads," she responded, her sharp blue eyes shining bright.

"And how's life on the farm Connie?"

"Fine, Malc, but I've got something to show you."

She fled upstairs, returning moments later with a rolled sheet of A3 paper, which she handed to him. He opened it out, holding it at arm's length, and his eyes opened wide in their turn.

"Who drew this?" he asked after some moments.

"I did. Have I done it right?" she responded, a hint of uncertainty in her voice as if awaiting some sort of judicial decision.

"Well. I'll need to check your measurements, but it certainly looks right."

He passed the drawing over to Jack, before turning back to her.

"How did you measure yourself, Connie?"

"Ralph helped me." She smiled and then added, "He also let me use his drawing board and instruments."

"I think we are in the presence of a very gifted young person, Jack," the frame builder said quietly. "It took me years to learn to draw as neatly as that."

Although Connie didn't know it, this was praise indeed. Malc had been a time-served engineering draughtsman before he'd been forced to reinvent himself as a bicycle frame builder.

Chapter Two

RADIUM Street, Ancoats, Manchester, could hardly be described as an attractive place, except by an industrial archaeologist. Situated on the first floor of an old cotton mill, Malc's frame building workshop was sub-let from a friend of his, namely Geoff Warby, who specialised in stove-enamelling bicycle frames and motorbike petrol tanks.

Their relationship was mutually advantageous. Malc needed the services of a stove enameller and Geoff, as well as being good at his job, was the only specialist in his field in Greater Manchester. The nearest alternative was C & G Finishes in Liverpool. At the same time, Geoff required the services of a frame builder.

Customers who decided to have their favourite frames re-enamelled sometimes asked for small modifications, requiring silver soldering and brazing, to be made. Those involved in crashes often required dents filled, tubes replaced and other repair work done that demanded the skills of a frame builder. Moreover, cyclists tended to renovate their frames during the winter months, when the demand for new frames was at its lowest.

The 27th of December was a Friday and Malc arrived at the premises at nine o'clock. He'd arranged that Jack O'Donnell should bring the two girls in at ten. In the meantime he decided to tidy up the workshop, a job he was prone to neglect.

"It looks as though there's been a war!"

Jack laughed. Ancoats came as a shock to many a Mancunian. Large sections of the area resembled a bombsite. To a young farmer's lass from rural Hayfield, a village whose own mills and textile printing works had long since been demolished or tarted up, it must have seemed extraordinarily dirty, ugly and neglected.

"It does a bit doesn't it, Connie? However, the fact is this is one of the most important sites in Britain's industrial history. It's a disgrace that it's been allowed ter fall in to such a state."

"What do you mean, Granddad?" Rosie asked

They were walking down Jersey Street. A wasteland of rubble to their left, obviously not the result of recent demolition, indicated long-term neglect. A complex of tall ancient and somewhat decrepit mills, some eight stories tall, shut out the light to their right. Then the scene changed, with equally tall mills on their left, plunging the narrow street in to deep shadow.

"These are McConnell's Mills," he informed them, nodding to his right. "They were built in 1790 by Scottish migrants. The next lot on this side were built shortly after by another Scottish family, the Murrays. They're the oldest cotton spinning mills still standing in Manchester, although they stopped spinning cotton here decades ago."

"But why are they so important Granddad?"

"Ancoats was the first industrial suburb in the world's first industrial city. This is where the Industrial Revolution really took off. The men, women and children who slaved in those mills propelled Britain to the forefront of world trade and world influence. It was on their backs that the Napoleonic Wars were financed and fought, and the British Empire was extended to the east. Thanks to mechanisation, by the 1840s the cotton masters were accumulating wealth on a scale hitherto unknown in all the history of all the peoples of the world. But those who designed and built and operated their mills and their machinery, and thus made it all possible, lived in abject poverty. Wages were so low all members of the family had to work, including children, some as young as six years of age up to the 1820s, when they raised the minimum age to nine. The cotton masters claimed it kept them off the streets!

"The Chartist movement - the fight of the common people to have the right to vote - began here in 1838 and in 1842 Manchester was the centre of Britain's first general strike and the struggle for the ten hour working day. The suffragette movement - the campaign for women's right to vote - began here. Such was the influence of this area by the 1860s, cotton textiles on every inhabited continent were known as Manchester cloth. The textile industry also led to Manchester and Salford becoming a major engineering, railway and chemical manufacturing centre. In many ways this area was the cradle of it all, and look at it now! The money grubbers have bled it dry and left it to its fate, just as they bled the workers dry in the so-called 'good old days.'"

He shook his mane of white hair in heart-felt disgust and then, having delivered his impromptu history lesson, turned in to a narrow lane between the two complexes comprising Murray's Mills. Half-way down this roadway, on their left, they came to a high arched gateway which led in to a large courtyard open to the sky. He led them across the yard to a flight of iron steps leading up to a closed wooden door in the far right-hand corner. They climbed to the top and Jack pushed the door open.

He led them in to a room, illuminated by fluorescent tubes. Two great metal cabinets, which the girls later learned were stove-enamelling ovens, stood to their left. Next to them, on overhead rails, an array of frames and forks in a variety of colours were suspended on hooks and, on two adjacent tables a collection of motorbike petrol tanks awaited attention. In the far corner, straight ahead, stood a wooden structure with a window and an open door, which had once comprised an office. Malc appeared and greeted them as if they were long-lost friends.

Back in Hayfield the sky was a clear pale wintery blue, the air crisp and frost abundant. Ralph and his father, assisted by Ralph's two elder brothers and their dogs, had been gathering their flock of Scottish Blackface sheep from the high plateau of Kinder Scout throughout the morning. In normal circumstances the sheep would have been left to make their own way down to the lower slopes as the winter cold began to take hold, but these were not normal times. Sheep thieves had been active in the area since the previous November and the Gartsides had not been exceptions to their depredations.

Ralph's Manchester terrier, Titch, had participated in the proceedings. Although the breed had been developed for the specific task of ratting, Titch's upbringing on the farm and his interactions with collies had made him as useful a work dog as any when necessity demanded his services. With the bulk of the flock safely grazing on the lower slopes where they could easily be seen from the farmyard, they finally made their way back home. Elsie looked up as they entered the kitchen.

"You look absolutely frozen lads. Get by the fire. Jed, put kettle on and I'll make a fresh brew."

The farmer did as instructed, but Jem shook his head.

"Ah'm goin' ter have ter go, Mother. Ah've been at it since five this mornin' an' Ah'm workin' ter neet in't quarry. Ah'm in need o' forty winks!"

"I can't stay either, Mum," Richard concurred. "I've promised to tek our lasses ter Buxton."

"All right," Elsie responded reluctantly, "But give my love to the kids, Richard, and to that lad of yours too, Jem. Tell Brenda and Dora we must get together soon."

Jem laughed. The whole family had spent Christmas day together, as they did every year. Nonetheless he knew his mother loved the role of grandmother and matriarch.

"What about New Year's Day? Let's all go ter the Rambler or th' Nag's Head fer a slap up lunch. My treat. You deserve a rest Mother and the kids will love it."

"Sounds good ter me!" Jed confirmed.

Young Ralph echoed his sentiments, as did Richard.

"I don't mind cooking. It's the least I can do for my family..." Elsie began to protest, but her eldest son's frown and rather stern expression stopped her in her tracks. She returned his look, shook her head and finally caved in.

"Okay. Have it your own way, Jem. I must admit it's something to look forward to."

With that Jem and Richard left to return to their respective families in Bradwell. Ralph meanwhile had taken the hint and was busy shovelling tea in to the pot as his father waited for the kettle to whistle. Titch had already retreated to his privileged place of honour on the flock mat in front of the fire, more than content with his lot after his earlier endeavours on the moor.

⁂

Jack O'Donnell and his two young charges were making their way back home, walking along Redhill Street, the Rochdale canal to their left. Malc accompanied them, pushing his bike. Connie had rather hoped he'd have been on the tandem, for then she'd have had a chance to persuade him to transport her back to Edgeley. Unfortunately, he'd cycled to work on his touring bike.

Both girls had learnt a lot from their visit, although Rosie hadn't spent much time in the mill. She'd persuaded Granddad to help her search for a particular church in Ancoats. When she was younger Granddad had read to her every night before she fell asleep and one of her favourite authors happened to be Alan Garner.

In one of his books, three children had travelled in to Manchester from their home in Burnage. They came across a large metal glass-fronted case containing a street map in Piccadilly, designed to provide visitors with detailed information as to their whereabouts. Having given the handle which scrolled the map up and down a spin, they'd discovered Every Street in Ancoats. The name had intrigued them and they'd gone on to find it. One of the lads had kicked his football which had sailed in to a derelict church. On entering to retrieve the ball they suddenly found themselves emerging in to a strange medieval world named Elidor.

The story had intrigued Rosie and the visit to Ancoats had refreshed her memory. Consequently she insisted Granddad should take her in search of Every Street. He had done as she asked, leaving Connie to learn some more of the art and science of bicycle frame construction without distraction. Unfortunately, although they eventually discovered Every Street, the church had disappeared - yet another victim of the decay and neglect prevalent in the area.

Connie had been more than happy with Rosie's desire to seek the entrance to the mysterious fantasy world of Elidor and thus leave her alone. She was determined take advantage of the situation presented to her. She needed to pick Malc's brains and take advantage of his practical skills if she was to advance her desire to build herself a bicycle frame. But there was more at stake than that. She was still smarting from being left out of Rosie's and Ralph's plans to make and sell sledges and walking sticks and was determined to show she too could play a useful and productive role. The frame builder's reaction to her first design drawing had been more than encouraging. He'd rechecked her body measurements and found those she'd detailed on the drawing to be accurate.

This hadn't surprised her too much because she'd followed the instructions in the book he had lent her very carefully. She had, however, made one simple mistake in the frame design, which Malc had pointed out to her. As a result he'd advised that the frame's top tube needed to be ten millimetres longer, which meant a slight change in both the frame's head angle and its fork rake. More importantly he'd explained in detail how she'd gone wrong, so now she not only knew what to avoid in future, but also realised that she had not been in error in the rest of her calculations. This in turn had given her greater confidence in her own abilities.

Despite this positive development, Malc had dealt one blow to her immediate ambitions. Much to her consternation he'd told her she would be wasting her time building a made to measure frame for her own use.

"Why not? It's the best way I can prove to the others I'll make a useful member of their team. I have to prove to them I can play a useful part in their enterprise! They just won't take me seriously."

He'd shaken his head, but smiled encouragement with his eyes.

"They'll want you to be part of the team; don't worry about that, Connie. But you're still growing and in the next couple of years you'll no doubt shoot upwards. What's the use of building a frame that will most probably be far too small for you before you've had chance to enjoy it? A made to measure frame, properly looked after, will last a lifetime. Wait 'til you're fully grown before you build it."

Connie had gazed at him, lost for words. She wanted to protest but she quickly realised his advice made sense.

"But what can I do? I don't just want to prove I can do the work. I want to be a cyclist like you. I can't wait until I've grown."

He'd laughed at that point, but then sought to calm her.

"I'm building a frame for a mate of mine. I'll pick you up on the tandem in the morning. You can help me and learn as you're going along. How long are you here for?"

"I'm going back to Hayfield on New Year's Eve."

"Right, that gives us until Monday night. Are you willing to work tomorrow and Sunday?"

"Yes, of course. I need to learn as much as I can."

He'd smiled once more.

"In that case, I'll phone Ralph on Monday evening and tell him how you've progressed. I'll also give you some test pieces to take back and I'll ask Ralph to teach you to bronze weld."

Naturally Connie had been over the moon, but Malc had a further card up his sleeve which he wasn't about to reveal.

When they reached the junction of Redhill Street and Great Ancoats Street, the frame builder announced he had to leave them.

They made their farewells and watched him cycle off before crossing the busy main road, heading for nearby Piccadilly railway station and the train back to Edgeley, both girls satisfied with their day out in the dismal industrial slum, although for differing reasons.

MURRAY'S MILLS, IN THE FOREGROUND AND MCCONNELL'S IN THE BACKGROUND; VIEWED FROM ROCHDALE CANAL BRIDGE, NEAR JUNCTION OF REDHILL STREET AND RADIUM STREET.

Chapter Three

"STOP rushing, Connie! I can't keep up!"

The younger girl turned, a big grin on her impish little face. "I can't wait to get home. I'm so excited; I need to tell Ralph all about it."

It was ten thirty in the morning and they'd disembarked from the bus a few minutes before. They were now making their way up the Kinder Road.

"All about what?"

"About everything I've learned. Malc's given me loads of ideas about useful things we can make that people will want to buy."

"Well, why don't you tell me? Why's it such a big secret?"

"I intend to tell you, but not until I tell Ralph. You and him are a team aren't you? It would be unfair to tell you and not him."

She laughed before adding, "We'd better call in to see Mikey. He'll need to be there when I reveal my business propositions."

She smiled once more and insisted Rosie stop dawdling. At the same time, however, she made a conciliatory gesture by putting her arm through the crook of the other girl's elbow.

"Come on Rosie. Let's go and see Mikey and Pearl. You can rest your weary legs and maybe have a cup of tea."

Rosie frowned and shook her head in disgust.

"My legs aren't weary," she responded with more than a touch of sharpness in her voice. "They just don't want to constantly race a one-legged cripple who seems to think life's just one long competition that she has to win at every stage."

She stopped in her tracks, looking at Connie, her face a portrait of dismay.

"I'm sorry. I didn't mean to say that! It came out all wrong."

The younger girl laughed.

"You didn't say anything wrong, Rosie. I am a one-legged cripple and I am competitive."

She paused for a moment as though searching for words, before adding, "That first time I went on the tandem with Malc we talked about the accident. He didn't say he was sorry for me, or any of that rubbish I find so embarrassing. Instead he told me life's a struggle and then we die, so we have to make the most of life while we can. I remember how relieved I felt when he said it. You see, I agree with that and have done for a long long time. It's just that he put my own thoughts in to words."

She gave her best friend's arm a reassuring squeeze.

"Come on, Rosie. You are far too serious sometimes. It's too cold to be hanging about."

A few minutes later they were knocking on the door of the Grimsditch's cottage. They didn't have to wait long before Mikey was ushering them in to the living room, the smile on his face indicating he was pleased to see them. His mother appeared in the doorway from the back kitchen.

"Hiya, you two. You look starved to death. Get by the fire. Mikey'll make us all a cup of tea won't you love."

The lad interpreted his mother's words as a command rather than a question, although he was more than happy to comply.

Connie, however, didn't join Rosie in front of the fire. Her attention had been drawn to a collection of wooden objects laid out haphazardly on the dining table. She picked one up and turned to Pearl.

"Did Mikey make these?" she asked.

Pearl smiled.

"Yes. He says they're for walking stick handles. He's been coming up with all kinds of hare brained schemes lately."

"But, this is beautiful Pearl. It's just what we need, and it's given me an idea."

She walked over to Rosie, urging her friend to examine it, before handing it to her. Then she turned back to study the others, a thoughtful look on her face. The pieces of wood were in various stages of development, the one she had passed to Rosie being the only one anywhere near finished. Most were blanks, obviously waiting to be carved, smoothed and varnished. Mikey had cut them out of flat sheets of wood, about 30mm thick in various shapes; some based on the curves of ram's horns, and some inspired by the head and neck silhouettes of various birds.

"So what have you learnt whilst you've been away Connie love?"

"Lots Mum, but I'm ever so glad to be back."
Elsie frowned.
"Didn't you like Stockport?"
"I liked staying with Rosie, and her mother and grandfather, and I enjoyed working with Malc, but I'm glad to be back."
Elsie looked even more puzzled, but Rosie added enlightenment.
"I think Connie's finally understood why Granddad and me think this place is so special."
"And why is that?"
"Because Stockport and Manchester are so dirty and so cramped. People need fresh air and wide open spaces. Granddad says we need to get out in to the great outdoors and submerge our roots in the natural world now and again if we're to be fully human and realise our true place in Nature's scheme of things."
Elsie laughed.
"Your granddad talks a great deal of sense young Rosie."
"The funny thing is Granddad loves Manchester and the surrounding towns. He knows all about its history. He's always talking about its people and what they've achieved and the way they've struggled, but he'll seize any chance to get away from it."
"Malc told me towns like Manchester are primarily made for toil, but people need time for self-education, leisure and recreation," Connie interjected. "He said sensible people realise they only work in order to win the means to live. He reckons only fools think they live in order to work."
"No doubt they are both right," Elsie conceded, "but in the meantime, fool or no fool, *I know* a woman's work is never done, and since you two are both fast becoming young women you can help me prepare a hot meal for Ralph and Jed."
Connie laughed.
"They must have heard you. They're crossing the yard now. I'll put the kettle on."
Rosie looked up expectantly and within moments the door opened and Titch came across the room at great speed, eager to greet her. He stood on his hind legs, ears erect, expecting his reward. The girl laughed, bent down and fondled his ears.
"How are you little one?"
The dog took a swipe at her face with his tongue and then went

scurrying over to Connie, pawing at her for attention in turn, as though bestowing a great honour on them both.

Jed Gartside took his place at the kitchen table opposite Rosie, removing his old battered flat cap as he did so, and carefully placing it on his knee. His eyes smiled a welcome from his weather-beaten face.

"You're lookin' well our Rosie. How are Jack and Alice?"

"They're fine Mr Gartside. They send their love."

Ralph meanwhile removed his jacket and placed it on the back of a chair next to his father, before sitting down in his turn.

"It's good to see you again Rosie," he said, a shy smile on his lips. "Has our Connie behaved herself?"

Before Rosie could respond, Connie darted across the room and, once behind his chair, put her arms around her favourite brother's neck, hugging him close.

"What a thing to ask! Whenever have you known me not behave?"

"Aye, true enough." he responded wryly. "You always do behave little sister. Sometimes well and sometimes badly. I just wanted to know which!"

She laughed, but before she could come up with a smart answer the whistle of the kettle called her back to her domestic duty.

Once the tea was brewed and they were all settled down at the table, Connie informed them, "Mikey's coming over after lunch."

She turned to Ralph.

"He's working on some handles for walking sticks. I told him you'll want to see them."

"They are really good," Rosie added.

Jed looked at Elsie through the vapour of his cup of tea.

"I reckon thee and me will be able ter retire soon," he said. "At this rate the kids will mek my humble efforts at sheep farmin' redundant."

Elsie chuckled.

"Maybe, but all work and no play turns kids in to sourpusses I reckon."

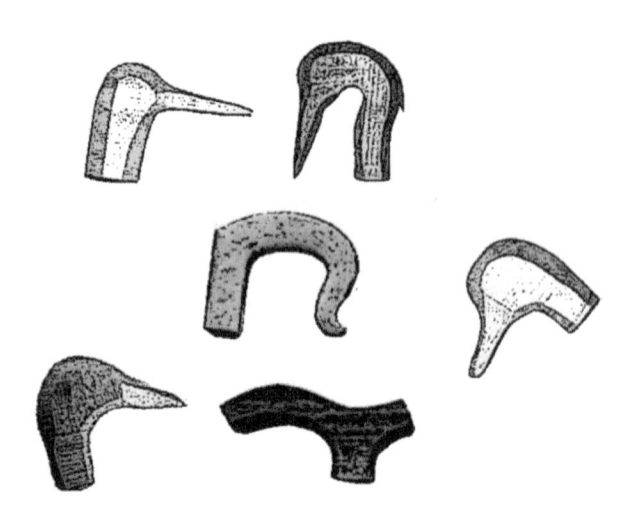

MIKEY'S PARTLY FINISHED HANDLES

Chapter Four

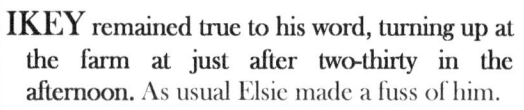

MIKEY remained true to his word, turning up at the farm at just after two-thirty in the afternoon. As usual Elsie made a fuss of him.
"Can you stop for the evening meal?" she asked.
He shook his head.
"Mam will be expecting me back, Mrs Gartside."
"Don't you worry about that young Mikey. I'll ring Pearl and invite her as well. It's New Year's Eve and you're near enough family!"
Without more ado she marched over to the phone.
Connie was eager to get down to business.
"Come on. Get that bag open, Mikey, and show Ralph your walking stick handles."
He did as she asked, placing his selection on the table in front of the older lad. Much to all their surprise, Jed had one in his hand before Ralph had his arm fully extended.
"Is this a heron's head?" he asked.
"Yes. I'm working on all the largish birds found in the area. That's a teal. The one with the long bill's a woodcock. The other's a mallard. I'm working on grouse and snipe and maybe a peregrine falcon."
"I wouldna mind one o' these. I've always liked herons. Are thee going ter paint 'em lad?"
"I hadn't thought about it, but I'm going to put eyes in them, once I've figured out how to make them, or where to get them from."
"There's a hobby shop in New Mills. They sell all kinds of doll's eyes," Connie informed him, with a smile. "Those for rag dolls and teddy bears might do it."
"How much do thee think yer can sell a walkin' stick fer?"
"Fifteen quid, Faither," Ralph intervened.
"Fifteen quid. That's more than I can get fer a yearling lamb!"
"That's the price they're selling them for in Castleton and they are cheap imported rubbish. Ours will be top quality, handmade out of locally sourced materials, and we are not about to sell our labour

cheap."

"But I'm family!"

"Family or no family, the labourer is worthy of his hire and we're beginning as we mean to go on."

Jed Gartside gazed around the table. His eyes were met by a circle of nodding heads. It seemed they all agreed with Ralph.

Ralph smiled at his parent's obvious dismay.

"Mind you, Faither, we could maybe do a deal if you were to provide us with some materials."

Jed's face brightened immediately.

"Now thee art talkin' lad! What materials?"

"Blackface or Woodland sheep horns. Collect all those you can find and we'll pay you the going market price."

The farmer frowned.

"And what exactly is the market price?"

"I'll have to work that out Faither. But you could test the water. All you have to do is find somebody nearby who wants to buy them. We don't mind competition."

"Who on earth would want ter buy 'em? I dunna know anyone! If there were any demand I'd have been sellin' 'em years ago. There wouldn't be a Scottish Blackface, ram or ewe, with a pair of horns on Kinder Scout!"

"In that case we won't have to pay you very much will we?" young Connie interjected. "It's all about supply and demand at the end of the day."

"Umph! Did yer hear that our Elsie? She talks like a Tory politician! She'll be quoting Adam Smith next and spouting Thatcher's stupid neo-liberalism. I might as well go off fer a walk I reckon. I'm wastin' me time bargainin' with this hard-faced lot."

"Well, you could go down to the village for me, love. I can always make use of a spare bag of sugar and more flour. Supplies are getting low."

"Nay lass. I'm goin' ter talk ter't sheep. I'll mebbe get more sense out o' them!"

Elsie laughed as he donned his ragged old coat and cap and made his way in to the yard.

She looked across at her son.

"You shouldn't wind your faither up, Ralph. He's really worried about the amount of sheep we've lost. He reckons getting on for thirty have gone."

"I know Mother. I was only pulling his leg. I've already started making him a stick for his birthday." He shook his head. "At least we now know which handle he likes," he pointed out.

"Right. I reckon we need a brew."

"I'll make it!"

Rosie was making her way to fill the kettle, before anybody else could respond.

"I think it's about time we got down to some serious business," Connie intervened. "I've got loads of new ideas how we could make some money!"

"New ideas?" Ralph sounded surprised. "I thought you were going to concentrate on building bike frames? Malc phoned last night and asked me to teach you how to braze."

"Did you agree?"

"Maybe."

"I'll take that as a yes. But it's going to take me ages to learn how to build frames. I'm going to have to make jigs and buy tools and that means I'm going to have to accumulate cash. I've discussed it with Malc. It's a long-term project. I'm aiming to be competent and equipped to do it by the time I leave school."

The kettle began to whistle.

"Can you organise cups, Connie?" Rosie asked.

The younger girl rose from her seat. Elsie looked across at Ralph. They were both used to Connie rushing in to things. Talking about the longer term was a completely novel development.

With the tea brewed and everybody settled once more, they all looked at Connie expectantly. She smiled.

"The problem as I see it," she began, "is how to build up sufficient funds. The walking sticks are a better idea then sledges, because materials are readily available and fairly cheap, and there's a steady all year round market. We can begin making money straight away and we can plough it back in to *our* co-operative."

She paused for breath. Nobody questioned her use of the word "our."

"I want to work with metal, not wood, but I need to make useful things that will sell all the year round. Something simple yet attractive."

Again she paused. Ralph looked at her, as if willing her to go on.

"Well come on Connie! What's your big idea?"

He was obviously becoming impatient. She bent down to root in the canvas bag she'd placed beneath the table.

"This!" she said, a note of triumph in her voice. She placed a strip of metal, approximately 25mm wide, 3mm thick and 30cms long, on the tabletop. It was shaped like a lazy S with a twist in the middle, and was painted matt black.

They all, without exception, looked at her as though she was as daft as a brush. Ralph was the first to recover his senses.

"What on earth are you talking about? How is that piece of scrap going to make us money?"

Connie bent down again, but this time lifted her bag and placed it in front of her. She extracted an identical strip of steel, and placed the two back to back.

"There," she said, "Don't you think that looks nice? And all I have to do is rivet or braze or weld them together."

She delved in to her bag once more and brought out two more strips of steel, this time shaped like a U, except that one upright was longer than the other. These were followed by a number of flat strips and more fancy scrolled shapes, and finally she produced a drawing showing how the parts could be assembled.

"A newspaper and magazine holder," she announced, "made with cheap materials, simply constructed, very attractive and bound to sell. Malc gave me the idea. I designed it, and I've loads more ideas and even more designs. Flower pot holders, window boxes, hanging baskets, table lamps, wall brackets. I've even worked out how to make a garden chair and a glass or wooden topped garden table."

She leant back in her seat, her green eyes shining as she took in their reactions. All remained lost for words. At last she got up.

"I'm going out for a walk. I maybe some time. When I return you can let me know if you want me to join *your* co-operative or whether I should form my own!"

COLDWELL CLOUGH

Chapter Five

"**F**AITHER! Don't do it!"

Jed turned round abruptly, startled by Connie's high pitched shout. Sat on a lump of errant gritstone, he'd been contemplating the vagaries of his life whilst staring in to the dark black waters of the Mermaid's Pool with unseeing eyes, until his youngest daughter's intervention.

"Do what, lass?" he asked, somewhat puzzled.

"Jump in!"

The black dog of gloom leapt off his shoulders and his face broke in to a broad smile as she walked towards him.

"Budge up, Faither. Make room for me."

"Life's not that desperate, yet," he said, as he shuffled his bum. "Anyway, I hate the thought o' bein' immersed in water. That's why I smell the way I do."

She took her place next to him and threaded her arm through his, hugging it close and leaning her cheek against his rough wool coat for a moment.

"You've always smelt nice to me, Faither," she replied softly. "You remind me of dry brown bracken and heather and bluebells."

"Bluebells!" He chuckled. "That's a bit far-fetched, love."

She shook her head.

"One of my first memories is about you and bluebells. I must have been four or five. I know I still had two legs then. I remember you carrying me down the lane and on to the bank of the Clough, under the trees, to pick them. It was a warm spring day. The whole bank was thick with them. I can still remember the sounds. The place was buzzing with bees and insects. The brook was splashing over the rocks. You told me it was chuckling because it was happy and free. We picked loads of flowers and took them back to Mum, and then we spent ages putting them in vases and old jam jars and milk bottles and anything else we could find. You tucked me in to bed that night. You smelt of flowers and you read to me. I think it was a *Mister Men* book and I felt happier than I'd ever felt before."

"You were always a happy little lass. Even when..."

"Even when I became a one-legged cripple!"

She hugged his arm against her waist once more. He remained silent, his brow furrowed, dark memories dancing through his head.

"You can say it, Faither. I wasn't so happy then, was I? In fact I was horribly miserable, but I soon got over it. You, Mum and Ralph saw to that. And look at all this," she continued with a sweep of her arm, taking in the great arc of the slopes up to Kinder and the clear pale grey-blue wintery sky above. "We couldn't hope to live in a better part of the world could we? We're ever so lucky."

Silence reigned once more, but this time Jed eventually broke it.

"Eh Connie, love. If the sky were covered with the blackest clouds and the mist were thick as sour ewes' milk thee'd find the silver lining. I'd bet me life on it."

He looked down at her and smiled, his old eyes watering.

"Come on. Let's mek a move, before we both freeze solid to this rock!"

"Okay Faither. But let's go higher. I need to stretch my legs and get the muck out of my lungs. I can still taste the car and lorry fumes from the last few days in the town."

"Aye lass. Gartside lungs are meant fer sheep dip an' cow muck."

"And heather and bracken."

"And bluebells love. Don't ferget the bluebells."

He shook his head and chuckled.

"Wait 'till I tell thee mother what yers said I stink of!"

⁂

"Ah! There you two are at last. Where've you been? It's gone six o'clock. It's been dark for ages."

Elsie was evidently not in the best of humours. The table was already set for the evening meal. Ralph, Rosie and Mikey and Pearl sat around it. Even Titch seemed subdued, for he hadn't come over to greet them, as he normally did when either father or daughter entered the kitchen.

"We've been communin' with nature, admirin' the moon, an' havin' a reet gradely chat," Jed responded.

"Communing with nature?"

"Yes Mum. We've been up on to Kinder. I was telling Faither how

181

lucky I feel to live out here, and he was telling me he wouldn't swap his life for all the riches in the world."

"Did he now! Well that's a big turnabout on what he were telling me this very morning over breakfast."

"Well. I guess Faither and me have had a really good talk and we've both realised how lucky we are. And guess what Mum? He told me you always remind him of primroses, violets and buttercups."

Elsie stared at her youngest in complete and utter disbelief. At last she managed to express her thoughts.

"He never! Never in a month of Sundays! Jed hasn't got a romantic bone in his body!"

Connie laughed, her sharp green eyes flashing under her carroty red hair.

"He did so! He told me how you always walked to school together, hand in hand, when you were a little girl and he was a young lad."

The farmer, meanwhile, had turned his back. He seemed to be taking an excessively long time to remove his old battered coat and hat, and then even longer to find somewhere to hang them. Whilst he was doing so his mind was attempting to cope with the totally unexpected outpourings of his daughter's highly creative mind. He determined to give her a ticking off at the first opportunity. He didn't approve of fibbing. At the same time he decided it would be counter-productive to let Elsie, or anyone else, in to their joint secret. The truth of the matter was that he'd only informed Connie those particular flowers were her mother's favourites, and that they had been so from ever since she was a young girl, when they *had* walked to the village school together, hand in hand.

Finally, he plucked up the courage to turn around and face his wife. By then, luckily for him, Elsie was squatting in front of the open oven door, her hands armed with oven-gloves, carefully removing a large lamb pot roast from its hot interior. He took his seat at the table opposite Pearl, whilst the going was good. Pearl smiled a sweet smile as though seeing him in a new and rather flattering light for the first time. Jed smiled back, his face a portrait of pure unadulterated innocence.

Ralph turned to his sister, who had taken her usual seat next to him. She returned his gaze, sensing he had something important to say.

"Whilst you were out, Rosie, Mikey and me have come to a decision."

"Go on then. What is it?"
"We've agreed you can become a member of our co-op."
"That's great!"
Her eyes lit up and she sounded genuinely excited.
"Well, the thing that finally decided it was something Rosie told me ages ago."
"Oh." A frown puckered her brow. "What do you mean?"
"Rosie's granddad reckons tea lubricates the wheels of productive industry."
"I've heard him say that. What's that got to do with anything?"
"We aim to be the most productive company in Derbyshire and you are without a doubt the best brewer-upper in the county!"
"And I was going to offer to set your old bike to rights, but now..."
At that point the phone rang its impatient summons.
"Can you get that for me please, Mikey? You're nearest," Elsie asked, as she lifted the lid and passed the pot roast over to Pearl, indicating she should help herself.
"It's for you Connie."

⁂

That evening the kids enjoyed a real treat. Jed was obviously in a good mood, because he invited Pearl and Elsie to the Sportsman to see in the New Year. Elsie had declined his offer, protesting she couldn't leave the children on their own. Pearl had quite naturally backed her up. However, Jed insisted. Moreover, he said the kids must go with them.

"It willna do 'em any harm to stay up late fer once. They dunna go back ter school 'til Monday, an' anyhow Mikey and Connie art both in their fourteenth year!"

This latter argument was, to put it mildly, stretching a point. The legal age for a child to accompany an adult in a pub was fourteen, and both were still only thirteen. However, Jed reasoned it was near enough. Connie and Mikey were well behaved. They knew better than show their parents up, and as long as the kids behaved themselves nobody had good reason to complain. Furthermore, it meant that once the midnight chimes had rung, Auld Lang Syne had been sung and handshakes shaken all round, Pearl and Mikey would only have a few hundred yards to walk home.

In the end, Elsie agreed, but also insisted Pearl and her son accompany them for the meal in the Nag's Head the following day. Rosie, Mikey and Connie were thus enabled to discover just how silly their supposedly sensible elders could be - for as soon as they had a modicum of alcohol inside them, the grown-ups' inhibitions seemingly dissolved. Consequently, they let their hair down and indulged in all manner of silly antics that particularly memorable night. The children, on the other hand, behaved extremely well, and 1991 gave way to 1992 without any great mishap.

However, two things stuck in Rosie Akroyd's mind. The number of young women attracted to Ralph's company like moths to a flame, and the fact that Connie, every time she found a bit of mistletoe, grabbed young Mikey and kissed him on the lips, seemingly oblivious to those around them.

VIEW TOWARDS KINDER

Chapter Six

NEW Year's Day dawned bright and clear, although young Rosie Akroyd remained oblivious to the fact. Tired out by the previous night's proceedings she lay curled up under her duvet, her long dark hair forming a fan against the white linen pillow, fast asleep.

However, Jed and Ralph were, as usual, up early. The cows had to be milked and the fact it was a bank holiday had escaped the bovines' attention. Connie had risen not too long after her father and brother, although, apart from checking for newly laid eggs in the hen house, she had no serious farm duties to fulfil.

She was, however, expecting a special visitor. The phone call she had received the previous evening, only part of which she had revealed to friends and family, had been from Malc. He had informed her, amongst other matters, to expect a well-known rambler, who would be delivering "something of interest" to her. In the meantime, she decided to ask her mother if she needed any help with her domestic duties.

Jed and Ralph returned to the warmth of the farm kitchen for breakfast, just after quarter to eight. Once they'd warmed themselves at the fire and taken their places at the table, Connie went in to action, ferrying food from her mother to them as and when required. She'd decided not to indulge in eating until Rosie had come back to life, but Ralph couldn't help noticing her green eyes seemed to keep darting towards the window and the yard beyond it. He decided she must be expecting Mikey.

By eight-thirty, Jed had taken possession of his armchair in front of the fire, Titch sprawled at his feet. Within another five minutes the farmer was snoring softly. Ralph had disappeared in to his workshop and Connie had departed to the bedroom to awake the slumbering Rosie. A knock on the kitchen door summoned Elsie from her brief respite at the kitchen table. She quickly crossed the floor, wondering who it could be so early in the morning.

"Benny Rothman and... is that you Lily! Happy New Year. What are you two doing here so early? Come in. Come in. There's tea in the pot.

Have you had breakfast?"

Benny grinned his impish grin.

"We've had food, but hot tea won't go amiss. It's a cold day."

"Well, don't just stand there. Sit here Lily. Make yourself comfortable. Young Rosie's with us. She'll be really pleased to see the both of you."

Man and wife took their indicated places at the table.

"Benny's treating me to a meal at the Nag's Head later," Lily informed her, "after we've been for a walk, but it's your Connie Benny's come to see."

Elsie looked up from pouring the tea.

"Our Connie? Why Benny?"

"Malc's sent something for her."

Elsie passed the cups of tea over, but before she could enquire further Connie and Rosie emerged in to the room. The eyes of both widened and big smiles illuminated their faces as they espied their visitors. As soon as the initial greetings were over, Connie decided it was time to get down to business.

"Did Malc send the wheel parts?"

"Yes. He's asked me to pick them up a week on Sunday. Is that all right?"

"Yes. I'll make a start today."

Benny shook his head.

"No. It's a bank holiday. Malc insists you enjoy it. He said you should be able to complete two wheels in a night, so there's no rush. He only wants three pairs. Anyway, Elsie and me thought you and Rosie might want to come for a walk this morning. There's a frost. The ground will be nice and hard on the tops."

"What's going on?" Rosie wanted to know, intrigued at the talk of wheels, to say the least.

"Malc needs to build some bike wheels, so he's asked me to lace them."

"Lace them? What does that mean?"

Connie laughed.

"I'll show you later. He gave me an illustrated pamphlet when I was in Manchester explaining how to build a bicycle wheel. Placing the spokes in position is called 'lacing'."

"Come on," Benny said, rising from his seat, "they're in the back of the car."

Both girls followed him, as did a curious Titch. Ralph emerged from his workshop as they crossed the yard. He greeted the elderly couple and after some brief chit-chat disappeared in to the farmhouse. The car was parked on the track behind the cattle byre. Benny opened the rear passenger door, bent inwards and began to pull out a large cardboard box, which he placed on the ground. It contained boxes of stainless steel spokes in various lengths, a box of nipples, rim tapes and four front and four rear hubs, complete with quick release levers, along with a spoke key.

Connie frowned. She thought Benny had said three pairs of wheels were needed. Again Benny leaned in to the vehicle, emerging with four pairs of aluminium rims. Before Connie could query the quantity he closed the car door and then positioned himself at the motor's rear and opened the boot.

"What do you think of this?" he asked.

Connie took her position by his side.

"Oh! It's beautiful."

Benny chuckled.

"It certainly is. The youngster he's put it together for is a very lucky person I reckon. Still, it's only my humble role to deliver it."

Connie gazed at the machine and even her relatively untutored eyes could see it was a work of art, as well as a product of craftsmanship.

"Where do you have to take it, Benny?"

He rubbed his chin, rooted in his inside jacket pocket, and extracted a rather grubby piece of paper. He held it up, peering at it, as though he needed spectacles, his brow puckered.

"Eh, I can hardly make this out, but I think it says..." The dimples formed under his cheeks, as he finally broke in to a smile. "Gartside Farm. Malc says it's yours, young Connie. Once you've laced his wheels and providing you do them right!"

Connie couldn't believe her ears.

"I don't know what to say. It's incredible! It's... it's just so beautiful."

Benny laughed.

"I think you've already said enough. I'll convey the message to Malc. Now be careful as you take it out, Connie. You don't want the bars swinging round. It's very lightweight and they'll dent the top tube if you're not careful."

Rosie looked on as Connie carefully extended her arms and leant forwards. She emerged, holding a bike frame and forks, complete with all the fittings, with the exception of mudguards and wheels. Benny extracted the mudguards and Connie finally realised why he'd brought sufficient components to build four pairs of wheels.

"Can you carry these?" he asked Rosie. "I'll get the box and the rims."

Once they'd returned to the kitchen, Benny suddenly remembered something.

"Connie. Can you go back to the car? There's a wheel-building jig on the floor behind the front passenger seat."

"A jig? I thought Malc only wanted the wheels lacing?"

"You'll need it to build your own wheels. He says you can have it on permanent loan. He's got another."

She passed the bike over to a bemused Ralph, instructing him not to allow the handlebars to swing under any circumstances, if he valued his life.

KINDER LOW FROM NEAR GARTSIDE FARM

Chapter Seven

"WHICH route shall we take Mr Rothman?"

Benny smiled at Mikey.

"The name is Benny young man. Unless you want me to call you Master Grimsditch? Is that it?"

Mikey shook his head.

"Right. Now we've sorted that out, the easiest way is up the clough and along the bridleway."

"I think we should cut across the flank of the hill," Connie intervened. "If we do that we can climb up behind Kinder Low and then either go up on to the Edge and descend down Grindsbrook in to Edale village, or, if the weather turns, go down onto the old bridleway just before Jacob's Ladder."

Benny consulted his map.

"There's no sign of a path," he finally said.

"Connie follows sheep tracks, not footpaths," Rosie informed him. "Don't worry. We won't get lost."

She bent down to fondle Titch's velvet ears.

"Will we?" she said softly. "And you'll get us home safe if Connie goes wrong won't you Titch?"

"Well," Benny retorted. "Connie and Mikey are the locals. We're in their hands. What do you say, Lily?"

"I'm up for it as long as you are, love."

Benny laughed.

"Right. Lead on Connie love, but don't start galloping on that special leg of yours. I'm not as young as I used to be."

They set off. The young lass and Mikey at the front, Connie armed with the ram's horn handled walking stick Ralph had made for her the previous year. Rosie stayed behind with Benny and Lily, keen to learn as much as possible about the preparations being made to celebrate the 60th anniversary of the Mass Trespass of Kinder Scout due to take place in April.

At first Titch remained content to walk alongside Rosie. She'd always paid him what he regarded as his due attention, whilst his master, Ralph, and mistress, Connie, both tended to take him for granted. However, as they gradually attained more height, his naturally inquisitive nature took over, and he soon overtook the other two youngsters.

The Hayfield end of the mass of Kinder Scout, the plateau of which comprised some fifteen square miles of open moorland, roughly faced south west. Its edge, high above the farm, swept round in a shallow concave curve, with Kinder Low, the summit of which was the highest point in the Peak District, projecting to their right. Connie's route climbed steadily in a diagonal. She was heading in a direction which would take them onto the plateau to the right of the Kinder Downfall and to the left of the Low. From there she intended either to carry on until she reached the well-defined track along the gritstone edge overlooking the Edale valley and stay on the high ground as long as possible, or, if the weather changed, drop down to the lower slopes behind the Low on to the well-worn bridleway.

As Benny had predicted earlier, the ground was hard and firm underfoot. The winter cold had ensured that. Consequently they made good progress. Neither Mikey nor Connie spoke, content to be in each other's company and to concentrate their energies on the long climb upwards. Rosie on the other hand, scarcely paused for breath as she fired one question after another at her companions. Apart from the Manchester girl's chatter and Benny's soft-spoken answers, the surrounding environment remained silent, save for the gentle sough of the chilly breeze, the rustle of grasses under their boots and the unceasing bleat of sheep below them.

Nearer the top they all suddenly ground to a halt, startled by an unexpected sight. An Arctic hare darted out of the tussock grass behind a rock at great speed. Titch followed hot on its heels, obviously determined on a chase, having flushed it from its form. Fast as the dog was, the hare was faster and they watched the flash of grey white as it zoomed across and up the hillside, before it finally disappeared in to a large patch of bracken interspersed with gritstone rocks. The dog followed and it too was lost to sight.

They waited with baited breath, wondering if he would flush the hare from its new hiding place, but Titch eventually emerged from the area where the animal had taken cover, having failed to find his quarry. He stood, ears erect and alert, fore-paws placed on a boulder, his dark liquid eyes fixed on them, as if to say, "Where were you when I needed you? What kind of pack have I been saddled with?"

The two adults and three kids recommenced their walk. Just before they reached his boulder, Titch had darted off once more. They'd soon be on the top and no doubt he might be able to find grouse or snipe to annoy, or an errant sheep to sniff at. Hares weren't the only creatures to have fun with and he had a chance of keeping up with the others.

Finally they reached the shoulder of the hill, joining Kinder Low to the Scout. Connie and Mikey stopped to admire the view. The Vale of Edale lay spread out below them, like a multicoloured illustrated map. Benny, Lily and Rosie joined them, all three glad of the chance to rest their legs. Benny slung his rucksack off his shoulder, opened a side pocket and took out an oilskin cycle cape.

"You should get one of these," he told Connie. "You can't beat them when you're cycling in the rain."

He opened it out and laid it flat on the ground. Lily immediately sat down on the yellow triangle and he followed suit.

"They're also very useful for sitting down on when the ground's cold or damp," he added, stating the obvious.

Lily chuckled.

"And for other things," she responded.

By now Connie was not only impressed but intrigued. Being an inquisitive child she asked the obvious question.

"How do you mean?"

"Well, whatever the weather any lady cyclist or rambler knows that a cape is her best friend."

Both Connie and Rosie frowned, obviously puzzled and wanting to know more. Even Benny seemed unsure as to what his beloved was getting at. Lily laughed, before enlightening them.

"When you are out cycling, or walking for that matter, nature can call at the most inopportune moments. You might be up on a hill or miles away in some rural area and you suddenly get the urge to have a pee. You're with a gang of men. Most embarrassing. But if you've a cape, all you have to do is walk a few yards away, put it on, squat down on the moor or in a field, as if you were in a tent with your head sticking out, and, hey presto - you can conclude your business, whilst preserving your feminine modesty!"

Benny gazed at his wife in disbelief and then turned to the girls, shaking his head.

"And I always thought she was sheltering from the wind. Now I discover I'm sitting on a portable lavatory!" He turned back to Lily. "First opportunity, I'm getting a new cape. You can have this one!" The girls giggled and Mikey, along with Lily, laughed. Benny remained quiet, content to enjoy the panorama laid out before him. Way over the valley, slightly to his right, Mam Tor stood sentinel over the head of the narrow steep sided glaciated vale, its ridge heading to his left, cut by the cleft of Hollin's Cross, before rising again to the summit of Lose Hill. He could make out the distinctive twisting road descending from Rushop Edge through the narrow cutting of Mam Nick, a snake of grey tarmac steeply twisting and turning as it made its way in to the valley bottom. Here it eventually ran alongside the Manchester to Sheffield railway line and the fast running River Noe, before entering the Hope Valley, some three miles beyond.

The old man's mind travelled back to when he was the same age Rosie had now attained - namely fourteen. That year he, like most of his working class generation, had given up on school, started work and embarked on his real education at the university of life. He'd managed to get a job in a garage. When he took his first wage packet home, and proudly handed it over to his mother, she'd told him he could keep it. She also told him to remember that, like his dad, she had first claim on every future wage packet, at least until he left the family home to forage for himself.

He spent his unexpected riches on a second hand bike and thereby learnt there was more to life than work and the cloying dirty atmosphere of an industrial town to seek amusement in. The first chance he got, he cycled to Snowdonia in North Wales, no mean feat for a fourteen year old new to cycling. Thus his love of the great outdoors in general and high country in particular began. He ended up sleeping in a shed on a farm, sharing it with a goat and her two kids. He still had photographs of himself to prove it, embracing the goat's offspring on his knee, which he'd treasured ever since. They'd been taken by the farmer's wife.

"There they are!"

Connie's treble voice and Titch's excited barking brought Benny back to the present with a bump. The farmer's daughter stood upright, excitedly pointing her walking stick down to the bridleway. He followed the line of its path. Down below a blue Land Rover, with a covered trailer hitched behind, stood near the old Edale Cross, two men leaning against it and looking back towards Jacob's Ladder.

"Who are they Connie? Why are you so excited?"

"The sheep thieves! We've got to catch them!"

Benny screwed his eyes up. The men were already climbing back in to their vehicle. Connie started downhill, Titch on her heels, followed by Mikey, but the vehicle was already on the move, heading towards Coldwell Clough and the tarmac lane.

"You don't stand a chance Connie," Rosie shouted. "We need to go to Edale and use a phone!"

The younger girl stopped in her tracks, knowing Rosie was all too right. Eventually she climbed back up the hill, consumed with anger and frustration. Her father's and her family's future was at stake. Young as she was, she was all too aware that hill farming was a hard way to earn a living at the best of times. The loss of any more sheep was the last thing they or any of their farming neighbours needed.

For Connie, the rest of the walk had been ruined, and her gloomy feelings inevitably descended upon them all, like a thick black storm cloud. It was her third sighting of the sheep thieves, and the third time she'd been absolutely powerless to do anything about it. The fact that on the first occasion, when the Land Rover and trailer had forced Rosie, Ralph and herself to seek refuge by the drystone wall in Coldwell Clough, there'd been no way any of them could have known what activities the men were engaged in, completely escaped her attention. Instead, no matter how illogical her thoughts, she inwardly blamed herself for the loss of the family's sheep.

Despite the near perfect weather conditions she abandoned her plan for a high level walk along Kinder Edge and insisted they descend to the farming hamlet of Upper Booth. Here she knocked on the door of Lee Farm, whose sheep she assumed would have been the latest victims. From there she'd phoned the police and then her father, before continuing on to the Nag's Head, leaving the farmer to phone his near neighbours and other farmers further afield.

Chapter Eight

CONNIE'S illogical mood of misery continued to pervade the atmosphere, to the point that the Gartside family's New Year celebratory dinner was seriously in danger of assuming the nature of a dreary and exceedingly gloomy wake, before the first course had been served. In the end the head of the family decided to intervene and take his daughter in hand.

"Connie, love, can thee come outside? I need yer help."

She followed him in to the beer garden at the rear of the pub. For once it was devoid of people, apart from one small group of hikers sat in the shelter of a wall.

"Here, Connie," Jed said, pointing to the corner furthest away from the wall. "Let's sit down fer a minute. I need ter talk ter yers."

She followed, wondering what could be so important. The youngster, normally so cheerful and lively, had been so consumed with her own thoughts she'd remained ignorant of Mikey and Rosie's unusually subdued mood and Ralph's ill-fated attempts at banter, let alone the frown of puzzlement on her mother's brow. They both took their places, sat opposite each other. Jed remained silent for a long moment, his old watery grey eyes looking straight in to her own, as if seeking to plumb the depths of her soul, whilst gathering his own thoughts.

"What is it Faither?"

"This is a very special day fer yer Mum, Connie. It's only a couple o' days in th' year she gets chance ter have all o' us tergether, and it's virtually the only day when she's guaranteed a day off from bakin' and cookin' an' lookin' after us all, waitin' on us hand and foot, an' I don't want it messed up fer her an' I reckon it's in danger o' bein' mucked up, an' you o' all o' us shouldna allow yerseln ter be the cause o' it. Yer Mum loves us all dearly, but you art very special to her. She thinks the world o' yers, as I do, an' all o' us do, so why art yers in such a despondent mood? What lurkin' dim and dismal darkness has getten inter thee lass? We've always relied on thee ter find the silver lining, not the cloud!"

It all came rushing out in a stream of quiet but heartfelt emotion with hardly a pause for breath; softly spoken, but no less shocking to Connie's ears. She gazed back at him, completely and utterly lost for words. At last she responded, or tried to.

"But, we're being robbed blind and I'm..."

"Ter blame!" he interjected. "Is that what yer sayin' Connie, because if yer are yer talkin' bloody nonsense and that's swearin'!"

She shook her head, shocked by her father's vehemence and his language. He'd never been one to swear, and certainly not in his youngest daughter's presence.

"But..."

"Look Connie Gartside. I'm th' head shepherd here. If I'd stood guard, watchin' me flocks throughout neet, like the Bible says the good shepherds did, do thee think it would have med any difference? We don't live in Biblical times. We art in the twentieth century, not the Bronze Age, whatever local parson or our superstitious bishop think. The biblical shepherds were plagued with sheep thieves, as sheep farmers always have been, but they didna have Land Rovers in them days an' they didna have slaughter houses an' wholesale merchants an' retail butchers who lived miles away an' who they ne'er met in their lives! I'm not ter blame fer what's happened an' I'm not goin' to beat meseln up about it coz it willna mek a scrap o' difference.

"More importantly, neither art thee ter blame. So I want thee ter go back inter that pub, put on a brave face an' be the normal good tempered fun lovin' girl yer Mum an' yer brothers and sister-in-laws expect yer ter be! We can worry about other things termorrer, but terday's a day dedicated ter yer mother's enjoyment. Put everythin' else out o' yer mind. Do yer understand?"

With that, he didn't bother to wait for a response. Instead he stood up, marched off and disappeared in to the pub without another word, leaving his rather shocked daughter to sort her head out on her own. Connie didn't watch him depart. She was sat with her back to the pub in any case. Nonetheless, her brain was reeling after what seemed to be an onslaught on it by her father's tongue.

Having already fallen in to the trap of blaming herself for the depredations of unknown thieves and villains she had no control over;

she now began to accuse herself of being a self-centred and uncaring source of unnecessary pain to her long suffering and ever-patient mother. Luckily for her, Ralph soon replaced his father at the beer garden table. However, he didn't sit opposite to her but next to her. Thus, when he placed his arm gently around her shoulder and asked her why she was so upset, she immediately embraced him, buried her head in his chest and burst in to tears.

Now it was Ralph's turn to be taken aback. Connie had never been one to bottle up her emotions, but crying was not a way she normally expressed herself. In fact, the only time he'd ever seen her break in to tears previously had been the day she'd had her artificial leg fitted and taken her first faltering steps, unaided by a crutch, following the accident which had robbed her of her lower right limb, and on that occasion they were tears of joy, having previously reconciled herself to never walking again unaided.

That had been the point when Ralph assured her she'd soon be able to run, let alone walk, providing she wanted to and was willing to work at it. The two had subsequently bonded in a very special and unique way; he becoming his younger sister's prime motivator, convincing her there was nothing any able-bodied person could do that she couldn't, providing she had the determination to succeed, whilst assuming the role of her principal defender and protector.

Thus, on the one hand he persuaded her to set herself targets and to take risks, and on the other he watched over her like a hen guarding her chicks, or a ewe guarding her lamb. There was a four year age difference between them and Connie was small of stature and therefore looked younger than her years. However, the very closeness of their relationship, over the seven years since the accident, had put a relatively old head on her young shoulders. Many in the local community viewed her as a somewhat giddy and reckless dare-devil and a bit of a Tom-boy, but Ralph knew there was much more to his normally fun-loving sibling than that.

He waited patiently for her tears to subside, holding her tight all the while, but saying nothing, as if sensing the time wasn't right for any pearls of comfort or wisdom from him. Eventually, Connie's sobs subsided. Then they talked, and slowly but surely Ralph worked his magic in the quiet and thoughtful way only he could. Connie's brain began to slip back in to a more realistic and sensible mode and not long after, in a much more positive frame of mind, she was ready to take her place with her family and friends, a little quieter than normal perhaps, but no longer the wet blanket she had been, not so long before. As she re-entered the room, Jed was on his way to the bar. He smiled, relieved she'd returned, and murmured an encouraging greeting to her.

Within moments, any remaining negative thoughts of sheep thieves were pushed firmly to the back of her mind. Richard's two youngsters, four year-old twins named Iris and Daisy, and the slightly older son of Jem, namely young Jed, saw to that. Aunty Connie, as they all called her, was a clear favourite of theirs and all were eager to share the teenager's company.

Following their meal, she, along with Ralph, Rosie and Mikey, agreed to accompany Benny and Lily back to Coldwell Clough. Jed and Elsie, along with Pearl Grimsditch, were being ferried back the way they'd come, by road, Jem having volunteered to be their driver in both directions. The weather conditions remained cold and dry; perfect for walking, as is so often the case at that particular time of year, with firm hard ground underfoot.

Having more or less reverted back to her normal good humour, Connie once more instinctively resumed her role of guide. She led her companions through the back of the pub and the beer garden and up the lane leading to the track marking the beginning of the Pennine Way, which took them up on to Kinder, via the steep and increasingly narrow cleft, known as Grindsbrook.

Their walk along Kinder Edge and back over the shoulder of Kinder Low passed without incident and all were in good spirits by the time they made their way across the yard and in to the warm welcoming kitchen of the farm and a fresh pot of tea.

By then Jed occupied his favourite armchair in front of the fire, snoring softly. Titch assumed his favourite position on the old flock mat. Elsie, cheered by the meal and invigorated by the company and attentions of her extended family greeted them all, urging them to take their places around the kitchen table with Pearl. Benny announced that he and Lily would be making their way home back to Timperley soon, but the farmer's wife insisted they stay for the evening meal.

"In fact," she said, "Why go home at all? You don't have to work anymore. Stay here tonight. You can take our Jed out for a pint at the Sportsman, Benny. The guest room's available. I thought we might have

197

people staying over the holiday, but things seem very quiet."

Benny and Lily exchanged glances. They didn't need much persuading and soon agreed to stay.

THE NAG'S HEAD, EDALE

Chapter Nine

"ART thee lookin' forward ter this year's celebrations, Benny?"

"Celebrations?"

"Aye. It's the sixtieth anniversary in April ain't it?"

"Oh. You mean the anniversary of the Mass Trespass."

The older man shook his head.

"I tend not to think about it too much, Jed. I leave all that to others. I'm content to wake up each morning. Every day's a bonus at my age."

"But you will be there?"

Benny smiled his quiet smile.

"Oh, I'll be there all right. I wouldn't miss it for the world. They're expecting me to speak again." He chuckled. "Anyhow, I'm guaranteed a free pint every five years and I get to meet old friends and new."

He looked at the farmer, his mischievous smile suddenly breaking out afresh.

"There are also new trespasses to be planned. The struggle for the freedom to roam isn't over yet - not by a long chalk!"

They were making their way down the narrow lane from the farm. It had just gone nine o'clock on a crisp cold frosty night, the sky above them a mass of twinkling stars and their way illuminated by a shining moon.

"Well, I'll be takin' advantage," his companion responded. "The work should be complete on our self-catering accommodation be then, and that mate of yours, Malc, is bringing his son up here. They're going ter camp in ower old paddock. He reckons he can get some o' his mates in his local cycling club ter come up too, so that's a bit more income fer us, an' Elsie's already got folks booked in fer bed an' breakfast."

"I thought you farmers were rolling in money?"

"Aye, a lot o' folks think that. There might even be some that are, but they ain't hill farmers an' that's a fact! The's no call fer wool no more and the's precious little call fer ower meat either. New Zealand lamb's dirt cheap an' that's all the supermarkets are interested in. If it wasn't fer subsidies we get from the Common Market we'd be out o' business fer certain."

"Well, that young lass of yours could change your fortunes. She's buzzing with ideas."

"Aye she is, and Ralph's pursuing his studies in engineering. I have great hopes fer both o' them, but it were young Rosie Akroyd that first put the idea of a manufacturin' enterprise in their heads. She's the catalyst."

He remained silent for a moment, but then continued.

"I were really worried about ower Ralph when he left school. He's always been a bright lad, an' I feared he'd leave the farm altergether, like Jem and Richard have. I couldna manage on me own an' yet I canna afford ter pay him as much as I should. If they get this co-operative off the ground, it could be the saving of the farm as well as the mekin' o' them. I'd hate ter know I was the last of the Gartsides at Coldwell Clough. We've farmed here fer o'er two-hundred and eighty years."

They continued in silence, before finding themselves standing at the brightly lit bar of the Sportsman involved in a slight disagreement as to who was to buy the first round. In the end Benny won and ordered two pints of best bitter.

They were still standing when they were ready for another. Jed placed their order, but on turning back to his friend suddenly grinned.

"Eh, we could be in fer a bit o' fun here," he said.

Two men had just entered the pub. They headed for the opposite end of the bar.

"Who are they?" Benny asked.

"The first one through the door is a recent incomer. Not short o' brass from all accounts, but you should recognise the second. His name's Jacob, John Jacob."

Benny frowned. The name rang a bell, but he couldn't figure out why. Jed decided to enlighten him.

"He were one o' the keepers who tried ter stop yer gettin' on ter Ashop Head!"

Benny nodded.

Having made his mind up to take advantage of the chance meeting, Jed immediately hailed the newcomers.

"Good evenin' John. Art thee lookin' for'ard ter April?"

John Jacob looked across, obviously surprised.

"Not particularly. It shouldna be allowed. The's nowt ter celebrate."

"You wouldn't be referring to the intended mass invasion of Manchester louts, would you?" his companion intervened.

"Louts? That's a harsh word, Mr..."

"Palfrey. Mr Palfrey. How else should I describe a horde of Manchester riff-raff and Communist agitators, intent on stirring things up and disturbing the peace? Hayfield residents don't want such disruption to their lives. People come to live here to enjoy the peace and quiet."

Jed smiled. Benny remained silent, sensing his companion would prefer to handle the situation without his assistance.

"I think folk who come to live here do so fer exactly the same reasons as workers from Manchester like ter spend time here. To escape the suffocatin' atmosphere of town and enjoy the hills and moors. Most o' those o' us who were born an' bred here have no quarrel with that."

"You're entitled to your point of view, but I think you are in a minority. There's a campaign to put pressure on the Parish Council to get the event banned this year, and if it isn't I think there will be a change in the membership of the PC at the May elections."

"Oh aye. That's very interestin'. An' who will be leadin' it?"

The gentleman drew himself up to his full height.

"I will," he retorted.

"Well. I wish thee the best o' luck, Palfrey. Yer gonna need it, I reckon, coz the's a lot of business people here who'll have nowt ter do with you or yer campaign, an' quite a few o' us farmers as well."

"Yer owt o' order, Jed," John Jacob intervened. "Mr Palfrey's a very respected self-made man."

"Is he now?" The farmer shook his head. "If he is, he's the first I ever met! How did thee go about it, Palfrey?"

The incomer frowned, not least because the farmer seemed intent on addressing him by his surname, bereft of any title.

"I made my money in business, through hard work," he replied with more than a touch of haughtiness in his tone.

"I weren't askin' thee about thy business. I'm not the pryin' type. I'm a sheep farmer. As such I'm knowledgeable about the business of begettin' and begattin', what you'd call reproduction. I were askin' thee how yer managed to arrange thy own conception. John said thee were a self-made man!"

Benny smiled. Jed had a way with words. Unfortunately, Mr Palfrey didn't seem to understand the joke. He knocked back his whisky and left without another word, leaving his companion alone.

"Aren't thee leavin' too, John?" the farmer asked. "I dunna like to share space wi' unrepentant lackey o' me old and unlamented landlord, the Duke o' Devonshire."

John Jacob glared at him, before making his own way to the door.

"You've a wonderful way of making friends," Benny observed. "And I thought I was the agitator."

Jed laughed, before taking a long sip of his beer.

"John's nowt but a toady and allus will be. That Palfrey's a man ter watch," he said, "but he'll ne'er do any good fert people o' Hayfield."

"How do you mean? What do you know about him?"

"Well, fer a start, he might be a prosperous man, but he spends precious little o' his money here. I'm surprised he came ter the pub terneet. He buys all his grub in some supermarket miles away. He's rarely seen in any o' Hayfield's shops. He's the worst kind o' incomer. He's bought two cottages in't same row as Pearl and Mikey live in. He's knockin' 'em inter one, no doubt to sell 'em. Likes o' him buy up properties, force house prices up, mekin' it impossible fer our kids to stay here, and now he seems determined ter mek village an unfriendly place fer tourists. Tek this pub fer example. It's isolated from rest o' village. Where would it be if it weren't fer ramblers and cyclists? There aren't enough locals ter keep it goin'. We need Palfrey's sort like we need plague I reckon!"

As if to underline his point, a group of laughing noisy young men and women, adorned in anoraks and boots, burst in to the pub, some heading for the bar and some to occupy tables near the fire. They were all camping a few yards up the road, on the site once occupied by the long closed Kinder Textile Printing Works, a timely reminder that the rural village of Hayfield was once a thriving mill-town, complete with its own working class riff-raff.

Chapter Ten

APRIL the 24th, 1992, happened to fall on a Friday. This was fortuitous for the organisers of the forthcoming 60th Anniversary Celebrations of the Mass Trespass of Kinder Scout. For Rambler's Association members and supporters the weekend would provide the opportunity to remember a great victory in the centuries' long struggle of the common people for the right to walk on uncultivated land in their own country - a right that most visitors to England, including those from Scotland, took for granted and were amazed the English didn't. No doubt the celebrations would remind them it was only a victory in one particular battle; that the war against the legacy of land theft was yet to be won. Hopefully they would be encouraged to continue their endeavours with renewed vigour and enthusiasm.

They would also provide a welcome respite from harsh reality. Ironically, the celebrations would take place at a time of recession and rapidly growing unemployment, all too reminiscent of the conditions appertaining in 1932. All who had dreamed that the replacement of Maggie Thatcher by John Major as Tory Prime Minister would herald a return to growth, were having their hopes well and truly dashed.

In the run up to Christmas a return to growth had been forecast by the Tory press. However, it proved to be the triumph of hope over experience. In the first week of January alone another 4,000 jobs were lost, 20 per cent of them being cut by the once mighty GEC. The deliberate and calculated murder of engineering, Manchester's principal manufacturing industry back in 1979 when Thatcher first came to power, was now virtually complete. East Manchester, along with Trafford Park, the world's largest industrial estate, and all the old industrial areas in and around the city, were now deserts populated by silent factories. The financial service industries, investment banks, assorted spivs and cowboys were firmly in the driving seat. Privatisation, de-mutualisation and de-regulation were the order of the day. The Thatcherite dream of an unskilled, compliant and docile workforce, enslaved by "cheap" credit and unaided by trade unions in defence of their working conditions and living standards, was being realised.

On the 20th February the Government's own figures ended any lingering hope of an early end to the economic crisis. They revealed that Gross Domestic product had fallen by a further 0.3 percent in the final quarter of 1991 - the fifth consecutive quarter recording a fall. Despite this, on the 23rd of February, the neo-liberal economists at the London Business School predicted that 1992 would experience a growth rate of 1.2 percent.

On being made aware of this assertion, Jack O' Donnell, in conversation with the frame builder, Malc Cowle, was heard to say, "That means Britain's children are in deep deep trouble. If you lay the proponents of Thatcherite laissez-faire capitalism head to toe they'll never reach a sensible or accurate conclusion! The idea we no longer need to manufacture useful commodities to pay our way in the world and we can rely on investment banking, finance and the service industries is a nonsense. The collapse of banks brought about the crisis in the 'thirties and the same thing brought about the Long Depression in the 1880s. We'll still be reaping the whirlwind of their backward economic policies in thirty years' time, unless we reverse them - mark my words."

On the 19th of March Jack's forebodings seemed more than justified. The Government announced unemployment had reached two-million six-hundred and forty-seven-thousand three-hundred, or 9.4% of the British workforce, the highest level since late 1987. On the latter date those out of work were at their highest since the Great Depression of the 'thirties, a mere four-hundred thousand below the 1932 figure. However, even Jack wouldn't have dared to predict that much worse was to follow.

Unfortunately, history would show that unemployment would continue to grow throughout the year, despite the Government's increasingly desperate tendency to massage the figures and its pathetic belief that "the hidden hand of the free market" would set everything to rights. And as the numbers thrown on the scrap-heap of unemployment crept up to three-million, so the politicians and gutter-press alike embarked on a campaign to vilify the victims as "work-shy" scroungers and parasites, content to live on benefit. How individuals who the day before had been hard-working souls could be transformed overnight in to such low forms of life was never addressed.

Despite all this doom and gloom, Rosie Akroyd, Connie and Ralph Gartside, along with young Mikey Grimsditch, were determined to enjoy life. Their hopes of a January and February dominated by snow had not come to fruition, as a result of which three hand-made sledges had been added to "stock in hand" in the ledger of the Kinder Low Manufacturing Co-operative Society, so carefully kept for them by Pearl Grimsditch.

Nonetheless, Connie had successfully completed her task for Malc and exceeded his expectations. Having successfully laced the wheels and then gone on to fully tension and thus complete the building of the wheels for her new bike, she'd proceeded to finish off Malc's as well. He'd been more than impressed with the work of his "apprentice." Consequently he made her a present of a quantity of stainless steel spokes in various lengths, "in case any off-road cyclists passing the farm find themselves with a broken spoke and a buckled wheel in need of emergency repair."

The bridleway up Coldwell Clough over to Edale was a favourite for many off-road cyclists, as well as walkers, and Ralph and Mikey had soon produced an eye-catching sign proclaiming "Emergency Bike Repairs and Sundry Metal Work Carried Out Here."

Hanging on one of Connie's handmade decorative wrought-iron brackets, it occupied a prominent position by the entrance to the farm. Not long after another neatly painted sign hung below the first. It read "Farm House Teas, Now Being Served." It didn't take long for word to get around, and Gartside's Farm soon became popular with ramblers and cyclists alike. And the more popular Elsie's teas and refreshments became, so the sales of hand-made walking sticks and fancy wrought-iron products flourished.

Elsie had worried that the more the children and Ralph became immersed in their enterprise, the more their concentration on school work and the enjoyment of their leisure time would suffer. She was a strong believer in education and that children should be free to enjoy their childhood as much as possible. She needn't have worried. At first they had perhaps devoted more time than strictly needed to build up stocks, but they had the opportunities for sales afforded by the anniversary celebrations, and the Easter school holidays preceding them, in mind and didn't want to be caught without products.

However, they still made plenty of time to enjoy themselves. Connie and Rosie in particular were always eager to go tramping over Kinder, determined to take advantage of the changing seasons of the year and the new delights each day produced, and wherever Connie went, Mikey wouldn't be far behind. True, they all now set out armed with a walking stick, and many was the time they returned without such aids, having sold them to admiring walkers they'd met by chance "at a bargain price!" In addition Connie took every opportunity, when Rosie wasn't present, to develop her cycling skills and the bike soon became her regular method of travelling to school.

The "income" side of Pearl Grimsditch's ledger, continued to record a far larger amount than the "expenditure" side. Thus the youngsters' collective capital accumulated, to be invested in raw materials, jigs and tools and the means to increase their productive forces. In less than two and a half years, Connie and Mikey would leave school. Rosie had just over a year to go. At that point it was agreed all would begin to draw a wage, according to the hours they worked. This latter point was all important, because Ralph had farm duties and they only expected Rosie to work full-time at first. Connie and Mikey's contribution would be limited until they finished their secondary education. In the meantime everything would be ploughed back in to the enterprise. They had no intention of having to go to a bank, cap in hand, for new capital and thus place themselves in debt.

Rosie's grandfather had successfully planted the principles of "self-help" and "co-operation" firmly in their young minds. They'd quickly grasped the concept that the accumulation of capital should not be an end in itself; that viewed properly capital was merely a tool to be used by labour to enable the production of useful goods, and thereby provide the labourers and their dependants with the means to live, and, as such, it should remain firmly subordinated to their democratic control.

As for education, their time at school had taken on a new lease of life. The more they engaged in manufacturing, the more they recognised the need to hone their mathematical, language and other skills, if they were to be an economic success. The need to design new products, to develop their drawing skills and to promote their products, all assisted their new found enthusiasm for schoolwork, an enthusiasm that more than surprised their teachers, particularly in the case of Mikey.

At first he had drawn out his bird's head and ram's horn silhouettes straight on to the wood, free-hand, but Connie had soon persuaded him to make templates for each design, thus enabling him to trace each on to his material in quantity, before cutting them out by fretsaw and then chiselling and filing and sanding them to their final shape. She'd also asked him to produce a number of shapes in the same material to her own design, which she was then able to use as formers around which to cold-bend her strips of mild steel in ever more intricate shapes. Mikey's math teacher had been astonished at the lad's sudden interest in geometry and trigonometry, an interest which quickly led to the lad leaping to the top of the class.

All four were learning fast. By working together they sparked each other off and the more they worked the more their individual skills flourished. When one had a problem, three other minds combined with his or hers to find a solution. A natural division of labour developed between them, but increasingly they all became familiar with each other's skills. An outside observer would have been struck by their obvious enthusiasm, the growing pride each had in their own individual work and the pride each took in the results of their collective labour. In short, work to them was not only a way of earning cash, but a source of pleasure.

Furthermore, if that same observer had any knowledge of normal production processes as carried out in a traditional capitalist enterprise they would have been struck by the fact that the youngsters had no need for supervisors to ensure they carried out their allotted tasks. There was no call for anyone to play the role of factory policeman in their enterprise, no doubt because each realised it was *their* enterprise. They had no employer to satisfy and no shareholders to cream off any profits. Only their own determination to provide themselves with a means to earn their future living and to achieve perfection drove them on. As Ralph had made clear at the outset, they had no intention of becoming anybody's wage slave. Any surplus they made, after meeting all their expenses, would remain theirs alone and they, and nobody else, would decide how it was distributed.

Rosie, who was without doubt the most politically aware of them all, confided to Granddad more than once that she felt that by setting an example that others could follow, they were striking a small blow against the capitalist system itself. Granddad had agreed, although he pointed out their enterprise wasn't unique and there were many pitfalls that could entrap them. Like it or not they lived in a capitalist world and could not fully escape its rules; this side of a political and economic revolution.

He remembered being shown a video of a documentary made by the BBC Horizon team in the early 1980s dealing with the experiences of those involved in developing worker's co-operatives in the Basque region of Spain during the mid-1950s. He remembered it was entitled the Mondragon Experiment [1] and determined to try and obtain a copy, so they could learn how to develop their enterprise and obtain knowledge of some of the principal mistakes they needed to avoid.

It was against this background and these developments that Malc and Tom would set out on their tandem on Saturday the 11th of April, the first weekend of the Easter school holidays, to camp on the farm. To say that the bicycle frame builder was likely to be amazed when Connie and Ralph showed him around their workshop and explained what they had achieved would be an understatement.

NOTE

[1] The Mondragon Experiment is available on You Tube. It can be viewed in full on the home page of www.malcsbooks.com

RIVER SETT - HAYFIELD

Chapter Eleven

FRIDAY, the 10th of April, had dawned with a fine drizzle making the pavements of Stockport glisten in the early morning light. In Hayfield it was raining heavily. However, by mid-day the sun had broken through and the weather forecast promised a fine weekend.

As Rosie disembarked from the bus in Hayfield that evening, Connie was waiting for her, accompanied by Titch and her bike.

"Are you going to give me a backie?" Rosie asked.

"No, but I am going to give you a treat!"

Before Rosie could enquire exactly what the "treat" involved, the younger girl said, "Come on. Mikey's saving us a table in the Three Trees. We can have an ice cream."

They set off, Connie pushing the bike. Titch walked ahead, stopping intermittently and turning towards them, his tail wagging, as if he was their guardian and leader. They crossed the main road and walked up the narrow passage by the church. The Three Trees faced them across the high street, next to the river bridge. Mikey occupied a seat by the window, his face one big smile as he spotted them. The girls crossed the road and Rosie entered the premises, as Connie placed her bike against another already leaning against the café window.

"Hiya, Mikey. How's your mam?"

"She's fine, Rosie. She's meeting me here as soon as she's finished work. She shouldn't be long."

Connie joined them. No sooner had she taken her seat, than a young woman appeared, small notepad in hand and pencil poised.

"Can I take your order?"

"Do you want ice cream?" Connie asked her friends.

Both agreed. The order was placed and duly served. It was now getting on for five-forty. Hayfield's streets were busy with men and women returning from work, making last minute visits to the shops to purchase food, intermingling with cyclists, walkers and other visitors, along with their children, making their way to bed and breakfast accommodation and the Kinder camp site. The café began to fill and within a few minutes a breathless and cheerful Pearl greeted her son and his friends, a big smile on her face, no doubt pleased that another five days of wage-slavery was ended and she had a weekend of freedom to enjoy.

She picked up the menu. Rosie interrupted her deliberations.

"This ice-cream's really good and it's Connie's treat!"

"Oh no it isn't! We are all buying our own."

"But you said..."

"Oh no I didn't. I said I had a treat for you, but it's not ice-cream."

"Well, what is it?"

Rosie was obviously puzzled.

"It's outside. My bike's leaning against it."

Rosie frowned, as she looked towards the window. Then enlightenment dawned.

"You mean that old bike?"

"It's not any old bike. It was Ralph's. It's a very good bike and it's the right size for you. Mikey and me have put it in good order so you can come cycling with us."

"Oh."

"You can ride a bike, can't you Rosie?"

"Course I can."

"Right. Hopefully you might be able to keep up with us! Male and Tom are coming up tomorrow and we are all going to Hathersage on Sunday."

Pearl laughed.

"Maybe I should get my old bike in good order again. I could do with losing some weight."

"Mam. That old sit up and beg's no good. You need a lightweight bike with drop handlebars!"

"Are you saying you wouldn't mind me coming with you? Wouldn't it ruin your street-cred, Mikey dear, to be accompanied by an old-maid like me?"

"Don't be daft, Pearl," Connie responded. "We could form a cycling club. Everybody welcome."

Mikey didn't look too sure.

"The Hayfield Wheelers," Rosie added.

"The Kinder Peregrines!" Connie retorted. "We need a really fast name. We can be a racing club."

"You just said everybody welcome. Not everybody wants to race," Mikey pointed out.

"Mikey Grimsditch! Are you afraid of being beat by a one-legged cripple?"

"Fat chance, Connie Gartside."

Pearl shook her head, wondering how such extremely close and fond friends could remain so competitive. She rose from her seat, having decided to go to the counter to order a pot of tea. The café's staff seemed to be overwhelmed by the influx of customers. If any of the youngsters had taken time to notice she had a thoughtful expression on her face as she crossed the room. The discussion about cycling had struck a chord.

One of her work colleagues had suggested earlier that day she needed to get out more. She was still only twenty-nine and life seemed to be passing her by. Maybe this was the answer. She resolved to ask the frame builder if he could recommend a bike shop in the area. Mikey's bike was a bit on the small side for him now. Perhaps she should treat him and herself to new machines. She'd loved cycling as a youngster.

༺༻

"Are you all right Rosie?"

As the incline up Kinder Road had increased, so the distance between the two girls had grown, although the lane had not been particularly steep at any point.

"Yes, but slow down. There's no need to rush."

The two girls had left Pearl and Mikey at their terraced cottage door and were now cycling to the farm. Connie had stopped at Bowden Bridge to allow her friend to catch up.

"You'll soon get your cycling legs. You're a good walker," she shouted back encouragingly.

Rosie only half-heard, her attention being drawn elsewhere.

"Just listen Connie. Isn't that wonderful?"

"What?"

"The curlew. It's Granddad's favourite bird. Oh, there it goes again."

Sure enough the bird's distinctive and joyful cry echoed across the valley. Connie smiled as her friend rode alongside.

"It's quite magical now you've drawn it to my attention. I suppose I just take it for granted. Bird song's part of my life. The chorus wakes me in the morning and the yip yip of owls sends me to sleep at night."

"It's a coughing of house sparrows that usually wakes me," Rosie responded, somewhat wryly.

Both girls now stood astride their machines, gazing in to the waters of the stream rushing and burbling over its rocky bed under the bridge beneath them on its way to Hayfield, before merging with the River Goyt at New Mills. From there the waters would eventually join up with the River Tame at Stockport, giving birth to the mighty Mersey, which flowed around the southern edge of Manchester to Liverpool and the Irish Sea.

"How's Ralph?" Rosie asked.

Connie's face broke in to a smile.

"Just as he always is. The best brother a girl could have."

The smile transformed in to a mischievous grin.

"I think there's a couple of older girls chasing him. You'll need to make your move soon Rosie or you'll lose him."

Rosie remained silent, but Connie noticed the frown that briefly crossed her brow. Having planted her seed of advice, she turned away, as if to study the waters of the brook.

It was one of those magical spring evenings. A slight breeze from the south-west was the harbinger of warmer weather. The hedgerows and trees were coming in to new leaf, with that quality of fresh pale translucent green that only new leaves enjoy. In a few weeks the hawthorn would provide a mass of May blossom, heralding a new summer. Further up the banks of Coldwell Clough, wherever trees provided shade, azure carpets of bluebells predominated.

The youngsters set off once more, Connie determined to reach their destination up the increasingly steep slope of the lane first, and Rosie equally determined to reach the farm without having to resort to the ignominy of walking. Once having left the noisy brook, every hedge and tree emitted the chirruping and song of birds, but the bleat of sheep dominated all. The Gartside's six Scottish Blackface tups, which had been put amongst the three hundred ewes the previous autumn, had clearly carried out their work successfully, for the first lambs were already born and the majority of sheep were close to giving birth.

They achieved their objective without incident, Connie a good twenty metres ahead of Rosie, but nonetheless impressed with the fact that Rosie had been able to keep up at all. Ralph was waiting for them, sat on the farm gate, and Titch sat alongside, his tail wagging in greeting. The dog ran across, as Rosie finally dismounted, as pleased to see her as Ralph was.

"Did you have a good journey, Rosie?"

"Yes, but my legs are aching." She looked at him as he clambered down from his perch, her bright blue eyes only being outshone by her smile, before adding, "And I'm out of breath."

He returned her smile, his white teeth contrasting with brown skin.

"That's where Connie has the clear advantage. Her artificial limb doesn't ache."

He paused, inwardly laughing at his sister's rapidly changing expression, but soon continued in slightly more serious mood.

"You shouldn't ride a bike with a rucksack on your back. Connie should have strapped it on to the pannier carrier. Use the bike to carry the weight. That's the first rule I was taught."

Both girls looked at each other. It made sense. Ralph's advice often did.

"Come on. Let me wheel the bike for you Rosie. Mother and Faither will be pleased to see you again."

They walked around the back and, after leaning the bikes against the cow-byre wall, made their way in to the kitchen. Elsie greeted Rosie with a fond embrace, as she always did, but then handed Connie a large titty bottle full of warm milk. Without a word her daughter marched over to the fireplace. Rosie turned in surprise. Titch was licking the face of a lamb curled up in a basket in front of the fire. The Mancunian watched in wonder as her friend squatted on the old flock mat. The orphaned lamb sucked eagerly at the bottle Connie held in her outstretched hand.

SCOTTISH BLACKFACE EWE WITH LAMB

Chapter Twelve

ANY motorist travelling up the A6 south of Manchester early on Saturday morning, the 11th of April 1992, who happened to come across a tandem from the rear could be forgiven for thinking they'd stumbled upon a pair of impoverished gypsies who'd had their caravan and car taken off them by creditors.

Hanging from its overfilled rear panniers was what at first glance could have been taken for a heap of scrap metal. It comprised an assorted collection of aluminium cooking implements and eating utensils, including a good sized frying pan, a mess tin, two enamelled mugs, a medium sized kettle, complete with whistle, and a zig bottle of paraffin; the latter two items swinging on the bike's off-side, as if deliberately positioned to scratch or dent any passing car that got too close.

Malc and Tom Cowle were back on the road again, doing what they did best and enjoyed most, much to the disgust of a few ill tempered and frustrated motorists and to the amusement of others. Both were in high spirits. They always were whenever they set out on a camping expedition, but this particular day had added spice for both of them. Tom was looking forward to spending the next week with his old friend, Rosie Akroyd, and his new friends, Connie Gartside and Mikey Grimsditch. Malc was looking forward to enjoying a break from toil, in pleasant surroundings and in good company, with plenty of fresh air and fun thrown in for good measure.

They'd just completed the long steady climb up the A6 that begins shortly after the Rising Sun in Hazel Grove, on the outskirts of Stockport, and ends just after the border of the villages of High Lane and Disley. Once on the flat they'd soon built up speed and were now travelling at a good twenty-two miles an hour as they swept around the long left-hand curve past the impressive gates at the entrance to Lyme Park on their right. From there the gently undulating road would take them through Disley village centre in to open country, above and alongside the wide open valley of the River Goyt, before turning off to descend in to New Mills. Then they would head up the valley of the River Sett in to Hayfield. Here they would take a break; enjoy a welcome cup of tea at the Three Trees café, purchase some food and then continue to their ultimate destination, Gartside's Farm.

Connie and Rosie were also heading for Hayfield on their bikes, having been despatched by Elsie on a food shopping expedition to the local bakery and the co-op. However, having passed the Sportsman at great speed, they were soon applying their brakes. Mikey and his mother were standing outside their cottage admiring a bike along with a near neighbour. The girls were soon over the road.

Mikey smiled a greeting.

"Mr Hodgson's offered to lend Mam his bike," he told them, "It's a real smasher."

Pearl turned at the sound of her son's voice.

"Hiya, you two. You've turned up just in time, young Connie. You might be able to help."

"Help? What kind of help?"

"A broken spoke," Mr Hodgson explained, "In the back wheel."

"Dished side, is it?" Connie asked.

Mr Hodgson looked surprised.

"Yes, but how did you guess?"

"It usually is," she said, with all the authority of an expert. "The spokes on the dished side are under the greatest tension. I bet it's a pulling spoke as well."

Mr Hodgson laughed.

"I never checked, but look for yourself."

Connie squatted down to inspect the offending spoke and discovered she'd been right.

"Can you fix it?" Pearl wanted to know.

"As long as I've got the right length of spokes. It's a 27 inch wheel, which is now old technology, but I'm sure we'll be all right. Malc gave me a good selection. If not, I can cycle in to New Mills. There's a good bike shop there. I'll take the bike up to the farm when we've finished Mum's shopping."

"I could pick some spokes up in the car," the bike's owner offered.

"I'm sure I'll have some Mr Hodgson, but can we phone you if I haven't?"

"Pearl's got my number. Phone any time."

Pearl smiled.

"Thanks George. You're a real pal."

"Don't thank me Pearl. You've been a good neighbour to me for many a year. It's my pleasure."

"This is quite a bike, Mr Hodgson," Connie interjected. "It's a curly Hetchin isn't it? How long have you had it?"

"Longer than I care to remember, lass. I used to be quite a cyclist in me time."

He looked at her once more. She was nowt but a youngster, and a farmer's daughter at that. He wondered where she'd heard about Hetchin from, and how she came to be so knowledgeable about wheel-building, but didn't ask.

Instead he said, "I'll tell you what Pearl. I'll run the bike up ter the farm." He turned to Connie. "You're Jed Gartside's lass aren't thee?"

"Yes. I'm Connie."

"Reet, Connie. I'll get it there and if you need spokes, or owt else fer it, just let me know. Pearl tells me you're all cycling to Hathersage termorrer. She might as well have a decent bike in good order, whilst she's at it."

Eventually, the two girls set off, this time with Mikey, who hadn't wasted any time extracting his own bike from its cubbyhole under the stairs. George and Pearl watched them as they speeded down the lane. At last George broke the silence.

"Isn't that the lass who lost her leg some years back?"

"Yes George. It was a terrible accident. They amputated just below the knee."

"Aye, but look at the way she rides. She's a natural. You wouldn't think there was owt wrong with her leg would thee?"

Pearl smiled.

"She's a wonderful young girl. She doesn't let anything get her down. Our Mikey thinks the world of her."

"She passed me on the lane the other day. She were accelerating uphill as if she were descending. She'd be good at racing I reckon."

Pearl chuckled, not least because she knew George had been quite a time-trialist and hill-climb champion in his day.

"Connie's not backward when it comes to competition. She'll take on all-comers, given half the chance."

⁂

Although her adult admirers didn't necessarily understand why, Connie had made a great discovery. She was in her true element on a bike. Whilst she was an intrepid walker and a good runner, cycling was a great joy to her. She, in common with all those who had discovered the bike as a means of transport and pleasure, enjoyed the speed and ease of travel, the wind in her hair and the fresh air on her face. However, for Connie in particular, cycling had an additional benefit. No matter how fit the individual - walking, let alone running, consumes considerably more energy using an artificial limb than is the case for an able-bodied person with two good legs.

When cycling, she'd soon realised, this particular effect was minimised to a great degree; the main reason being that the bike carries the rider's weight, leaving the legs free to power the machine through the pedals and drive chain. Moreover, because the pedalling motion is rotary, the strain on muscles and joints is far less than when walking or running. Luckily, the hip and knee joints of her right leg, along with the upper muscles, had not suffered as a result of the accident. Thus, despite the fact her lower limb and foot were artificial, she was still able to deliver almost as much power to the right-hand pedal as to the left.

It had taken her years of hard graft and determination to learn to walk and run sufficiently fast to keep up with her contemporaries. In contrast, once she'd mastered the art of riding a bike the rest was an easy matter. The energy deficit resulting from any slight loss of natural pedalling power was easily overcome by her highly-honed competitive nature, and that was more than sufficient to give her the edge she needed. If she came across any cyclists on her travels, her instinct was to overtake them, and if she was overtaken in turn a chase was guaranteed.

As a result of the latter circumstance, she'd soon learnt the advantage of getting as close as possible to the leading rider's back wheel. That way she remained protected from the cyclist's biggest enemy - namely air resistance - particularly when faced with a head wind. As a result she found herself resting, whilst speeding along in the other's wake.

Then, when a suitable occasion arose, particularly a hill climb, she'd nip around her erstwhile and often unsuspecting human windbreak and shoot uphill, with muscles nicely refreshed and re-oxygenated, taking the person she'd slipstreamed so quietly behind by surprise. Few caught the youngster, no matter how hard they tried, for as well as being determined, she was small and light, a winning combination when faced with a climb.

Moreover, the Peak District of Derbyshire is not an area bereft of good climbs, and to a girl with Connie's temperament the steepest specimens acted as a magnet. The next time she cycled up the infamous Winnats Pass, which climbs a total of 188 metres in a distance of 1.6 km., that is exactly one mile, with a leg breaking 20% incline in parts, wouldn't be the first, nor the last.

"There they are. Quick Mikey. Shout them over!"

Connie, Rosie and Mikey occupied their favourite table in their favourite café and they'd just spotted Tom and his dad. However, it proved unnecessary for the young lad to leave his seat. The two had disembarked from the tandem by the church and were wheeling it across the road towards them, their smiles showing they'd spotted the youngsters. Within moments the tandem nestled alongside their three bikes and Tom had taken his place at the table with them, leaving his father to find a seat at the next. After saying hi to the young lad, Connie immediately rose from her seat, eager to talk to her older mentor, who after his initial greeting was now perusing the menu.

"How are things, Malc?" Connie asked.

He looked up and smiled.

"Fine. We've had a good journey. How's tricks with you?"

"Good, but I might need your help."

He looked across the table in anticipation.

"I've a wheel to repair when I get back to the farm. It's a simple job if I've got the right length spoke, but I've realised I'm going to have to remove the block. I think it's a Maillard six-speed, but I'm not sure. The thing is, the last time I tried to remove a block I had a real struggle, it was on so tight, and this is a very old bike."

"Did you put the block remover in the vice before turning the wheel and using the rim as a lever?"

"Yes. And I kept the tyre on to ensure maximum grip, but I couldn't do it on my own. Luckily Ralph was about and he's ever so strong."

"Well, being a little bloke, I'm not that strong either, but I'm sure we'll manage between us."

"It's a Hetchin," Connie added.

"Curly or straight?"

"Curly and it's got the Tottenham head badge, not Southend."

Malc shook his head and smiled.

"You've been doing your homework since I saw you last."

"There are some interesting books in the local library and I get *Cycling Weekly* from our newsagent."

"But do you do any cycling? That's what's most important."

"Of course I do. I use the bike every day and now the nights are lighter, most evenings too. It's really wonderful Malc. I'll never be able to thank you enough. And we've fixed Rosie up with a bike."

"You don't have to thank me young Connie. All you have to do is build wheels for me for the rest of your sweet life!"

At that point the waitress approached and asked if he'd like to order. Connie wondered if he could possibly be serious with regard to wheel building, but not for too long.

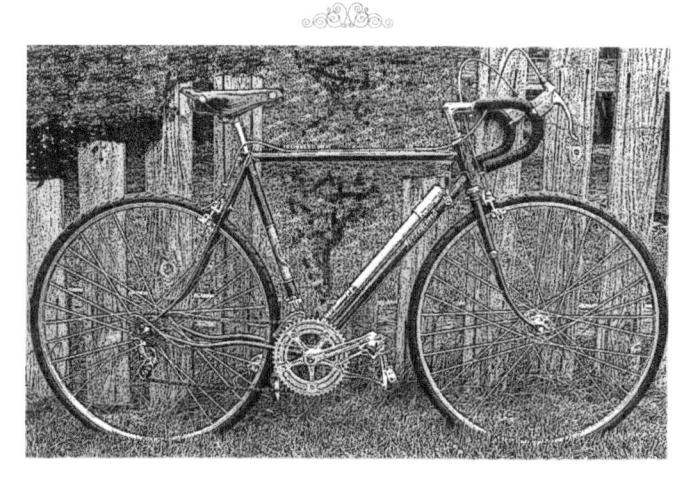

"CURLY" HETCHIN
[NOTE THE REAR SEAT AND CHAIN STAYS]

Chapter Thirteen

CONNIE'S fear that the removal of the six speed block would test her strength, proved to be over-pessimistic. Having clamped the remover firmly in to the vice in Ralph's workshop, and having placed the wheel in to position, she'd gripped the rim and tyre firmly with both hands and with one good twist she discovered she was able to wind it free quite easily.

Rather sensibly she had Malc standing by just in case and he'd supervised her efforts.

"Whoever put this on knew what they were doing," he pointed out, as he inspected the threads of the freewheel.

He wiped the grease with the end of his finger and showed it to her.

"It looks as though it's full of rust!"

"No, Connie. Quite the opposite. It's copper-slip grease. That's why it's a golden-brown colour."

"Copper-slip?"

She looked up at him, her green eyes a question.

"Yes. It's usually used on the seat post. It prevents aluminium bonding to steel, by introducing a third metal, namely copper. That prevents the electrolytic action between steel and aluminium which results in cold-welding. Some greases, like lithium grease which is used to lubricate bearings, tend to promote bonding. Then you end up with a seized-in seat post, which isn't a good idea."

She nodded her head, indicating she understood. She made a mental note to ask Ralph if he had supplies and to obtain them if he hadn't. She remained silent for a long moment. Malc anticipated a question and eventually she said, "I wish you lived here. You know all about bikes and I need to learn so much."

He laughed.

"I'm only a telephone away Connie. You can get in touch anytime. You know I'll always try and answer any questions you might have."

"There is one you could help me with."

"Go on. What is it?"

"Mr Hodgson's bike. The lugs are so beautiful. How do they make them like that, and why?"

"Why do you spend so much time designing new shapes for your wrought-iron work? After all you can make a hanging bracket that will do its job efficiently by bending a strip of steel in to a right angle and then putting a strut in place to form a triangle. That's all it needs for rigidity and strength. Instead, you go to great lengths to come up with more and more fancy designs. Why's that?"

"To make them eye-catching and attractive."

"Exactly, and each one's distinctive to you, isn't it? Each is a unique design. It's as good as putting your signature on them, and that's pretty much the reason why some bicycle frame builders do the same. They spend hours, drilling and cutting and filing the lugs in to fancy shapes, because they want to make their work distinctive, instead of looking like some mass-produced object from any old factory. In effect they and you are the heirs to William Morris."

"William Morris? Who was he?"

"A man of many parts. He's most famous for his wallpaper designs, but in his day he was an author, a socialist and revolutionary, as well as being a translator. Thanks to him many of the old Norse sagas can now be read in English and he wrote *News From Nowhere*. He was also a founder of the arts and crafts movement. He was a friend of Eleanor Marx and approved of her father's thoughts on alienation. To cut a long story short he was appalled by capitalism's waste of natural resources and the artificial division of labour between production and design, craftsmanship and art, mechanisation had introduced. He was against the inbuilt obsolescence, brought in by businessmen to ensure maximum profits. He believed that useful objects should be made to last, not thrown away after a short time, and that they could and should be made beautiful and not merely functional goods. Something that both the producer and the subsequent owner could take pride in."

Malc was never one to use two words when a score would do. Nonetheless, Connie listened with patience and the message wasn't wasted.

"Could you show me how to do it?"

"Do what exactly?"

"Cut out the lugs. I noticed those on the tandem are quite fancy."

"Are you still intent on building yourself a bike frame? I thought you'd be content with your wrought-iron work."

She smiled.

"No. That's just a means to an end. Our sales of them are helping us build up capital for tools and raw materials. I still want to build frames when I leave school. Ralph's been showing me how to braze as he promised, and that's how I put my wrought-iron work together now, instead of riveting, but I could be building up a stock of lugs and fittings in the meantime, couldn't I?"

The frame builder nodded, a thoughtful expression on his face.

It hadn't taken Connie long to finish the job of putting the wheel back in good order. Malc had then given the bike a final look over, and, after checking the gears were functioning properly, following the removal and refitting of the wheel, and giving a final check to the brakes, pronounced all was well.

Both had departed to the kitchen for a welcome cup of tea. Connie phoned Pearl to let her know the bike was ready and then asked her mother if the lamb needed feeding. In the meantime Malc had filled the kettle and set it on the stove, much to Elsie's approval.

The farmer's wife had taken a liking to the Mancunian, not least because of the way he encouraged her daughter, but it had really been Tom who had impressed her most. Elsie believed that children are often a greater indicator of their parent's true characters than many adults might care to admit. She was also quite aware that although Tom had a good relationship with his mother, for he was always talking about her and did so with affection, it was his father whom he lived with, and it was his father who had shouldered the day to day responsibilities for bringing the lad up from when he still wore nappies. In Elsie's eyes, going on the strength of her own interactions with the young lad and Rosie Akroyd's tales of him, Malc seemed to have made a pretty good job of it. One thing was for sure. Whatever differences Tom's parents had with each other, they certainly hadn't allowed them to affect their child.

True, the bicycle frame builder wasn't much to look at, save when he broke in to a smile which, perhaps luckily for him, wasn't infrequent. Nonetheless, he was good humoured and good company. Now that

Pearl had decided to take up cycling - well, maybe they might get together. She wondered if she should act the role of match-maker, or leave things to take their natural course.

Her thoughts on a possible romance found their echo elsewhere, although they had nothing to do with Pearl or Malc. As soon as the Mancunian had made the brew and Connie had joined them at the table, the youngster suddenly asked, "Where's Rosie got to?"

"I think she's gone for a walk with Ralph. I think your brother suggested they might pick some bluebells for the guest room. I'm expecting visitors tonight."

Connie smiled. Elsie was not slow to notice the amused look on her face.

"All right, Connie, my love. Tell us what you are thinking."

"The spring is sprung. Romance is in the air."

"You're talking in riddles. Anyhow that's not how it goes; it goes like this -

>The spring is sprung,
>The grass is riss.
>I wonder where the birdie is?
>The bird is on the wing,
>But that's absurd!
>The wing is on the bird."

Her daughter and the frame builder laughed, but then Connie said, "You know what I mean, Mum. I told Rosie a couple of older girls were chasing Ralph and she'd have to make a move soon if he wasn't to escape her clutches."

Elsie shook her head.

"You shouldn't wind young Rosie up," she admonished. "I've told you before; affairs of the heart are not to be taken lightly. Anyway, I'm quite sure our Ralph knows on which side his bread's buttered. Rosie doesn't need to chase him, I can assure you. And, before you say another word, young Tom's gone along to keep an eye on both of them!"

Connie gazed in to her mother's eyes in wonder. She seemed to know a lot more about Rosie's relationship with Ralph than she'd ever expected. Indeed, she seemed to know a lot more than Connie did.

MALC COWLE

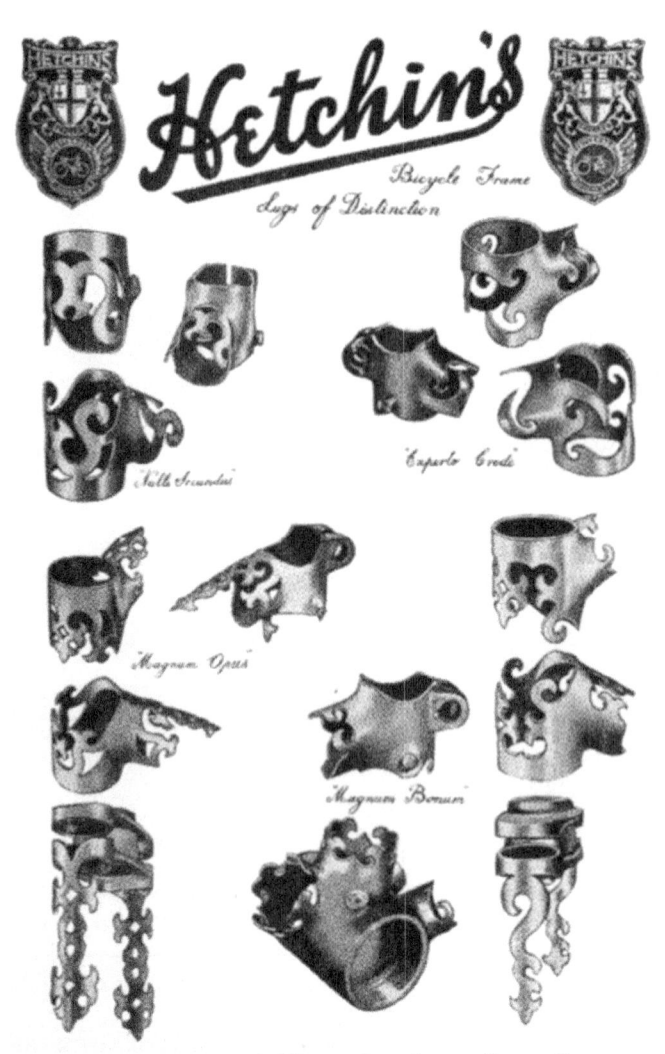

SELECTION OF HETCHIN'S HAND-CUT LUGS, FORK CROWNS AND BOTTOM BRACKET SHELL [FROM 1964 CATALOGUE]

Chapter Fourteen

"MALC, here's a cup of tea for you."

"What? Oh, it's you Connie. Where's Tom?"

The youngster grinned at the head popping out of the tent, obviously only half-awake.

"He's tucking in to a proper breakfast."

He finally had the entrance to the flysheet of the mountain tent fastened back and the cup of tea Connie offered him firmly in his hand. He took a sip and looked up at her.

"What time is it?"

"Almost nine."

She laughed, before saying, "Tom told me you needed a lie in."

He gazed at her through the vapour from his cup.

"I bet he told you I never feed him either."

He looked serious, but his hazel eyes were smiling.

"Does he do that a lot?"

"Only when we're camping. He's usually cadged at least one breakfast before I'm awake. That's why he leaves me to have a lie-in. There are people throughout the British Isles and one or two in France who think I neglect him."

"Well, get that down you and come inside. I'll make your breakfast."

Before he could protest, she was off, leaving him to sort himself out. Pearl and Mikey would be expecting them soon and Connie was looking forward to her day out.

Mikey Grimsditch and his mother had finished breakfast long ago. Unlike Mikey, Pearl was far from calm. She'd already taken the bike out for a run down to the village and back, concerned she might not be able to keep up with the youngsters. She'd checked the tyres were hard, checked the brake and gear cables were in good condition and then double-checked everything again. It had been a long time since she'd been on a bike ride of any distance, although she regularly used her old bone-shaker to visit the local shops and friends. When they'd first informed her of their plans to visit Hathersage it hadn't fazed her, but now she was about to embark on the expedition the thought of all the hills on the way made her question her original decision to accompany them.

"Do you want a cup of tea Mam?"

She turned towards her son.

"Yes. That will be nice. But what time are they coming?"

"Mam. How many more times? Ten o'clock. It's only half-past nine."

"Well, we don't want to hold them up."

"We won't, unless you wear that bike out just looking at it!"

Connie, Rosie, Malc and Tom were knocking on the Grimsditch's door at nine-fifty-seven precisely. Mikey ushered them in to the small front room of the terraced cottage. Mr Hodgson's bike occupied centre stage, its handlebars and saddle leaning against the wall under the window looking out on the Kinder Road.

Not long after, having refused the offer of a cup of tea, the six members of the newly inaugurated Kinder Peregrine Road Club, led by Connie and Mikey, were riding down the lane in to Hayfield. Their route, planned by Malc and Connie in advance, would take them to the outskirts of Chinley, where they would traverse a series of lanes to cut across to Rushop Edge and from their head up to Mam Tor and descend in to Edale. Malc and Tom brought up the rear on the tandem, the frame builder keeping an eye on his less experienced companions, like a sheepdog watching the flock. The A624, Glossop to Chinley road, can be busy at the best of times, and at weekends even more so. Luckily, for the first part of its journey, a lane known as Highgate Road runs out of the village, following the contours of the valley side, parallel with and above the main road, before joining the latter just before Chinley Head. It was this route Connie led them on to.

The sky was clear; the south-westerly wind little more than a slight breeze as they climbed up the narrow lane, bounded on both sides by drystone walls, in the lee of Highgate Head. Finally they reached the junction with the main road. Luckily it was clear of traffic and within a short distance they'd passed Peep o' Day and entered the cutting taking them over the summit at Chinley Head. Pearl breathed a sigh of relief. The first climb of the morning and it hadn't troubled her too much. Rosie Akroyd was having similar thoughts.

The pace increased as they began the descent in to Chinley, Connie leaning low over her handlebars to reduce air-resistance and young Mikey hanging in, close to her back-wheel, as she'd advised him to do, assuming he didn't wish to be left behind. He'd treated her advice with disdain at the time she'd voiced it, but he wasn't daft enough not to take it. They were now descending rapidly as the road dropped towards the valley bottom; so much so that Malc wondered if Connie had forgotten the need to take the lane off to the left before the main road plunged under the Manchester-Sheffield railway.

He needn't have worried. Connie signalled left in good time, turning back briefly to shout over her shoulder to Mikey to follow suit. They all followed in her wake as she turned in to the small hamlet of New Smithy, climbing gently once more alongside a tree-lined stream. After an initial sharp bend to the left the narrow lane curved around the hillside and then Connie took another right hand junction, ignoring the signpost for Slack House and Beet Farm. Once more they were climbing, this time between Gorsty Low and Breck Head, before descending to the T junction at Breckend, having finally crossed the railway. Here Connie halted and waited for all to catch up, much to Malc's approval.

He'd recognised that Connie's temperament might lead her to assume that everybody was as fast as herself and, as a consequence, she might have a tendency to unwittingly leave others behind. As a result, he'd advised her that it was important not to allow the group to be split and to always ensure nobody was left behind at every major junction. The youngster had obviously remembered his advice.

Satisfied all her companions were present, she turned left and carried on up the lane, now so narrow it was scarcely wide enough for a car. Shortly after the lane split and she took the right hand curve descending until they'd crossed a bridge taking them over a fast running brook in to the tiny hamlet of Wash. The steep-banked hedge-row lined lane now climbed steeply and the gap between the riders steadily increased as their young leader forced her machine onwards and upwards over Bowden Head. Finally, she came to a halt outside the open gates of the Ford Hall estate at Slackhall, next to the junction with the main road which would take them up Rushop Edge. The Ford Hall estate houses an impressive Otter and Owl Centre. It also has a café which acts as a magnet, attracting cyclists and walkers from many miles further afield.

Malc and Tom eventually rode alongside Connie and Mikey. The frame builder advised the youngsters it was a good place to have a break and to let the others rest their legs and get their breath back, pointing out they had a long climb up the Edge before them. Nobody disagreed. Rosie and Pearl were more than relieved, although their earlier fears they might be left behind, or hold the group up, were receding fast as their confidence increased.

Once suitably refreshed the six commenced the climb up Rushup Edge, but this time Malc took the lead. Tandems are slow uphill which made the pace easy for Rosie and Pearl. At first the road climbs steeply, following the contours of a tree-lined hill to their right, the valley to their left shelving steeply below them the higher they climbed. After the first mile or so the terrain began to change dramatically as they achieved higher ground. The trees disappeared and they found themselves with the distinctive ridge of Rushop Edge to their left and the valley sloping gently down to their right. Views of open sky and an expanding vista of rolling hills and wild country unfolded before them.

They were now travelling along the divide between the gritstone of the Dark Peak, marked by Rushop Edge itself, and the limestone of the White Peak. The incline gradually eased and within another mile the road levelled out. Connie had made her move long before and was streaking off alone, heading for the junction where the lane headed off to the left over Mam Nick to provide access to the Vale of Edale. Mikey let her go, content to remain on the tandem's rear wheel as Malc speeded up in pursuit of Connie, egged on by Tom. Rosie and Pearl did their best to keep up and at least had the assistance of a following wind.

By the time they were within one-hundred metres of the junction Connie had disappeared. Malc was only too well aware that to those not familiar with the road the lane off to the left could come as a shock. It climbed steeply to cross the narrow divide between the ridge of Rushup Edge and the soaring bulk of Mam Tor, before descending just as steeply down the other side. He expected Connie to be waiting at the top of the initial climb. As it happened he was right.

Just before the turn off the main road he asked Tom if the rest were in sight and, after a quick look over his shoulder the lad confirmed they were. Malc nodded, turned left and immediately climbed out of the saddle, dancing in the pedals, using the combined strength of arms and legs to force the tandem up towards the top of Mam Nick. Tom stayed in the saddle, whilst redoubling his own pedalling efforts. Connie was waiting at the summit, as Malc had expected. He forced his way over the final metre, grunting instructions to Connie to wait for the others as he passed by.

With Tom's concentrated assistance he kept on going, and then they were accelerating at great speed, braking on the curves as the narrow road snaked down to the valley bottom below. Tom was in his element, urging his dad to go faster, as they reaped the benefits of their previous fight against gravity. The road was clear of traffic and Malc ironed out the bends, crossing the white centre markings as the road curved to the right, and cutting the corners as it twisted left. Meanwhile Connie did as he'd asked, letting the others begin their descent, before setting off in their wake.

Nonetheless, by the time Rosie, Pearl and Mikey were half-way down the hill, she'd gleefully swooped her way to the front again and was powering after the tandem. Unluckily for her Malc had taken advantage of the straight immediately before the road levelled out and had reached a breathtaking fifty miles an hour. The momentum of the speeding tandem carried father and son over the gentle rises of the now undulating valley bottom and by the time Connie got close the tandem had come to a halt, just before the junction with the lane leading off to Grindsbrook Booth, the given name of what is known by tourists as Edale village. Tom sat in his place, looking back towards her, with a big grin splitting his mischievous little face.

As Connie approached he shouted, "See you at Cooper's café!" and before she could respond, the tandem was on the move once more, heading up the tree-lined lane, under the railway, past the Rambler on the left and the National Park Information Centre to the right, before turning left in to Coopers Farm, immediately before the Nag's Head.

The road out of Edale, heading towards Hope, is fairly flat, the one steep rise, near the entrance to Clough Farm, being quite short. The road itself runs parallel with the railway line, crossing from side to side as the terrain dictates. Shortly after Clough Farm there's a short straight stretch with the railway on the right. Three cars were parked by the railway embankment and a number of people with cameras lay in wait. Malc noticed them, but it was Tom who urged him to stop.

"I bet it's a steam special," he informed his dad, remembering a similar situation the previous year.

Sure enough, the lad proved to be correct and all were rewarded with the sight of the streamlined Sir Nigel Gresley, in its distinctive blue livery, pulling eight coaches full of railway enthusiasts on its excursion from Sheffield. The locomotive driver sounded the engine's steam whistle, as if in greeting to the enthusiasts who had bothered to wait at this remote spot to gain a photograph or two, and so it passed them in a cloud of swirling white vapour, a chuff of steam power, the acrid smell of anthracite smoke and a clickety-clickety-clack of carriage wheels speeding over rail joints.

They recommenced their ride. The River Noe, which up to then had flowed to the right of the railway, was now on their left. The valley opened out as it swung to the right to make its way towards the Hope Valley. They were soon swinging under a railway bridge, emerging to find the river on their right again. They made good speed around the eastern flank of Lose Hill, the steep sided slopes of Win Hill rising impressively from the flat valley floor on their left.

The fields of the valley were now lined with hedgerows, as well as drystone walls, their lush grass noticeably a brighter green than the herbage of those they'd left behind. Not so long after they crossed the river once more, and, after riding past the Cheshire Cheese pub on their right, were pulling up at the crossroads opposite St Peter's church in Hope village. The colour of the stone used for building materials had changed to a light whitish grey. They were in limestone country and the River Noe had disappeared in to the waters of the Derwent.

A quick check that all were together and Connie took the lead again, taking the left on to the main road, closely followed by the tandem. Mikey dropped back to talk to Rosie and to encourage his mother. He needn't have worried about Pearl. Having never forsaken her old sit up and beg, she'd not really lost her cycling legs. Moreover, she'd found the ride exhilarating, not least because the Hetchin was a light sleek state of the art machine, especially when compared to the old heavy tank she was used to.

Perhaps more importantly, her youthful memories of the bike rides she'd participated in before "getting caught" by being put in the family way at sixteen, and the great pleasure she'd derived from them, had come back to her mind as fresh as though they'd only taken place the day before. Like born-again Christians, born-again cyclists tend to be zealots and Pearl was fast becoming one.

Rosie, on the other hand, was beginning to feel tired, and her legs were starting to ache, although she didn't confide this information to anyone. She'd been hanging on to Pearl's back wheel for some time and the foremost thought in her mind was how long would it take before they reached Hathersage and lunch. The signpost at the crossroads indicated it was four miles. Rosie hadn't noticed. She might have been cheered if she'd been aware they'd now cycled over sixteen miles since leaving Pearl's. On the other hand, the knowledge she had another four to go, and then at least another twenty before the day was done, might have proved disheartening.

No such thoughts were troubling young Connie. She was as happy as the skylark trilling so enthusiastically high above the adjacent river meadow. It was only three short months since the frame builder had given her the bike, but in those three months her world had been transformed. Malc had confided to her that a bike had been his passport to freedom and pleasure since he'd been ten years of age and that he couldn't imagine life without it. It provided transport for him in the town and also his principal means of escape from that self-same town and urban drudgery. Connie was beginning to realise what he'd meant.

She didn't have a dirty town to escape from, but she did have a whole new world to explore and she intended to visit every little nook and cranny. She upped the pace slightly, full of confidence in her own prowess and knowing it was a straight road in to Hathersage, so none of the others were likely to get lost. About a couple of miles up the road, just past the junction to the left heading for Bamford, Ladybower and the Snake Pass, a group of cyclists, who, Malc informed her later, were no doubt a "chain-gang" of racing cyclists from Sheffield on a fast training ride, flashed past in a whirr of freewheels and shining spokes on stripped down gleaming enamelled machines; a uniformed array of brightly coloured tops and black lycra shorts, riding two-a-breast.

The temptation proved too much for the youngster. Her competitive spirit aroused she set off in hot pursuit and, much to the frame builder's astonishment, had jumped on the back wheel of the last of the group within thirty metres. The frame builder instinctively followed, having momentarily taken his right hand off the handlebars to snake it behind his back to give Tom's right hand a squeeze. His son recognised the signal and commenced pedalling hard. He enjoyed a chase as much as anybody.

The tandem accelerated and within a quarter of a mile they were on Connie's tail. Contented, Malc awaited the right time to make his next move. Maybe he could still teach Connie a thing or two. He looked down at his computer. Twenty-six miles an hour. Not bad on the flat for a fit adult - but brilliant for a thirteen year old one-legged cripple!

Tom took a look behind. The rest were in sight in the far distance, but only just. Pearl had taken the lead and, rather sensibly, she showed no sign of attempting to join the chase. Malc glanced to his left. They were passing the sign denoting they were entering the parish of Hathersage.

He prepared himself to move out to the right to launch his attack, but as he did so, so did Connie. Almost before he could take it in, she was out of the saddle powering forward alongside the group, who'd towed her along for so long without being aware of her presence. The rider to whose wheel she'd first attached herself attempted to follow, only to find a tandem alongside him, preventing his egress.

Tom smiled in to his startled eyes, as if to say, "This is how you do it. Just watch and learn!"

By now Connie was overtaking the lead pair of riders. She redoubled her efforts, finding she still had power in her legs. Thus she sprinted in to the village high street, arms held high like a professional, her face a portrait of triumph, with Malc and Tom trailing a poor second in her wake. She looked around, anticipating she'd be able to silently crow to the racing lads she assumed were still following, only to witness them taking the lane for Calver and Sheffield she'd just passed.

Malc grinned at her and led the way to the Hathersage Outside shop, above which was rather a good snack bar, frequented by walkers and cyclists alike.

Kinder Edge and Vale of Edale from Mam Nick

Chapter Fifteen

"ARE you sure you don't want anything else?"

All shook their heads.

"I think we should have a look round. I've never been here before," Rosie added.

Again all concurred and Pearl took the lead in rising from her place at the table.

Hathersage is an attractive and compact village, which like many in what is now deemed to be "wild" upland country was once highly industrialised. In the nineteenth century its water powered mills were replaced by steam and any visitor approaching it would have found it shrouded in dirty evil smelling smoke. Prior to the industrial revolution it remained a small agricultural settlement, with many inhabitants employed in handicraft industry in their own cottage homes, manufacturing brass buttons and wire, whilst others were engaged in quarrying, the high gritstone edges to its east and north being a major source of millstones, used for milling corn and grinding metal.

In 1750, the Atlas Works was opened and wire manufacture was mechanised. Thus the village became a major manufacturer of needles and pins. Later a paper mill was built to supply the wrappers for those self-same products. Both factories were water powered, until steam power was introduced in the early nineteenth century. The division of labour, so crucial to the efficient manufacture of needles and pins was documented and made famous by the plagiarist, Adam Smith, in his *Wealth of Nations*.

What he didn't document was the terrible price paid by the workers in the industry. The needles and pins had to be ground using grinding wheels made from the local gritstone. As a consequence the atmosphere and the worker's lungs were filled with fine metal and gritstone particles. The life expectancy of those who toiled and produced the factory owner's wealth plummeted to thirty and ended up being the subject of a major public health enquiry. Unlike the *Wealth of Nations* its report is long-forgotten, just as it was largely ignored at the time of its publication.

By 1992, well after the village's demise as an industrial centre, the village had become a magnet for hill walkers, rock climbers and cyclists alike, attracted by the nearby gritstone edges, high moorland wastes and the contrasting verdant valley of the River Derwent, which flows from the upper regions of the Hope Valley, beyond Hope village and its adjoining neighbour, Castleton. Despite the attractiveness of the village, it wasn't long before the Kinder Peregrines were eager to be awheel once more. Cycling is a peculiar form of transport in many ways, one of its peculiarities being that the reaching of a destination is not necessarily of primary importance, whilst the nature of the journey to that destination is of the utmost importance. Unlike a motorist, the cyclist doesn't just move through the landscape. He or she is part of that landscape, fully exposed to the elements of wind, rain, sun, frost and snow.

Moreover, unlike a motorised vehicle which you sit in, or on in the case of a motorbike, the machine between their legs becomes a direct extension of the cyclist's limbs and muscles. As such it remains subject to the rider's control, its speed completely dependent on the cyclist's whims; its performance limited only by the rider's skill and the degree to which they are able to provide it with sufficient power to overcome air and rolling resistance, and the forces of gravity. Their ability to see, hear and smell all the delights that nature provides remains unrestricted by a metal casing, windscreens and soundproofing, or a full-face helmet.

When they struggle uphill, there is no engine to put under load, save the engine that is their body delivering power through their own legs. This is why the cyclist's brain enjoys such a buzz when the summit is finally reached and the pain of effort subsides. Then the rider can take pleasure in the views provided, and anticipate the sheer joy of the reward to follow, the rapid easy descent aided by gravity.

Only walking for pleasure can come anywhere near matching cycling in this sense. Indeed, some would argue that properly defined, cycling is merely a "mechanised method of walking" with knobs on. But cycling enjoys the extra bonuses of speed and the ability to cover relatively long distances.

Amongst our intrepid group, Malc was the one who had studied these attributes of cycling most analytically. Such was only to be expected. Not only was he the most experienced, having indulged in the past-time for most of his life, succumbing to the addiction - and it is an addiction - when a mere lad of ten. He had also studied the art and science of manufacturing the machines to meet not only the individual customer's riding requirements, whether it be for touring, road or track racing, but to match their physical measurements, in the same way a bespoke tailor manufactures a made to measure suit.

Nonetheless, all his companions were on a fast learning curve, and each, including young Rosie after obtaining sustenance and resting her weary limbs, had thoroughly enjoyed the trip to Hathersage. All were now eager to sample further delights on the agreed return route to Hayfield. This would take them back to Hope the way they had come. From there, however, they would forsake the road in to Edale, with the intention of accessing Mam Tor and ultimately Rushup Edge by a somewhat interesting alternative.

"What's that?"

"The cement works, Rosie," Connie responded. "That's where our Richard works. Our Jem works in a limestone quarry way over the other side of the hill."

Rosie wondered why she hadn't noticed the large towering white structure with its extremely tall slender chimney, dominating the hillside above the village to their left, when they'd first arrived at the crossroads by the church earlier that day.

They were now cycling through Hope village, Connie and Mikey in the lead and riding two abreast, with Pearl and Rosie immediately behind them and the tandem bringing up the rear.

"Another mile-and-a-half and we can have a break," Malc suggested. "I don't know about you Pearl, but I could murder a cup of tea."

They were soon through the small village and in open country again. The road, now almost level, meandered gently following the course of the Derwent, a tree-lined remnant of the glacier's melt waters that had carved out this valley at the end of the last Ice Age, bounded on the one side by the dark heather-clad gritstone hills separating it from Edale and on the other by limestone peaks, the source of valuable minerals and essential building materials. Then they were entering the rather "twee" village of Castleton, once a quarrying and lead mining village, but now completely dedicated to tourism; some would say to the point of vulgarity, whilst others would profoundly disagree.

Faced with a noticeable increase in traffic in both directions, Connie accelerated ahead of Mikey and they all slipped in to single file. They quickly found a café where they could sit outside in comfort, enjoy a brew, and watch the multitude of tourists hurrying and scurrying between the ruins of Peveril's Norman castle and the famous Peak Cavern; peering in to shops selling all manner of souvenirs, semi-precious blue-john stone artefacts, outdoor clothing, walking boots, waterproof hats and other requisites; some of great value and some of no use whatsoever, except as a reminder of the visit.

Once they'd ordered a pot of tea for six and supplies of fruit cake Connie asked if they were going to climb up Winnats Pass or take the old road along the flank of Mam Tor.

"I think we should avoid Winnats," Malc responded.

"Do you think I can't make it?" Connie countered.

"No. I'm sure you can Connie, but I don't think you'll enjoy it. Just look at the traffic on the road. Winnats will be full of cars heading in both directions. Your lungs will be full of petrol fumes before you're half-way up."

Pearl smiled.

"I don't think I could do it without getting off and walking, cars or no cars."

"I've done it with Dad more than once," Tom informed them, "but I think we should go up the old road. Winnats wears Dad out and then I end up having to get him home. Being a tandem stoker's a form of hard labour sometimes!"

Suitably refreshed, the Peregrines were on the move once more. Malc and Tom led the way. The traffic was so dense heading towards Winnats it was down to a crawl. He quickly found a space and moved to the centre of the road, overtaking the cars, all of which he knew would be turning left within a quarter of a mile. The rest followed his example, Pearl bringing up the rear, keeping her eye on the youngsters. They'd soon safely passed the entrance to the steep limestone cliff-lined pass and the road ahead was clear, climbing fairly steadily and at an easy incline initially.

Before long a five barred gate forced Malc to halt. Tom immediately dismounted to let his father and the rest through, before closing the gate behind him and remounting. They were now beginning the ascent of "the broken road," the gate having been placed there to prevent access by motorists, with the sole exception of those requiring entrance and egress to and from Mam Farm.

By the time the tandem was on the move again, Connie was already powering her way up to the first left-hand hairpin bend. The others were following, but not without difficulty. They were no longer faced with an easy climb. Shortly after the first bend the tandem riders had caught Pearl, Rosie and Mikey. Malc, only too conscious of the fact he had to keep up his momentum, or give up and walk, moved out to their right and overtook them. By now Connie was well ahead, but the frame builder and his son knew she would be climbing off her bike soon enough.

Sure enough she dismounted, looked back to see where her companions were and decided to wait for them. Malc and Tom eventually pulled up alongside.

"What's up, Connie? You're not going to allow a small crack in the tarmac stop you surely?"

"Small crack!"

She looked at Tom in a way that indicated she thought he'd lost his marbles.

The lad laughed.

The fact was the road had slipped and two thirds of its width at this point was a good three metres below its once adjoining surface. Furthermore, for the next one hundred metres at least the situation was repeated. Indeed, at points there was scarcely a metre of the old highway adjacent to the hillside to walk along, with any degree of safety, and even then there were sections where they had to lift their bikes bodily to cross a jagged crack and step up a good metre onto the next bit of tarmac. For Malc and Tom, the sheer weight of the tandem, combined with its long wheelbase, presented additional problems. As a result they remained in the rear, so as not to impede the progress of the rest.

Eventually they'd completed the obstacle course Nature had placed in their way, as if She were laughing at mankind and his puny works. Connie opened the gate to access the good bit of road left and allowed her fellows through, before joining them in contemplating the view back towards Castleton, now reduced to a small miniature of a village down in the valley far below.

The Broken Road, Mam Tor

Chapter Sixteen

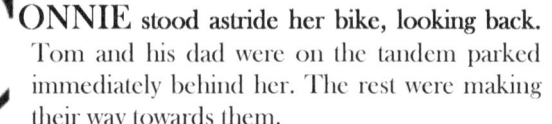

CONNIE stood astride her bike, looking back. Tom and his dad were on the tandem parked immediately behind her. The rest were making their way towards them.

They were now on the last leg of their journey, having regained the Rushup Edge road and reached its highest point.

"Right. They've almost caught up."

"Okay, start off Connie but stay close in. There's a car turning out of the lane from Mam Nick. It will be passing us soon."

She set off. Malc waited for a second and then followed suit. His timing was such that young Mikey had jumped on his back wheel. By the time they'd built up speed at the beginning of the long downhill stretch a car towing a caravan had joined the first vehicle in overtaking them. Not so long after Malc rode alongside Connie and reminded her they'd need to be prepared for the right turn in to the lane to Wash by the Otter Centre. She nodded agreement and he drifted back to his original position in her wake. The pace continued to increase and the riders began to string out behind. Another vehicle overtook them - this time a Land Rover towing a trailer. The effect on Connie was electric.

She turned her head, shouting at Malc and gesticulating, before beginning to sprint. He only caught the words "sheep thieves!" but they were sufficient. He set off in pursuit, more concerned about Connie's safety than catching sheep thieves, an animated Tom sensing his extra efforts were also needed.

The frame builder's initial reaction had been that they had no chance of getting anywhere near close to the Land Rover. If they'd been further down the hill, where the road was at its steepest and descended in a series of sweeping bends it would have been different. He soon caught Connie and rode alongside intending to persuade her to slow down, but she pointed ahead triumphantly.

"We can catch them if we try. Quick Malc!"

He doubted she was right. The Land Rover was a good two-hundred metres away, but Connie had realised something he hadn't. Once again she redoubled her efforts and once again she began to leave him as she accelerated downhill.

He sprinted forward in hot pursuit and finally caught and overtook her. Connie expertly jumped on his back wheel, to take advantage of his slipstream. Malc now realised the youngster had been right. The Land Rover had visibly slowed down. The gap between them had noticeably decreased. Maybe they could catch it? But what then? An idea began to form in the frame builder's mind.

The gap was now reducing fast, the Land Rover's way ahead impaired by the car and caravan. Moreover, cars travelling in the opposite direction made it impossible for it to overtake the obstacle, assuming its driver might want to. He, presumably, would have no knowledge he was being chased. By the time the road began to curve around the bends, Malc was having to brake just to remain behind the vehicle. Much to his alarm, Connie pulled out and appeared on his offside.

"We must get past them," she urged.

"No!" he shouted back. "There are three different sets of junctions coming up. We don't know which way they're heading."

Connie frowned, but drifted behind him again. Nonetheless she had a peculiar look in her green eyes. They'd narrowed to slits like those of a particularly angry and frustrated wildcat. Malc's head momentarily turned to Tom for a second and he said something over his shoulder. Tom nodded. Connie began to pull out once more, intent on making a move, whatever her elder mentor advised.

Much to her consternation, she realised Malc was braking again. He had no alternative. The trailer's brake lights were glowing a bright red. The Land Rover was slowing down fast. She decided to overtake, but as soon as she began to accelerate the Land Rover's indicator lights begin to flash. It was preparing to take the right hander to Wash. She could see the driver's eyes glaring at her in his wing mirror. Undeterred, she shot forward, certain she could get in front of the vehicle, enter the lane first and hold it up.

Malc looked on in horror, feeling completely helpless. The Land Rover was beginning to turn right and Connie was now alongside it. A collision seemed certain, but Connie wasn't beaten yet. The entrance to the lane is quite wide, so as to enable farm tractors and long trailers to access it from the main road in both directions. In the middle of this meeting point is a small green with a large old tree at its centre. The young girl swooped in to the lane to the right of the tree, much to the annoyance of a motorist exiting the Otter Centre. The Land Rover and trailer went to the left.

Unfortunately, or perhaps luckily for the youngster, depending on your point of view, the lane divides in to two again on the other side of this small green, the entrance to Slackhall Farm lying in between. Malc knew the two lanes eventually met again before Wash, but only after climbing steeply. The Land Rover took the left, ploughing its way up the single track road, scraping the errant branches of the overhanging hedgerows. Connie tried to follow, but having gone to the right, she'd had to brake hard before turning in front of the farm. She'd lost all momentum and finally gave up the chase, realising that despite all her efforts any chance of catching the vehicle and its thieving occupants had disappeared. No matter how fast she was uphill, the Land Rover was faster. Malc and Tom quickly joined her.

"Don't look so downhearted, Connie. We'll go in the café."

He pointed through the open gates of the Otter Centre.

"I don't need any tea!" she exploded. "I need to catch the thieves."

"And so you shall!"

"What do you mean? How can I? They've got clean away - again! That's the fourth time!"

"Tell her Tom."

"AKJF."

"AKJF! What are you talking about?"

Malc laughed.

"Put 853 after the J and before the F and tell the police. It's the Land Rover's registration number. There's a phone in the café. Ask them if you can use it! Dial 999."

He held out his hand for her bike. Connie handed it over and began to run. Tom clambered off the tandem and followed, more than a little excited. Dad had told him he was intent on enjoying a nice quiet day before they'd set out.

Meanwhile, Malc, his legs straddling the tandem and holding Connie's bike, remained stuck in the lane, until the others caught up and rescued him from his predicament, or another vehicle heading for Wash appeared on the scene. He hoped, if it should be a motorist first, it wouldn't be one of those whose brain switched off whenever the car's ignition key was turned on!

Somewhere high above the burbling cry of a curlew echoed across the valley.

CURLEW

Chapter Seventeen

TUESDAY evening, and a meeting was to be held in the upper room of the George in Hayfield village. Jed Gartside had promised Malc Cowle some rare entertainment and insisted he be present. He'd also persuaded Benny Rothman and Jack O'Donnell to attend as well.

He deemed that three representatives of Manchester's working class riff-raff would be sufficient to witness the proceedings, not least because all three were notorious "reds!"

The meeting had been called for eight o' clock prompt to mobilise opposition to the celebrations of the Mass Trespass due to commence a week the following Friday. The main speaker was to have been a Mr Palfrey, but unfortunately unexpected business had detained him elsewhere. As Jed had been one of the first people to be made aware of this unexpected development, he, being a public spirited individual, had contacted the Clerk to the Parish Council, who happened to be billed to chair the meeting in his "personal" capacity, and offered to stand in as speaker at short notice.

The Clerk to the PC naturally accepted this offer with alacrity. Jed Gartside was a well-known and well-respected member of the local community. His family had farmed in the area for untold generations. His offer appeared to be a god-send. If anybody could rally the villagers and rout the despicable Manchester workers and Communist insurgents he was the man.

The Clerk was known to be a thoroughly nice fellow and a gentleman. He was also, like all too many of his breed, extremely naive.

At half-past six that evening, Jed Gartside, Elsie, Ralph and Connie began their walk from the farm, accompanied by Malc and Tom and Benny Rothman. They would pick Pearl and Mikey up on the way. Jack O'Donnell and young Rosie were already ensconced in a side parlour in the George Hotel, which was already buzzing with life. Jack had suffered from bronchitis the previous winter. He was still having trouble with his chest and his ability to walk had deteriorated. Consequently, Benny had dropped him off in the village earlier, having picked him up in Edgeley, and Rosie had decided to keep her beloved Granddad company.

"So what's going on?" Benny asked.

"You know very well what's going on," Jed responded. "We're going ter a public meeting ter sort out once and fer all whether you and yer allies should continue ter celebrate the Mass Trespass, and, according ter some, continue ter disturb the peace of ower village."

Benny shook his head. Malc smiled.

"But how come you are the main speaker?"

"Because I'm a verra respectable man, with a great deal of influence and insider knowledge."

Elsie gave her husband a look, her eyebrows raised a good half-inch. Malc smiled again and so did Connie. Benny didn't notice their reactions, or else he might have addressed his next question elsewhere.

"Insider knowledge? Knowledge of what?"

"Ah, Benny, my friend. That is the key question. And all will be revealed, but not 'til we are sat in the George with me auld mate, Jack O'Donnell!"

The diminutive white-haired rambler looked up at him, but before he had chance to frame another question, Malc was knocking on Pearl's door.

"How's Mam, Granddad?"

The old man, put his pint pot on to the round table top and licked the froth from the bottom of his top lip.

"Workin' too hard as usual. She sends her love, Rosie."

"Is she still coming up for Easter?"

He nodded.

"You can meet her off the bus, Thursday neet."

"I've missed her, Granddad." She looked up at him, her bright blue eyes shining beneath her mop of long dark hair. "And I've missed you."

He chuckled before saying, "And I've missed thee as well. But I'm here now and I'm staying. What mischief have yers been up ter?"

"We went on a brilliant bike ride, and..."

She got no further. Jed and the rest crowded in to the room.

Greetings were exchanged, enquiries as to who wanted what to drink made and Jed and Malc despatched to the bar, whilst the rest found seats and made themselves comfortable. Ralph moved next to Rosie, whilst Connie pulled out a seat for Mikey. Elsie made way for Malc, thus ensuring the frame builder sat between herself and Pearl. Tom moved to find a place by Granddad.

Eventually, all were sat and sorted. Benny decided it was time to renew the enquiries he'd commenced earlier.

Jed beamed a smile, as if relishing being the centre of attention for once in a while.

"I had a phone call from the police early this mornin'," he informed them. He looked directly at Benny. "As you know, we've been plagued with sheep thieves of late. It's been goin' on fer well o'er two years an' every sheep farmer with flocks on Bleaklow and Kinder and most moors roundabout have been affected. They've teken a few here an' a few there, and they usually start about October-November, when the ewes are pregnant. This year they've got greedy an' teken ewes in lamb and with lamb."

He paused for a moment to take breath and a swallow from his beer. Benny found this very interesting, but what it had to do with the mass trespass, and the meeting soon to start, he hadn't a clue. Nonetheless, he curbed his tongue, sure he was about to find out. Jed put down his pint and resumed his narrative.

"Ter cut a long story short, late Sunday afternoon, we made a breakthrough, or at least ower Connie did."

"And Malc and Tom!" Connie intervened. "They were the ones who got the Land Rover's number!"

"Aye. Thee art reet lass." He smiled and then said, "Anyhow, Connie phoned the police Sunday and they phoned me this mornin'. They've tracked the thieves down ter a farm. A farm near a place called Prestbury in Cheshire. A farm that's listed as a dairy farm, with a prize Friesian herd, but in latter years has also specialised in fattening up sheep for slaughter on the side."

Tom looked at his Dad. They'd cycled through Prestbury more than once and they'd taken shelter in one of its pubs, the Admiral Rodney, when caught in a sudden thunder storm. It was part of the area known as the Golden Triangle, reputed to have more millionaires per acre than any other area of Britain.

Benny could contain himself no longer.

"This is all very interesting and I'm pleased they've caught the thieves, but what has it got to do with our celebrations. We've a public meeting in ten minutes!"

Jed laughed and took another sip - a very long drawn out sip - from his pint of Robinson's best bitter. At last he carefully put his pot back on the table.

"Everythin'!" he announced. "It's a cast iron guarantee the celebrations will go ahead. I'm about ter mek an important public announcement on the very subject. Yer sees Benny, the Cheshire farm is jointly owned by one of Manchester's biggest meat wholesalers and his sons. Yer've already met the elder of the family. Their name happens ter be Palfrey!"

∘⋄⊙⋄∘

The result of the public meeting turned out to be very much as Jed expected it to be, having taken the trouble to ensure local business people attended, including the proprietors of the Three Trees café, the Kinder campsite, various pubs and guest houses, food and souvenir shops and similar establishments with a vested interest. The result was a decision to send a message of greeting and welcome to the ramblers attending the celebrations, coupled with an instruction to the Clerk of the Parish Council to deliver the message personally and in his "official" capacity.

They then all retreated back to the front parlour of the George to be treated to a remarkable rendition by Jed himself of an old Lancashire dialect poem by Samuel Laycock, which, despite being written over a century before, seemed to contain a message for those seeking to circumvent the people's Freedom to Roam.

Appropriately enough it was entitled *Th' Peers An' Th' People* and went like this -

"CLEAR us a ring, lads, an' let's have a feight,
An' we'll soon have it settled whoa's wrong an' whoa's reight;
Th' People or th' Peers - which is it to be?
Let's have a reawnd or two, then we shall see.

"Must these preawd Peers tak' possession o' th' helm,
An' quietly say whoa's to govern this realm?
Are th' Bees to eat th' lean, an' th' Drones to eat th' fat,
For ever an' ever? We'll see abeawt that.

"Widen that ring, lads; neaw up wi' your sleeves,
An' we'll soon mak' short wark o' these lordlins an' thieves;
Lancashire lads can march up to their graves,
But can never be ceawards, or traitors, or slaves!

"Comrades an' friends, shall we give up for nowt
That freedom for which eawr brave forefathers fowt?
Nay, never, so long as these feet are well shod,
We'll oither win th' battle, or dee upo' th' clod!

"But why talk o' deein', or have ony fears
While there's nowt i' eawr way but a hon'ful o' Peers?
Let 'em only feel th' tips o' eawr famed wooden shoon,
An' they'll look for a road eawt o' th' field, an' soon.

"Clear us a ring, then, an' let's have a feight,
An' we'll jolly soon settle it, whoa's wrong an' whoa's reight.
Th' People or th' Peers - which is it to be?
Let's have a tussle, an' th' world shall soon see!"

    Benny Rothman, Malc and Jack congratulated the Derbyshire farmer on his grasp of the Lancashire dialect.
    Elsie pointed out that her mother had been a spinner at a mill in Little Hayfield and that it was she who had taught Jed the poem, "When he were nowt but a lad." Furthermore, she added, "Mam was originally from Ancoats."

THE TANDEM BUILT BY MALC FOR TOM,
NOW PUT TO GOOD USE BY
DAVE ROLLINSON AND HIS YOUNG CHILDREN [2010].

Postscript to The Bicycle Frame Builder's Apprentice

WHEN I embarked on this tale of the continuing adventures of the teenagers associated with Gartside's farm, I was in two minds as to whether my portrayal of the kids as entrepreneurs would be taken seriously by adults. I had no such worry about child readers. I've always had a great belief in the ability of children to overcome difficulties and to find solutions to problems, especially when they are a member of a "gang" - a much abused term - and are used to playing or acting together as part of a cohesive group. I too, was a child once upon a time, a long time ago.

In this case my own son, Thomas, provided inspiration. As a result of my association with the Communist Party of Great Britain, and its successor, Democratic Left, when Tom was ten years of age he used to attend meetings with me at the offices the latter organisation rented in Mount Street, not far from my bicycle frame building workshop in Ancoats. Here he came in to contact with and learned to use the office AppleMac.

By the age of fourteen he'd begun to interest himself in computer science, a subject not taught in school for some strange reason - a reason perhaps associated with Thatcher's daft idea we no longer needed to manufacture anything. In my opinion, for what it's worth, I.T. studies are largely a farce and totally inadequate. The year he embarked on his "A" levels, he designed me a website and began to take on work for other people. The rest is history. He became a highly successful and sort after self-employed website designer, before being head-hunted by a major promotion company.

Whether the producer co-operative founded by Ralph, Rosie, Mikey and Connie will survive, we have yet to see. They were soon to be shown the BBC video detailing the trials, tribulations and triumphs of those involved in the Mondragon Experiment in the mountainous Basque region of Spain. Perhaps it would inspire them and move them to pursue their objectives with renewed vigour.

Malc Cowle
Manchester, 2012

Postscript to Trespassers!

Benny Rothman continued to trespass. He died in January 2002, three months before the 70th anniversary of the 1932 Mass Trespass. As I shared his politics, being like him a member of the Communist Party of Great Britain up to its termination I will leave it to what was once the nearest thing to an official Tory press mouthpiece - the *Daily Telegraph* - to make the final comments on the man who gave me welcome advice and encouragement at a certain stage of my life.

Daily Telegraph
Obituaries - January 25th 2002

"**BENNY ROTHMAN**, *who has died aged 90, led the Kinder Scout Mass Trespass of 1932, the first significant event in the movement demanding public access to the countryside; within three years it had inspired the formation of the Ramblers' Association.*

"*Then as now, the countryside represented an escape from urban drudgery for many city dwellers; but others saw it as land to be defended from intrusion. At Easter 1932, Rothman and half a dozen members of the British Workers' Sports Federation (a subsidiary of the Young Communist League) were chased off Bleaklow in Derbyshire by gamekeepers. They determined that they would return to try to get up Kinder Scout, the highest hill in the Peak District and a privately-owned sporting estate, known to be heavily patrolled by keepers.*

"*Several weeks later, Rothman and his colleagues called a rally at a quarry in Hayfield, Derbyshire, expecting around 200 people. In the event, nearly 500 turned up, as well as a large contingent of policemen.*

"*When the intended speaker dropped out under pressure from the police, Rothman took his place. Tiny in stature - well under five feet tall - but with passionate moral conviction, he harangued the crowd with a stirring attack on the laws of trespass. Then, having warned his audience against using violence towards the keepers, he led the 500-strong crowd up Kinder Scout. 'Kinder was thick with keepers,' Rothman recalled. 'The professional ones just shouted and waved their sticks. It was the silly buggers that waded in.' In the inevitable melee that followed, one* keeper sprained his ankle and a trespasser was arrested. A 'riotous assembly' was then deemed to be taking place, more arrests were made, and six participants, including Rothman, were sent for trial.

"At Derby Assizes, the jury, composed largely of military men and landowners, had no hesitation in finding all six defendants guilty. They were sentenced to various terms of imprisonment for riotous behaviour; Rothman's term was four months in Leicester jail. The rambler movement had its first martyrs.

"In immediate terms, the Mass Trespass of 1932 represented a defeat for the Manchester ramblers. But it turned out to be a catalyst for change. Publicity about the affair led to the formation in 1935 of the Ramblers' Association. The 1949 National Parks and Countryside Act gained access to the moors of Kinder Scout and the Peak District.

"Bernard Rothman was born on June 1 1911 to Jewish Romanian parents who had come to Britain via America at the turn of the century. He won a scholarship to the Central High School for Boys in Manchester, but had to leave at the age of 14 to earn his living.

"He became an errand boy at a city garage and soon earned enough to buy a bicycle, on which he set off, in 1925, for his first solo expedition to the countryside - in Snowdonia.

"At the garage he befriended a Scottish mechanic who invited his young workmate to Sunday night debates in the Clarion Cafe on Market Street, Manchester, a favourite haunt of Trotskyists, ILP members, Socialists, Communists and other assorted Leftists.

"Rothman joined the Young Communist League and became involved in advertising the party's new publication, the Daily Worker, chalking slogans on walls and pavements round the city. On one occasion he unwisely wrote a slogan on the pavement outside a police station and was promptly arrested and charged with causing an obstruction: 'I was fined seven-and-sixpence - a week's wages,' he recalled. 'That was my first taste of justice.'

"In the 1920s the YCL and its subsidiary, the British Workers' Sports Federation, began organising weekend camps in the Derbyshire countryside - morally and physically bracing affairs of 'spuds, blankets and canvas' - and Rothman became an enthusiastic participant. 'We'd have 50 or 60 people a weekend,' he recalled, 'all ages from 15 to over 50. Our weekend activities were mainly rambling, with sing-songs round the campfire at night.' One of Rothman's jobs was segregating the sexes, or 'keeping the buggers apart' as he put it.

"In 1932 Rothman and a group staying at a camp held at Rowarth went for a ramble on Bleaklow where they were driven off by keepers. 'It was not at all unusual for ramblers to get very, very badly beaten by them,' Rothman claimed, 'and of course if you were working-class there was no redress.' Back at the camp Rothman and his friends set to work to plan the mass trespass at Kinder Scout.

"By the time he was released from jail, Rothman had lost his job; so he decided to become a full-time political activist. Moving to Burnley, he worked for the YCL in helping to organise the unsuccessful Moor Loom strike in the Lancashire textile industry.

"Later he returned to Manchester, where he found work as a garage mechanic. As the decade wore on, Rothman became involved in attempts to disrupt meetings of Sir Oswald Mosley's blackshirts. On one occasion, after throwing anti-fascist leaflets from a meeting hall balcony, he was set upon by half a dozen blackshirts, who threw him over the balcony in to the crowd. 'That night Mosley travelled down to London in a first-class carriage with the Chief Constable of Manchester,' Rothman recalled.

"In the mid 1930s he found work at A V Roe's aircraft factory but his Communism brought him in to conflict with management; so he moved on to Metropolitan Vickers in Trafford Park, where there was a more unionised workforce.

"He volunteered for the Army at the outbreak of war in 1939, but was rejected as being in a reserved occupation. After the war he became active in the trades union movement.

"Little more was heard of Rothman until the 1980s, when he resurfaced at the head of protests against Conservative countryside legislation; among other achievements, he was credited with winning concessions for ramblers during the passage of the Bill to privatise the water industry.

"Rothman lived in a neat semi-detached house in the Manchester suburb of Timperley, took a daily walk in his allotment, and enjoyed weekend drives to the moors in his Lada with his wife, Lily.

"In 1992 he led a commemorative ramble up Kinder Scout to mark the 60th anniversary of the first mass trespass.

"Benny Rothman's wife Lily died last year; he is survived by their son and daughter."

In the two years prior to his death Benny had the satisfaction of knowing that the primary objective that he and his working-class comrades had fought for, the right of ordinary people to roam freely on uncultivated land in their own country, had at last been largely won - thanks to the CRoW Act providing access to all uncultivated upland land in England and Wales enacted by another Labour Government in the year 2000. Amongst other things the Act provides a new right of public access on foot to areas of open land comprising mountain, moor, heath, down, and registered common land, and contains provisions for extending the right to coastal land.

The Act also provides safeguards which take in to account the needs of landowners and occupiers, and of other interests, including and, perhaps most importantly in my view, wildlife. I must at this point declare an interest, for the next drinker in the Railway on Lapwing Lane in West Didsbury who declares I am a member of the latter category, won't be the first!

Perhaps the event most likely to have put a wry smile on Benny Rothman's face, if only he'd lived to witness it, occurred at the 70th Anniversary when the present Duke of Devonshire, the eleventh of that line, apologised for the actions of his grandfather, calling it "a great wrong" and a "shaming event in my family".

However, the Devonshires still hold vast estates. Although Kinder Scout has been bought by the National Trust, Chatsworth is not their only stately home. They own Bolton Abbey, and Lismore Castle and its estates in Ireland. Furthermore, the poor of Hayfield have little chance of an early return of the forty-acres once known as Poor Man's Piece and Poor Man's Wood.

In other parts of the world acts of land theft continue on a daily and sustained basis, whether it be in the rain forests of Amazonia, the mineral rich outback of Australia, the rural areas of China and India, the savannahs and forests of Africa, the cold regions of Alaska, northern Canada and Siberia, or the ice-shrouded Arctic wastes. Thus people continue to be thrown off the land, their traditional ways of life destroyed, wildlife persecuted, and the needs of majorities are constantly subordinated to the greed and immorality of wealthy minorities in pursuance of ever more profit.

So the age old struggle continues, but our rulers should beware. Working people and toilers everywhere are like grains of gunpowder. A single grain is of no consequence, but amass the grains together, first in to grams and then in to kilograms and then in to tonnes, and the fireworks are likely to begin.

On a final cautionary note to the rich and powerful, the First Earl of Devonshire, Sir John Cavendish, (1345-1381) became Chief Justice of the King's Bench. In this capacity he helped suppress the Peasant's Revolt. One of its leaders, Wat Tyler, was summoned to parley with the authorities and during the course of the negotiations, the Mayor of London, William Wallworth, struck at him with a sword, delivering a severe wound to Tyler's neck.

The cowardly second son of the judicial Earl of Devonshire, another John Cavendish, not content with this, took his own sword to Tyler, killing him on the spot. However, Sir John Cavendish the father paid the price for his son's disgraceful act. Peasants pursued him relentlessly, determined to avenge their leader. They finally caught him and he was taken to the market place at Bury St Edmunds, tried, found guilty of land theft and murder and subsequently beheaded by an orderly and sober crowd led by Jack Straw on 15 June 1381. His remains are buried in the town where he was executed.

Brought to you by the publisher
to celebrate the
80th Anniversary of the Mass Trespass of Kinder Scout
24th April 2012

NORTHEN GROVE
PUBLISHING PROJECT

27 Northen Grove
West Didsbury, Manchester, M20 2NL
www.malcsbooks.com

Take Nothing But Photographs
Leave Nothing But Footprints

Educate, Agitate And Organise
You Still Have Your Chains to Lose
And A World To Win

NORTHEN GROVE PUBLISHING PROJECT
27 Northen Grove, Manchester M20 2NL

The mission of the Northen Grove Publishing Project is to publish works by writers, who would not normally be published, and those out of print and out of copyright, which have a bearing on the struggle for a democratic Britain and advance the cause of working people. Other works already published include:-

Dirty Politics - Hard Times by Malc Cowle
Dirty Politics - Famine Times by Malc Cowle
Born To Annoy - Book One by Malc Cowle
The Manchester Man by Mrs George Linnaeus Banks
Mary Barton by Elizabeth Gaskell
North and South by Elizabeth Gaskell
Ruth by Elizabeth Gaskell
The Working Class Movement in England by Eleanor Marx
News from Nowhere by William Morris
Utopia by Sir Thomas More
The Life and Adventures of Michael Armstrong, the Factory Boy by Frances Trollope;
Self-Help by the People - The History of the Rochdale Pioneers by George Jacob Holyoake
The History of David Grieve, by Mrs Humphry Ward
A Memoir of Robert Blincoe by John Brown
The Life, Times and Labours of Robert Owen by Lloyd Jones

All can be downloaded free of charge at www.malcsbooks.com

Printed in Great Britain
by Amazon